Praise for USA TOD...
Kasey Michaels

"Kasey Michaels aims for the heart and never misses."
—*New York Times* bestselling author Nora Roberts

"Michaels holds the reader in her clutches and doesn't let go."
—*RT Book Reviews* on *What a Gentleman Desires,*
4½ stars, Top Pick

"Michaels' beloved Regency romances are witty and smart,
and the second volume in her Redgrave series is no different.
The lively banter, intriguing plot, fascinating twists and
turns...sheer delight."
—*RT Book Reviews* on *What a Lady Needs,* 4½ stars

"A multilayered tale.... Here is a novel that holds attention
because of the intricate story, engaging characters and
wonderful writing."
—*RT Book Reviews* on *What an Earl Wants,*
4½ stars, Top Pick

"The historical elements...imbue the novel with powerful
realism that will keep readers coming back."
—*Publishers Weekly* on *A Midsummer Night's Sin*

"A poignant and highly satisfying read...
filled with simmering sensuality, subtle touches of repartee,
a hero out for revenge and a heroine ripe for adventure.
You'll enjoy the ride."
—*RT Book Reviews* on *How to Tame a Lady*

"Michaels' new Regency miniseries is a joy.... You will laugh
and even shed a tear over this touching romance."
—*RT Book Reviews* on *How to Tempt a Duke*

"Michaels has done it again....
Witty dialogue peppers a plot full of delectable details
exposing the foibles and follies of the age."
—*Publishers Weekly* on *The Butler Did It* (starred review)

KASEY MICHAELS

What a Hero Dares

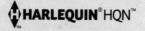

Recycling programs
for this product may
not exist in your area.

ISBN-13: 978-0-373-77860-7

WHAT A HERO DARES

Copyright ● 2014 by Kathryn Seidick

Printed in U.S.A.

Dear Reader,

I've spent three books listening to Maximilien Redgrave's siblings talk about him, drop snippets about him here and there for me to pick up on—for readers to pick up on. Now it's time to see what all the fuss has been about.

He's a handsome fellow, this Max Redgrave, not to mention cocky. Bright, outwardly confident, determined, daring. But he isn't perfect. He's been betrayed, had his heart badly broken and his trust in his own judgment shaken by one Zoé Charbonneau, the French beauty who made him the man he is today: deadly dangerous.

Now Zoé's back, just as Max is up to his neck in intrigue. She's got a score of her own to settle, and doesn't care if she's in his way—not as long as he stays out of hers. Which isn't as easy as it sounds, not when they can't seem to keep their hands off each other, enemies or not.

All I have to do now is sit here at my computer and let Max lead me where he wants to go…everywhere a hero dares!

Please visit me online on Facebook or my website to catch up on all my news.

Kasey

www.KaseyMichaels.com

To Mike, with all my love.
In good times and bad these past fifty years,
you've always been there for me.

Lord, I wonder what fool it was that first invented kissing!
—Jonathan Swift

PROLOGUE

SOMETIME IN THE mid-1700s, Charles Redgrave, six-teenth earl of Saltwood, took it into his head that the amount of royal Stuart blood in his veins trumped that flowing in the Hanovers now (erroneously, obviously) occupying the English throne.

Charles did not like sharing what he perceived as his power, but realized he did need a few reasonably intelligent aides, inferiors who would obey his every command and help secure those goals (no matter their own petty motives).

And thus the Society, a most unique hellfire club, was born.

Charles handpicked his inner circle, the Devil's Thir-teen as they were then dubbed, offering them, if not the sun and the moon, a secret world of more earthly de-lights, along with wealth and power such as they'd never dreamed could be theirs. Once he had his chosen ones, like-minded traitors all, they sought out their minions, as all the best courts had minions, sycophants, useful, loyal, yet expendable.

He outfitted a hidden pleasure palace on Saltwood land geared to satisfying every desire, indulging every carnal pleasure, encouraging every vice, from women (always a grand draw, Charles knew), to heady opium pipes. There was also the promise of intellectual discourse in there somewhere, and the lofty goal of a more justly ruled England, but mostly the more minor members were there for the silly costumes and the diddling.

It was only after their desires were met, even exceeded, and the first demands were voiced that they truly realized this particular hellfire club, this Society, now owned them—them and their reputations, with Charles's every wish suddenly their command.

Charles knew he needed one thing more: an army. For that he turned to France, and struck yet another devil's bargain, truly believing he was about to embark on the path that would lead him to the throne.

Instead, Charles turned up quite dead one morning (a plate of bad fish, so sad), before the French army could be launched, its destination the welcoming shores of Redgrave Manor. The Devil's Thirteen and the minions melted back into a more humdrum society, hopeful the masks they'd worn during ceremonies, the code names they'd used, would protect their identities.

Whispers of debauchery and perhaps sedition to one side, the Society might have been forgotten, if not for one thing. Charles had decreed every member keep a journal. Those journals were yearly turned over to the Keeper to update the bible, the key to everything about the Society.

When the time was considered ripe, the Keeper had dutifully turned over the journals and bible to Charles's only son. Barry Redgrave, as hoped, had *oohed* and *aahed* in sincere appreciation, and apparently decided his late sire had been nothing less than a bloody genius. Along with an almost eerie resemblance, Barry had inherited an attraction to the more perverse delights life had to offer. Although Barry believed himself to be more handsome than his father, and most definitely smarter.

And that plate of bad fish? The Keeper had another tale to tell about *that!*

Even before he reached his majority, Barry had clearly taken over the running of Redgrave Manor, cajoling his doting yet oddly nervous mother, winning her over with his smiles, his outward affection, while operating quite secretly behind her back. The morning he turned one-and-twenty, after a long night of revelry with his chums in Town, he flung his unsteady, drunken self into his mother's chambers in the family's Cavendish Square mansion, to rouse the woman with a cruel slap followed by a boozy, punishing kiss on her mouth.

He was followed by a trail of maids and footmen prepared to "Pack you up, you murdering whore," and denied her an allowance unless she limited her visits to the Manor to one month out of each year.

He then paid a covert visit to Grosvenor Square. He politely thanked the aging Keeper and mentor in the ways of the Society for all he'd done, and told him to say hello to Charles a moment before tossing the old fool down the marble stairs.

Two weeks later, he purchased that same Grosvenor

Square mansion, leaving his father's outrageous monstrosity in Cavendish Square for his mama's use. Let her live with the ghosts there.

And let the games begin!

While his still young and beautiful mother traveled on the Continent or partied in Mayfair, he appointed his very best friend, Turner Collier, to act as the group's Keeper, guardian of the bible. They then went about gathering up any of the original Devil's Thirteen and minions still aboveground, and the Society was soon back in business. He met and married a barely royal Spanish beauty he deemed a suitable broodmare, put a child in her as often as he could, enlarged both the Manor house and its lands. And plotted. And schemed. And added more and more like thinkers and helpful minions to *his* Society.

All within the confines of his first and truly only love, Redgrave Manor.

For nearly ten years of planning and conniving and bribing, all seemed to go quite swimmingly. His negotiations with the French king would soon come to fruition. Until the fall of the Bastille dealt the first crushing blow to Barry's ambitions. That was closely followed by his drunken decision to stand up in a duel against his wife's French lover, only to fall on his handsome face when a weapon fired from the trees put a bullet hole in his back and a period to his existence. The new widow, smoking pistol supposedly still in her hand, promptly deserted her four young children and ran off to France with her lover.

What followed was open conjecture throughout the *ton* concerning some sort of salacious hellfire club, and even speculation that Barry Redgrave had been whoring out his wife to his devil-worshipping friends, and that was really why she shot him. There were whispers of sedition and treason as people remembered his father and those rumors, dragging them out for another airing. But, mostly, it was the titillating scandal of the murder, the reason behind it, and the insult to those who deemed the Redgraves immoral, unsuited to retain the earldom (or the Manor, or all that lovely money).

It was as if Barry was more of a danger dead than he'd been while alive. The Redgraves were about to lose everything…including control of their secrets.

Enter the determined Beatrix, Dowager Countess of Saltwood, and fiercely protective grandmother to Barry's four good-as-orphaned children. The by now deliciously notorious Trixie, who had spent her entire widowhood playing May games with society, most especially the men—those she loathed, those she admired, and those she might someday be able to use.

She'd learned a lot from Charles….

Perhaps because she had more brass than a chamber pot, but most probably because she knew more than most men would like the world (and especially their wives) to know, she managed to make it through the scandal. She spent decades tenaciously (and perhaps more cleverly than legally), holding on to the earldom for her eldest grandson, Gideon, who had been only nine when his father was hastily interred in the family mausoleum.

Her husband's Society, her son's intention to follow in his father's footsteps—these were never mentioned within earshot of the grandchildren. Trixie would rather die a thousand deaths than reveal what had gone on within the Society, the part Charles had forced her to play those long years ago. Her grandchildren knew of the scandal caused by their parents' actions, yes—that would be impossible to hide from them as they matured and traveled to London, but with the Society long since gone, there was no reason for them to know anything else.

In truth, they seemed to delight in being *those scandalous Redgraves*. Welcomed everywhere, because to deny them would be folly. Quick, intelligent, *dangerous,* no door was shut to them. Who'd dare?

But now, suddenly, the Society was back for a third go-round, even using Redgrave land as its headquarters. Its methods the same, its *partner* this time none but the upstart new French emperor himself, Napoleon Bonaparte. For years, he had longed to add England to his long list of conquered countries. The Society would be more than eager to assist him in that endeavor in exchange for—God, what *did* they want? Certainly not the Crown; that silly Stuart business could only be gained through the Redgraves, and they certainly had no part in this new incarnation of the Society.

No, the methods might be the same, but the aims were different. Still, at the end of the day, if the Crown got so much as a whiff of what was going on, the Red-graves would pay the price, and this time no amount of Trixie's machinations would save them.

Gideon, already suspicious that something odd was going on at Redgrave Manor, had learned about the resurrected Society through Turner Collier's daughter, Jessica. He immediately confronted Trixie, demanding she tell him everything she knew. Consulting with his siblings, they then decided they were left with no other choice than to secretly, quietly ferret out the members and this time bury the Society too deep for it ever to be raised again.

First and foremost, of course, the Redgraves were all loyal to the Crown. But they were also loyal to the Redgrave name, and to the incredibly brave woman who had raised and protected them. They knew neither could survive the possibility of being connected to this or any earlier incarnation of the Society.

Plus, even with some early quick successes, they knew they were running out of time, having been forced to bring Prime Minister Spencer Perceval in on what they'd learned about Society efforts to sabotage troops and supplies heading to Wellington on the Peninsula.

Gideon's sister, Lady Katherine, had scoured Red-grave Manor, locating the journals from both her grand-father's and father's time but not, alas, the all-important bible, the tome having been reduced to ashes by the Keeper. His brother Valentine, following clues found in those journals, had dared to infiltrate a portion of the

Society, nearly losing his life in the process, but adding to their knowledge.

They were getting ever closer to the core of the Society and these new, unknown leaders who hid behind masks and code names while going about their dirty business.

Unfortunately, these successes also alerted the Society that the Redgraves were onto them, most certainly fueled by information given to them by the dowager countess.

Only a few short days ago, following a nearly successful arson in the mansion in Cavendish Square with a bold attempt on Trixie's life on the streets of London, the hunters had suddenly become the hunted.

There couldn't be a better time for Maximillien Redgrave, currently doing his own investigating from the other side of the Channel, to return to the estate where, unbeknownst to him, his family was all already gathered, and under siege.

Max also didn't know his own past was sailing to Redgrave Manor with him.

But he was about to find out.

CHAPTER ONE

MAXIMILLIEN REDGRAVE had last seen his birthplace from the seat of his curricle as he set off to London and a quiet meeting in a small office tucked away in the bowels of the Royal Admiralty. He felt he'd been traveling ever since, going about the king's business, with only a few, flying visits to London. It was during one of those visits that he'd learned about the Society, so that his work on the Continent now included searching out anyone who might be affiliated with the treasonous hellfire group.

This very night he was returning to Redgrave Manor, the magnificent estate that sprawled nearly to the size of a small English county. Sneaking home, as it were, via the back door.

Not that he'd expected to ride through the front gates heralded by fanfares of trumpets in any case, a roasted boar turning on the spit in the massive kitchen fireplace. A few hearty claps on the back from his brothers, an excited hug from his sister, a half-dozen dogs slobbering on his boots. That would be more than sufficient.

Except for the necessary addition of his irascible grandmother reclining at her ease on her favorite chaise longue, hoisting a wineglass as she sent him a knowing wink. It wouldn't be a proper homecoming without her.

After all, who else but Trixie Redgrave would have thought setting her grandson up as an agent for the Crown held less pitfalls than allowing him to roam Mayfair, wealthy, bored and hot for adventure? To either her credit or as the result of grandmotherly niggles of guilt, she'd then commissioned her own agents to watch over him, report his every move, his every mission to her. According to Gideon, they all had discreet keepers following them about, guardian angels who happened to be wide as barn doors and carry small arsenals with them. Poor Kate, still living on the estate, had everyone from the potboy to the butler to the tenants sworn to keeping her safe.

Not that Trixie would admit to any such thing.

Not that Max would so accuse her, either, or tell her the number of times he'd escaped those same keepers from the first day they'd set off to Eton with him, employing both fair means and foul. Oh, no, he would simply continue as he'd begun all those years ago, and thus wouldn't tease Trixie later tonight about how their new friend Richard Borders had crossed the Channel and somehow located that one tavern out of dozens lining the water in Gravelines, France, probably to inform him he'd just been whistled to heel by his true master.

Not now, Trixie, he'd whispered inside his head, pulling his hat down far enough to cover his distinctive low, winglike brows and long-lashed, sherry-brown eyes as he sidled out the side door and into an alley smelling of everything foul the human body could produce.

There were occasions his almost startling handsomeness was a boon, but not at times like this; right now Max craved anonymity, and having Richard calling out his name or asking the barmaid if she'd seen him could get both the seeker and the sought filleted. *Besides, I've got fish of my own to fry, thank you. I'll be kissing the dear lady's powdered cheek soon enough.*

Max didn't applaud himself as he melted into the darkness, as it had been easy enough avoiding Richard. The man would be looking for someone who appeared very different from the Max Redgrave who had been slouching in a dark corner of the taproom, his hair and beard unkempt, his clothes not much more than several layers of rags beneath a long, greasy cloak, his wide-brimmed hat filthy and sagging over his face. He did have a gold earring, but any bit of sweepings found roaming Gravelines could use his sticker to slit a drunken seaman's ear and help himself to a bit of gold. It was almost expected of them.

"And who was that fine, fair, fat gentleman you just left behind, *mon ami?*"

Max answered Anton Boucher without bothering to turn his head. "Who? You didn't have to follow me. I only came out here to relieve myself," and turned to the wall and unbuttoned his homespun trousers. "You've been at this too long, Anton. You've turned into an old woman, seeing trouble everywhere. It may be prudent of you to step back. The wind, you know."

"It is picking up, isn't it," the man said, retreating a few paces. "And the rain, as well. As long as we're out here and already drenched, we may as well get on with it. Perhaps they won't sail, as a full moon does no one any good when it's hidden behind clouds."

"Admit it, Anton, you're a timid sailor. There's no need for you to travel with me tonight. I won't be returning with you in any case."

"Nonsense, as if I'd leave you with no one to guard your back. Besides, I've gained their trust. Only the one ship tonight, and they won't let you board without me."

Max deliberately kept his tone light. "Braggart. But I suppose you're right. And you're confident they'll have the same destination as last time?"

"Same godforsaken destination *every* time, just as I told you." Anton smiled, his pale blue eyes seeming to twinkle in the reflection from a streak of lightning overhead. "Missed all the fun then, didn't we, sailing in the trailing boat? Pirates, the captain swore as we turned and raced back here, as if he'd know a pirate from a pickle. Probably just other smugglers, thinking to make an easy profit without the trouble of having to cross the Channel. Can't trust the English, Max, you know that, being one of them."

"The same stands for you, concerning your fellow Frenchmen," Max returned, and Anton's smile vanished.

"Touché. But we don't speak of such things. The past is the past, and the guilty one punished does not bring back the dead, does it?"

Max wished he hadn't spoken. This was no night for unpleasant memories. "No, it doesn't."

They made their way along the docks to the rather questionable-looking vessel their so-called employers had chosen for the run across the Channel. *Borrowed* from a band of English owlers their French hosts were currently entertaining at one of the inns expressly built for their comfort by none other than the emperor himself. Like so many others, having delivered their cargo of wool, all they'd wanted was full tankards and some sweet *mam'zelles* warming their laps before loading up their cargos of brandy, tea and silk for the return to the beaches of Romney Marsh or perhaps Folkestone before daybreak.

Max had watched from the corner of the taproom as the unsuspecting crew drank down their ale, neatly doctored with laudanum. The fools were now blissfully asleep with their heads fallen forward onto the tabletops, unaware their vessel was about to take a second run across the Channel yet this night. They'd wake to find a friendly gang of ships' carpenters repairing damage they'd discovered on the hull. Not to worry yourselves, my good *messieurs,* they would be told, you can sail for home tonight, and in the meantime, please enjoy the hospitality of these lovely young buds of springtime whose only wish is to please you.

Clever. Bonaparte and the Society, working together for their mutual advantage. God only knew what headed to England, God only knowing what returned with them to Gravelines.

Max wished he'd discovered the truth on his own, but that hadn't been the case. It was only after running down Anton in Ostend that he'd learned about the tactics, if not the cargo or the destination. And it was only when he and Anton had sailed from Gravelines with the Society that he'd glimpsed the familiar shorelines of Redgrave Manor just before the sloop sailing ahead of them was attacked and their mission had been aborted, rescheduled for tonight.

A real piece of work, Anton Boucher, this Frenchman who had thrown in his lot with the English. Never revealing more than he had to, and if not a friend, at least trustworthy. To a point. Max had told him only what he'd wished him to know when he'd asked for his assistance…but never called the Society by name or let on that he'd recognized the area of English coastline that had been and was now again their destination. As far as Anton was concerned, Max was simply carrying out another mission for the Crown.

No matter how much you trust them, tell them only what they need to know and, if you can manage it, only half of that. Max had earned that lesson the hardest way possible.

"Are you regretting escaping your watchdogs in Ostend?" the Frenchman asked as he squinted through the downpour, looking up and down the pier. "Don't you miss them?"

"I never miss them for long, unfortunately, as they've somehow made their way here. As far as they know, however, I'm still at my hotel, sleeping off an afternoon of melancholy drinking, just as if the place had only a front door. You're not supposed to notice them at any rate, as my behemoths rather pride themselves on their stealth."

"And now you're about to leave them on the other side of the Channel. Poor fellows. Even hounds can't follow a scent across the water."

"They can make their own way home," Max grumbled as they each loaded yokes holding a pair of small brandy kegs onto their shoulders and advanced up the narrow, dangerously swaying gangplank. *Along with Richard, who'd obviously already found them guarding that same front door.* "Damn, man, we haven't cast off yet, and already you're turning green. It's only a storm, not Armageddon. Don't worry, all we can do is drown."

"Sometimes I do not so much like you, *mon ami.* French stomachs are delicate, not like those of you English, who would eat shoe leather, and probably do."

"Only on Sundays, with quite lovely burnt carrots and turnips. Find yourself a dark corner, why don't you, as I help the others finish the loading."

Ten minutes later they were pushing away from the dock, and ten minutes after that Anton was leaning over the rail, alternately cursing and casting up his accounts.

At least the wind was with them, and they'd be off-shore at Redgrave Manor in a matter of hours. Unless the unknown captain's skill faltered, in which case they'd all be at the bottom of the Channel. There was always that. Years ago, Max had been able to brag of being not only the youngest coxswain in the Royal

Navy, but had been aboard the *Trafalgar* when the mighty Nelson was mortally struck down. But those who'd been there never spoke of that fateful day, even in whispers.

Just as he could not betray himself now by conking the inept captain over the head with a belaying pin and taking control of the ship.

Cursing the foul weather under his breath, Max leaned against a portion of lashed-together kegs as the sloop seemed to climb skyward on each wave, only for the hull to then slap down on black water turned hard as any board.

There came the sound of tearing sail high in the rigging, and Anton's curses grew louder. A French royalist intent on defeating Bonaparte and returning the monarchy to the throne in Paris, Anton had been secretly working for the English for close to a decade, and he and Max had more than once joined ranks in ferreting out information valuable to the Crown. Worked together, gotten roaring drunk together, laughed together...mourned together.

It was only natural that he would contact Anton for his assistance, and it was Anton who'd first suggested English traitors could be making themselves at home in any of the hotels Bonaparte had ordered built to house English smugglers along the coast, many of them at Dunkirk and Gravelines. Anton had taken out a gold coin and flipped it, with him picking Gravelines when he won.

Max had seen that trick from Anton and his two-headed coin before, but had never called him on it, just as Max had some small tricks of his own. Anton had information he wasn't sharing, and had made sure Gravelines was their destination. As long as they both knew each other's tricks they could both pretend ignorance in certain things. It was safer that way, as long as the mission succeeded.

Which, hopefully, it was about to do.

Once in the seaside town, watching and careful listening had resulted in information about one small group of men and their *borrowed* ships. Their runs were infrequent, and loaded with quite singular cargo. Yes, they loaded brandy meant for England, unloaded wool that came from England. But there was something more.

"Men going to England, but not returning with the ship," Anton had informed Max. "My contact told me it's the damndest thing. Sometimes two, three dozen seamen sailing off along with the kegs, but only a handful returning on the next tide."

He'd laughed then, that full-throated laugh of his that rose all the way to his pale eyes. "You don't suppose Boney is invading a score or so at a time? Piecemeal building himself an army on English shores? I always told you, Max, these revolutionists toss words like *liberté, égalité, fraternité* into the dustbin every time they sniff a whiff of power. Drop a crown on their heads, like Boney, and they're even worse, gobbling up other countries like sugar treats. Why else are you here, with the English so concerned about Bonaparte's business, yes?"

Remembering Anton's words, Max squinted into

the darkness along the deck, attempting to single out
bodies that didn't belong, anyone who seemed out of
place. It was impossible to recognize faces from his
other crossing, save for a magnificently tall and leanly
muscled man with skin the shade of wild honey and
eyes the color of sand that stared straight back at him.
Max acknowledged him with a ragtag salute, and the
man nodded in return, then both looked away.

Friend? Foe? Interested bystander? The man would
bear watching.

Other than the crew, he then counted the other men
clinging to the ropes, hired from the docks to assist in
the off-loading of the contraband once they reached the
shoreline. Expendable bodies, like his, and Anton's,
hired to do a job of work, or drown in the process.

Except there were too many of them.

There were more than a dozen Frenchmen, four quiet
men dressed as Dutchmen. A trio of Spaniards who
could be dockside lingerers or hired mercenaries, but
currently fully occupied with their rosaries. A short,
fairly rotund fellow engulfed head-to-foot in a worse
cloak than Max's own and currently hanging over the
railing next to Anton, apparently feeding the fish with
whatever he'd had for supper.

Lastly, his gaze alit on a slim figure wrapped all in
black: black leather trousers, black tunic, overly large
black hooded cloak, black gloves, black boots, black
muffler covering all but a pair of narrowly slitted eyes.

Not one of the crew. Definitely not hired to wade
through the choppy waters to the beach, a brace of kegs

tied over his shoulders. Which meant one thing… Max was looking at another part of the cargo, most likely a spy.

And spies could be valuable.

He spent the next three hours making and discarding plans. He knew he wasn't returning to Gravelines; that had never been part of his plan. But now, on top of successfully stealing away from the shore on his own, he would have to lug an unwilling companion along with him.

There was no other possible conclusion: he had to enlist Anton's help once they reached their destination.

He reminded himself yet again that he trusted Boucher. As much as he trusted any man. Or woman.

Which, Max acknowledged silently, wasn't much. For instance, he still didn't quite understand why Anton, such a sorry sailor, would insist upon escorting him to England in this storm when he could have vouched for him to get him on board, and then waved his farewell from the dock. That didn't quite make sense.

The Frenchman hadn't led him astray yet; his information had all been spot-on. But loyalties could change, especially if money was involved, just as easily as the direction of the wind now blowing toward England, at last leaving the storm behind them. Trust was at a premium in these tumultuous times. It was all too easy to end up betrayed and dead. Both Anton and Max knew that. *But we don't speak of such things. The past is the past, and the guilty one punished does not bring back the dead....*

"Open the shutter, boy," the captain suddenly commanded. "Once, then again, and watch for the all clear from shore. Ah, there it is! Lower the longboats, and be quick about it."

It was time. His decision made, Max scrambled to his feet with the others, and headed for Anton, who was still standing at the rail.

"We part ways now, yes?" Anton whispered close beside Max's ear, his breath foul, so that Max covered his own mouth and nose. "Me to follow our return cargo once it lands, and you to chase after those who remain on the shore. Don't attempt to sneak away empty-handed. I think it best you heft a brace of kegs, like the others. The longboats are down. Here, let me help hoist a yoke onto your shoulders."

Max nodded, remaining where he was, his forearms on the rail, leaning forward, straining to see the shore as Anton went to retrieve the yoke and kegs. Then Max would tell him about the possible spy.

He never got the chance.

"Anton! Another smuggler's lantern, signaling onshore. Could be unwelcome company portside," he said, turning toward the man, so that the belaying pin that came down on his head only grazed his skull rather than rendering him totally unconscious.

All he would ever remember after that was a hard body barreling into him with force sufficient to knock his breath from him, and helplessly falling through the air, heading for the dark water that was suddenly lit by the flash of a cannon broadside that seemed to have come out of nowhere to crash through the rigging of the sloop.

"RELEASE ME, YOU FOOL, I'm all right. *Let me go!*"

Zoé Charbonneau's words were closely followed by a kick that landed in the most tender spot of her unnecessary rescuer's pudgy anatomy. He seemed to go unconscious with the pain. Her arm was freed at once and she was up and running, stumbling, only to fall to her knees on the sharp shingle beside Maximillien Redgrave.

Max. Her Max. But not any longer.

She spared only a moment to look into his well-remembered face, still misbelieving what she was seeing even after staring at him for hours, before she pushed him over onto his belly with all her might, and then straddled him.

"Breathe, damn you," she commanded, bracing her arms against him, slamming the sides of her fists into his back over and over again. "Don't you dare die again!"

"Like this, *mademoiselle,*" came an unfamiliar voice from behind her.

Zoé felt herself being picked up and tossed aside like so much flotsam and looked up to see the towering Arabic man from the smuggler's sloop. "No, don't, I have to—"

"Many apologies. I am called Tariq, and promise you

I am harmless. If you would please to turn his head to one side? His nose in the sand aids nothing."

She did as instructed, and saw Tariq pushing on Max's back with twice the strength she had been able to muster.

"Is he past saving?" she asked, her voice maddeningly tremulous, her hands clasped tightly together at her chest so that she wouldn't give in to the urge to push his sodden hair back from his face.

"Only a fool would leave a young lady so eager to keep him here," the man said, grinning, showing off a splendid set of strong white teeth. "Is your man a fool?"

Zoé shook her head, ordering herself to be calm. Hysteria aided nothing; she'd learned that long ago. Even if she were dying inside, she had trained herself to remain outwardly calm, even detached. Perhaps she'd succeeded too well, especially in these last months, and was no longer capable of feeling even what she should. But, then, how else to survive in this treacherous world she'd chosen to live in? "No, just stubborn."

"Then he'll live. Stubborn is good."

As if to prove the man's point, Max began to cough and choke, and then rise on his elbows and knees to begin vomiting up half the Channel.

Zoé immediately scrambled backward, away from him, then stood up to assess her surroundings. It would be disastrous for Max to see her, even as it would kill her to walk away.

"Take care of him please, Tariq, and then trust him to take care of you. But you never saw me, did you?"

Max's savior winked at her. "The pale-haired angel in the devil's clothes? Who would believe me?"

"*Shukran,* Tariq. Thank you," she responded, dredging up some of her limited Arabic.

"*Alla ysallmak,* miss, may God keep you safe."

"Until I get my bearings, He'll have to, won't He?"

There was light enough to see where she was, thanks to the bright flames shooting up from the sails of the smuggling craft, its hull slowly listing to port as a dozen or more grappling hooks thrown from a nearby ship attempted to heave it to starboard, intent on keeping it afloat until it could be dragged closer to shore.

There was yelling somewhere in the distance, pistol fire and the sound of clashing swords, but no one else was visible besides Max, Tariq and the still-unconscious stranger. Just the beach, some abandoned-looking cottages with a steep hill and darkness behind them. An impressively high, clearly impassable rock jetty jutted out into the water to her left; another grassy hill rose to her right, beyond which she could see a distant outcropping of land, dim lights telling her it was clearly home to some sort of town. Anyone attempting escape from the beach would surely head toward the lights, and most certainly be easily captured.

Which was why she knew she had one way to go: up.

Climbing. Like all trapped, desperate animals.

No, she wouldn't think about that.

With one more assessing look toward Max, barely resisting the urge to touch him just one last time, she headed for what was possibly a path that would lead her up the faintly visible hillside behind the cottages. He could take care of himself, the man who called himself Tariq could assist him, and if Boucher still breathed, he also would have no other choice but to navigate the steep hillside in order to escape in the current chaos.

Unless he was responsible for it. No, no, that was impossible. Anton would never willingly put himself in a position of danger by ordering someone to fire on a ship while he was still aboard.

For her own safety and now Max's, as well, she had to presume Anton'd survived the attack. More, she had to *know*.

It had taken her many weeks to ferret the Frenchman out, only to almost lose him earlier on the docks. If she lost track of him now, it might be years before she could locate him again, now that he was in England. Even worse if he had seen her; then he'd be the one in pursuit. Her entire future lay in finding him first. Only with him dead could she walk away, hope to begin her life anew.

Or so she'd thought when she'd first boarded the smuggling vessel.

But Max was alive. Against all information, against all hope, Max was alive. Even disguised, she'd always known him; how he walked, the tilt of his head.

This changed everything.

Her own head felt ready to explode with questions.

She'd taken no more than a few steps before a grip very like iron closed around her arm and she was whirled about, going chest to chest with her unwanted rescuer, who apparently had more recovery power than she'd given him credit for. Again, she aimed a knee toward his crotch, but what had succeeded the first time was neatly countered this time.

"Now, lass, where do you thinking you'd be heading in such a hurry?" the older man said, twisting her arm about to bring it up behind her. "Seems to me, tossing away your cloak and leaping in after the lad and me like you did? Smacks of concern, I'd say."

"Someone was firing on us. I was saving myself, you fool. He means nothing to me."

"Of course you were. Of course he doesn't. He means nothing to either of us."

Zoé stopped struggling, knowing she didn't have the power needed to escape this grinning old man. She hadn't slept in days, couldn't remember the last time she'd eaten. She'd expended nearly all of her energy making her way to shore; she simply had nothing left to fight with. She'd have to outthink him while formulating a better plan. There was always the knife in her boot, if she could only reach it, but she'd never killed for no reason, not if her wits could save her. "After you pushed him overboard, I would imagine he means *something* to you."

"Ah, but only after one of those Frenchies nearly put him to sleep with that belaying pin, and just before the cannon shot whistled through the rigging. There's all that to consider, don't you think? So much going on. Now, let's go see the lad, shall we?"

Zoé felt panic rising in her throat even as her knees,

already wobbly, turned to mush. "I'll pay you to let me go. Pay you well, in English coin."

"And there's a pity for you and a blessing for me, as I once would have welcomed the coin but no longer need it. Tell me now, miss, before you run off—do you know where you are, where you're heading? I'd want to know that before I traveled too far. Let me enlighten you. Behind you, the Channel, so not really a choice at all. To your left, to your right, and for as far as you can see ahead of you and leagues beyond that, is Redgrave land. All of it, more than you could imagine. And with every man-jack on it loyal to the Redgraves. Exhausted, forced to travel on foot, and with only that fetching but rather singular rig-out? Still so anxious to be off?"

"Mon dieu." Zoé's entire body sagged at this devastating news. But she shouldn't have been surprised, just as she shouldn't have been so quick to believe him dead. It was inevitable. One way or another, Max Redgrave always won.

"He'll more than likely turn me over to be hanged now that we're on this side of the Channel," she said quietly as she looked Max's way, to see him now only as a shadow sitting on the beach, his forearms resting on his bent knees, still unaware of her presence. "And it will be on your head."

"Truly? A gentleman like Max? You must have been a very naughty girl."

"I'm certain he believes as much. Please, if you have any compassion…"

"Fresh out, I'm afraid. But a bit of advice, young

lady. Never whimper. Men loathe whimpering. Face him head-on."

"Something to consider, I suppose." She continued to watch as Max, with Tariq's help, staggered to his feet, one hand held to the side of his head. Zoé wanted to turn away, not see the hate and hurt in his eyes when he at last recognized her, but she forced herself to raise her chin while praying neither that chin nor her voice would wobble. "Maximillien, my congratulations," she dared as he drew nearer. "I thought never to see you again, but you seem to have more lives than a litter of cats."

He halted where he was, still supported by Tariq. He looked at her for a long time, taking in her bedraggled mane of blond, seawater-stiff hair, her sodden clothing clinging tightly to her body, before holding his cold dark gaze with her own soft brown one. His answer came in a maddening drawl of disinterest. "My, my, will wonders never cease. It's been months."

"Has it?" she returned coolly, as if she hadn't counted the days. There was such a hardness in his eyes as he looked at her, which was no real surprise. She felt naked standing in front of him, vulnerable, which was an unwelcome realization. Some fires clearly didn't die, no matter how many tears you'd shed over them.

He merely shrugged, as if her words were of no matter to him. Down, but never out—that was Max. "I was told you were in prison."

Anger, quick and hot, betrayed her. "I was told you were dead. But you'd simply walked away. As if we never existed, you and me, together."

"But there never was a you and me, was there? No, don't bother to lie. On to more important matters, if you please. It was you on the ship. That business of bad pennies and all of that. I should have known," he said, pulling himself more upright, showing he could stand on his own two feet even if he fainted in the process, the idiot. Brave, strong, stubborn...but not always smart.

"You should have known a lot of things." *No, no. I have to stop, now. To say anything else would only make things worse. I can't let the shock of seeing him trick me into showing him he still has the power to hurt me.* "But, yes, let's move on."

"I suppose I have you to thank for this blasted bump on my head."

"Yes, of course. I already proved I'm the embodiment of all things evil."

"I believe the lady considers herself insulted, and has good reason," the man who still held tight to her arm interrupted. "It's one of the frogs you have to thank for the bump. Oh, and I'm the one who pushed you over the rail, so you can thank me for that."

"Richard?" Max leaned forward, squinting in the dying light from the burning rigging, clearly seeing the other man for the first time. "How...?"

"How else could I boost you out the back door more efficiently than by so clumsily coming in through the front door dressed in all my now thoroughly ruined finery? You may be quicker than this harmless old fat man, but I've been around longer than you, and know more tricks. You should look behind you more often, although I admit the rain was more a boon to me than it was to you. In any event, welcome home. This young lady you've been glaring daggers at thinks you're going to have her hanged. Is that right?"

They were speaking of her as if she weren't there, listening to every word. Max looked like hell, maybe worse than hell, but was still the most handsome, compelling man she'd ever met. Her last and best lover. The man who'd held her in his arms and told her about Redgrave Manor and his own estate, about his family and how they would welcome her. The children they would have together. She'd loved him so much. She'd fallen into jagged, devastated bits on the floor of her cell when told he was dead.

"I hadn't considered the matter, but, yes, she deserves at least that. Don't you, Zoé? But the ladies might not approve. Perhaps we'll put it to a vote tomorrow, over tea and cakes. Are they here, Richard, or scattered all over London and the countryside?"

"Every last one of them here, yes. As you've probably gathered, I was sent to fetch you, which wasn't particularly easy. It took me two trips across the Channel to find you, as you were no longer in Ostend when I got there, and when I returned to London for more information it was to find out there'd been an attempt on— No, that can wait. What's of first importance is that the Society is all but figuratively knocking on the Manor gates and ready to smash them down. There's trouble, lad, deadly serious trouble, and you're just what Trixie thinks is needed. I didn't know our destination tonight when I invited myself onboard, but sometimes a man gets lucky, doesn't he?"

Max looked again at Zoé, who couldn't help but flinch under that intense gaze. "Does he?" Then he raised his head as if sniffing the air to locate the noise that still came to them on the breeze. "What in bloody hell is going on, Richard? There aren't really pirates, are there? Somehow the family already knew about the smuggling runs? They would have saved me a mountain of trouble if someone had bothered to get a message to me."

"If you'll excuse me for pointing this out, I *am* the message."

Zoé hadn't been paying much heed to the noise still coming to them across the dark distance, or to anything but her own perilous position, and how every second that passed was taking Anton further from her reach. But Max had her attention now.

"There's even more to this beyond a smuggling run? I should have known, with Anton aboard," she said.

Max looked at her rather curiously, as if she'd just spoken in Greek or some such thing. "Richard, since the women are here, may I assume my brothers are the cause of that commotion we're hearing?"

"Currently occupied on the far side of that impressive pile of rocks, yes, by now undoubtedly just finishing up their business. Oh, and there may be a few, um, gentlemen of the skull and crossbones persuasion in attendance at the party, as well, but we don't ask questions, as it concerns a private arrangement between the marquis and his secretive friend."

Max lifted a hand to his head once more and then took it away, looking curiously at the dark wet stain on his palm. "We'll leave that for now, whatever in holy hell that meant, or who this marquis is. Tariq, what do you say we all make our way up the path. From there, we can look down on the beach on the other side of the jetty. It's safest you remain with me, and I wouldn't be averse to a helping hand."

"No need for climbing," Richard told him. "Follow me."

Zoé didn't resist as Richard let go of her arm and took hold of her hand instead as he walked her toward the jetty, grateful for his assistance over the slippery mix of sand and shingle as she attempted yet again to marshal her thoughts. Max was in some sort of trouble? His beloved family was in some sort of trouble? If he wasn't going to immediately turn her over to the authorities in Dover to be measured for her hanging chains, perhaps she could convince him to let her help, prove she could be trusted.

No. Thanks to Anton, it was too late for that.

"Give me a minute, if you please. It's here somewhere," Richard said, letting go of Zoé as he used his fingertips to probe at the edges of the solid rock wall now in front of them while Tariq took hold of her shoulders, anchoring her gently but firmly where she stood. "There's one on either side. I don't know how he discovered them, but I watched carefully as Simon showed me. Perhaps it's too dark to— Ah, there's the handholds."

He stepped back as Zoé heard the scrape of rock against rock and a section of the stone in front of her somehow turned into a door that swung open as the man called Richard held out one arm in a flourish and took a bow. "Metal hinges replacing brittle, ancient leather, and liberally greased. Repeated at the other end. Amazing, isn't it, considering it's probably old as Caesar's war horse."

"A passageway through the rocks? I'll be damned," Max said from behind her. "I've fished from these beaches all of my life…. Where does it lead?"

"There's only one way to find out," Zoé said, taking the initiative, pushing her fear of dark places behind her determination to save herself. After all, what did she have to lose? And once Max was surrounded by his family, she might find a way to gain a pistol and make her escape. She hadn't precisely given her word she wouldn't try.

As Tariq released his grip and she stepped through the narrow opening, she deftly gathered up her mane of betraying blond hair and twisted it into a knot, then slipped a black toque out of her trouser pocket and covered her head with it. There was a small torch burning against the wall to her right as she moved forward in what must be a cave hollowed out of the mass of jumbled rocks by the tides. The cave seemed to be heading uphill. If she just kept her head, became as inconspicuous as possible, and then slowly melted away from the others and back into the tunnel…

"Ah, I think not, Zoé," Max growled, grabbing her arm. "For some strange reason, I'd prefer you alive for the moment, and the best way to accomplish that is for you to let me go first."

"Perhaps I want to die, because you hate me so," she said, shrugging her shoulders in a purely Gallic gesture she already knew would bounce off him like a dried pea dropped on a drumhead. She needed to keep him more angry than interested.

"While you love me so," he bit out, proving her point, and then rudely shoved her behind him while Richard and Tariq forged ahead.

"You don't know the meaning of love. And neither did I. Young and reckless, the pair of us, believing ourselves invincible. But no longer. Have you ever been in a Paris cell, Max? Have you ever been so cold and hungry you'd do most anything for a blanket and a crust of stale bread? Most *anything*."

Max very nearly winced, but he'd never so betray himself, she knew that. "You knew what you were doing. That things didn't work out the way you'd planned isn't any concern of mine."

"How very *English* of you."

"Now's not the time or place for this conversation."

"Yet I'll dare one thing more. Until I stepped on that blasted boat and saw you, I believed you dead."

Now he was forced to look at her. "Boucher? You were following Anton? Why?"

She'd said enough to, hopefully, make him suspicious. Keep him alive. "That's a question you might want to ask him, while you let me be on my way, which would probably bother your conscience less than turning me over to the Crown. Now, as it would seem whatever battle was raging is over, it's time your family gets to welcome the prodigal home. Do you think they'll all be there? Gideon, Valentine and perhaps even your darling, daring Kate? Yes, I remember all their names. How delighted they will be. Or are we to stay here in this strange damp passageway until we all drown?"

Max looked down at his booted feet and the seawater sloshing around his ankles. "Damn. Tide's coming in. The whole other side of the beach will be underwater in an hour. Let's go."

"Brilliant suggestion. Do you perhaps have a white handkerchief hidden in that mass of rags you're wearing? It would be highly embarrassing, wouldn't it, if one of your own brothers mistook you for the enemy and shot you."

"That won't happen." As if to prove his point, Max took a few more steps, and then put two fingers to his mouth and whistled. The sound seemed to bounce off the stone walls.

The same melancholy birdsong of a whistle he'd taught her, the one the two of them had employed many times in the past. She instantly remembered the lessons in whistling, and the kisses they'd shared as he showed her how to pucker her lips *just so*.

Maybe she did want to die. Seeing him again, knowing what she'd gambled and lost, was so bloody hard.

There was a short silence, and then an answering whistle, closely followed by a shout. "Max? Max, you son of a hound! Where are you? Everyone—weapons down. My brother's out here somewhere, damn him!"

"That's big brother Gideon. This could prove interesting. He'll either hug me or knock me down. Perhaps both. Richard, Tariq—you two watch her if you please, until I call the all clear. She's rather anxious to leave us," Max warned before running a hand through his wet, unkempt hair, and then sloshing off downhill against the rising tide, toward the end of the tunnel.

"Forgive me for overhearing, but it was rather impossible not to catch at least a few words. Echos, you understand. More than a lovers' spat between the two of you, clearly," Richard said, stepping forward to pull Zoé's arm through his.

"Nonsense, sir, we're the best of good chums, as you English say it," she responded dully.

Behind her, Tariq chuckled softly.

"Much more than that at one time, I would think. I'm an observant man. Part of him wanted to throttle you, while part of him wanted to pull you close to his heart and cover your face with kisses, if I might be so romantical. Men can be difficult, especially where their hearts are involved."

"His head is the problem. It's very hard. A pig's head."

"I think you mean he's pigheaded, stubborn. But you

love him. You nearly maimed me to get to him when you though he'd drowned, remember?"

"We should all forget that. It was but an aberration. My mind was temporarily muddled at the shock of seeing him again."

"I won't argue with you. Tell me, did he ever mention Trixie to you?"

Zoé turned to peer at the man inquisitively. She'd yet to attempt to place this Richard person with Max, let alone with the rest of the Redgraves. She could easily have looked at him and dismissed him; just another pudgy white-haired old man. Except for his physical strength. Except for his quick, incisive mind. That second look made it easier for her to believe this man had survived on his wits more than once. "His grandmother? Yes, he did. Several times. To hear him tell it, she's quite extraordinary."

"She's considerably more than simply extraordinary. I do believe the two of you should have a small talk. In fact, I'm quite certain she'll demand it."

"Why?"

"Because even on such short acquaintance, I dare to say you two may be very much alike. Just don't lie to her, because she'll know."

"I may be an exemplary liar," Zoé said, one ear open to the sounds from beyond the cave, but hearing nothing more than muffled voices.

"The ability to lie convincingly is only a minor talent. Eleanor of Aquitaine could have taken lessons in family intrigue from the dowager countess. You'd have to live another forty years for even the hope of being a patch on Trixie Redgrave, young lady. Only remember this, as the dowager countess goes, so go the Redgraves."

She turned back to face the man, studying his features in the flickering light from the small torch. "Why are you telling me this? For all you know, I could use such information against Max, against all of you."

"I'm not quite certain why. Perhaps it was the way you reached out your hand as if to touch him and then turned away before he might see you. Or it might have been the tears in your eyes that blinded you to my approach. You've both been quite interesting to watch these past minutes. When you stand at a distance, see only the gestures, without hearing the words? Sometimes, young lady, that's when the heart hears more clearly than the ears ever will."

Zoé looked at Richard levelly. "Your heart and eyes deceive you, sir. Max has no heart, and neither do I. We're cold, fairly terrible people, intent only on survival."

"And the game," Richard added, raising one eyebrow. "I lived by my wits at the card tables for the majority of my life, young lady, traveling all of England and the Continent. Always in search of the next adventure. To win, yes, winning is always important, as one can become accustomed to regular meals and a dry bed. But it isn't paramount for people like us. We're different from most of the world, aren't we? For people like us, it's the thrill of the hunt, the chances you take. The risks that make your blood pump hot in your veins, always skating on the thin ice of detection and even death—and *feeding* off that danger. *That's* what I see in you, in Max. Together, you must have been pure beauty to watch in action."

A hundred memories came crashing unbidden into Zoé's mind. "Yes, we were both quite good at what we did. Thank you, Richard, for reminding me," she said simply before heading toward the end of the tunnel, eager to get out from beneath the crushing confinement of the boulders overhead. "I'd say it's time to go meet the family."

CHAPTER TWO

MAX LAY BACK in his bath, his injured head propped against a thick, soft length of toweling. He'd vowed never to see her again, never ask about her, never think about her. He'd willed his heart and mind to forget her.

And then, there she was. Here she is. Under his brother's roof and his grandmother's at least temporary protection thanks to Richard Borders, and disturbingly back in his life. Clearly not forgotten.

Zoé. Blonde, beautiful, courageous, passionate, daring, clever. Lying, cold-hearted, devious, deadly Zoé Charbonneau.

From the beginning they'd been inseparable, paired together by the Crown and sent off to the Continent. First as wary partners, then as friends, then as lovers; they'd variously played the parts of siblings, husband and wife, priest and holy sister.

They'd even been so daring as to attend one of Bonaparte's luxurious fetes as minor Flemish royalty, Max standing guard outside Boney's private office after midnight while Zoé rifled through the drawers of his desk. She'd committed two dispatches from his field marshals to memory and then pocketed a small crystal paperweight bearing a gold eagle, just so the man would know someone had breeched his supposed impenetrable security—yet have no idea *what* information had been compromised.

Max's contribution, a week later, had been to wrap up the paperweight and post it back to Paris, even as Zoé scolded him that such an action might be considered rubbing salt into an open wound.

And then she'd laughed, and he'd laughed, and they'd made love in the hayloft of a barn just outside Marseilles.

They'd been so good together. In every way.

They'd come together in passion in more than a dozen countries, sometimes in rainy meadows, sometimes on silken sheets, at times in leisure and other times in haste, to rejoice, or to conquer unspoken fear after near disaster.

They were two. They were one. They thought alike, anticipated each other's every move, guarded each other's back.

How many times had Max begged her to give up the game and allow him to take her to Redgrave Manor? Where she'd be safe, where he would visit her when he could, where he wouldn't have to worry about her.

And how many times had she told him no, she couldn't live not knowing where he was, the dangers he faced. They'd begun together and they would finish together, only when Bonaparte accepted true terms of truce, and proved his word. Until then, with war formally declared or not, they would live out their oath to the king.

Besides, if they'd only admit it, they were having themselves the adventure of a lifetime. Existing on the edge of danger and heart-pounding tension, loving freely and fiercely, relishing each new challenge, each victory, applauding each other for their combined brilliance. Were any other two people ever so *alive?*

Was any one fool ever so badly hoodwinked and betrayed?

"Dozing, or fading into unconsciousness again?"

Max opened his eyes, grateful to be rescued from his thoughts. "Gideon," he said flatly. "If you're referring to that moment climbing the hill to the horses, I did *not* swoon. I stumbled."

"And quite gracefully at that. In either event, it's a good thing your new friend was behind you. You'll have to tell me more about him."

"I'll do that, just as soon as I know more than that I woke on the beach with him looming over me with that extraordinary grin of his, as if I'd just mightily delighted him. Now, can I safely assume you're it as far as unwanted company tonight, or is Trixie close on your heels?"

"She's otherwise occupied, welcoming home her new husband," Gideon said as he shifted Max's clothing from chair to floor and sat down. "You've missed a lot, Max, but you can hear it all tomorrow, after Jessica and I have departed for London."

"You have a meeting with Perceval?"

"No, not this time. In fact, we're rather avoiding each other, the prime minster and I. He nearly had Valentine clapped in irons, a sentiment I've shared more than once, but that also is another story, and I won't deny our youngest brother the delight I'm sure he'll bathe in as he tells it. Only then should you allow Kate to corner you and tell you all about how wonderful love with her marquis is, which can be damned embarrassing when we're more used to her challenging us to races."

"Kate and Simon Ravenhill. Kate with *anybody* for that matter. It will be a while until I get used to that, although Val being conked on the head by Cupid's shovel, as he explained the thing to me, probably is the news that really bears off the palm. I'm on the Continent, risking my life, and all anyone here has been doing is billing and cooing."

"You underestimate your siblings. I'd say we've been doing a trifle more than that since last you and I spoke. As have you."

Gideon's tone told Max that, athough there would be questions to come concerning how and why he'd been on the smuggling craft, he and Zoé would be the only topic of discussion tonight. "Just ask your questions and then leave me to my misery. My head's pounding as it is."

"And you look like hell, there's also that."

"While you're always impeccable," Max said, "even when running about on a moonlit beach like some revenue officer, rounding up smugglers."

"I don't know about that, but I do manage to shave."

"I shave," Max protested, rubbing his face. *Zoé used to shave him. He'd actually trusted her with a straight razor.*

"If you say so, although I'd be interested in hearing how you do that, and yet always look as if you haven't. Although I will admit you look less the too-pretty young Greek god with half your face fuzzy. Is that your hope?"

"I won't deny that. But as I said, I do shave. Every three or four days."

"Such a pity I've yet to be in your company on any of those glorious days."

"Are you finished now? Or is this leading us somewhere?"

"No," Gideon said, tugging lightly at his shirt cuffs. "I'd just realized we hadn't yet welcomed you home in our usual loving, brotherly way." He smiled at his brother. "Welcome home, Max."

His older brother bore the closest resemblance to their Spanish mother. Dark, smoldering, his bearing both aristocratic and intimidating. Max had visited the bullring while in Spain, and had no trouble visualizing Gideon dressed all in gold and black, standing with his long legs tightly together, his spine bent gracefully back as he swirled the red-lined cape daringly, encouraging the bull to charge. With Gideon, however, it was the *ton* he dared, the *ton* he ruled, seemingly with no effort on his part. If Max had a hero when he was growing up, it had been Gideon.

Now he wished he'd just go away. But he'd really

like to hear more about Richard Borders, the man Max knew only as a friend of Jessica, Gideon's recent bride.

"Before you launch your inquisition—tell me about Richard Borders and Trixie. That's going to take some getting used to, as well, you know. I thought she hated men...on general principles, I mean, which had nothing to do with bedding every last man in England." Max had already stepped out of the tub and wrapped the toweling sheet around his waist. "Here, give me those," he said, motioning toward the clothes on the floor. "They may be two years away from the latest style, but that doesn't mean they deserve such shabby treatment."

"Four years, at the least. It's been a long time since you've graced Redgrave Manor with your presence." Gideon handed over the clothes. "Oh, and not every last man. Only those she thought useful, trainable, biddable, and—is this a word? Blackmailable?"

"Probably more of a description." Having drawn on a pair of tan breeches, Max shoved his damp arms into a white shirt with flowing sleeves, the unturned cuffs sliding down to his fingertips, the shirttails hanging. He didn't bother to close more than a few of the buttons before adding a red and black paisley waistcoat, also left open.

"Always the epitome of style and precise grooming. It still amazes me why women are so drawn to you," Gideon said, shaking his head. "All that's missing, other than hose and shoes—and underdrawers— are those damn blue-lens spectacles you were wearing last I saw you in London. For which, may I say, you have my enormous gratitude. The scruffy facial hair is more than sufficient."

"Don't be too grateful. They're around here somewhere, not cracked or even slightly bent. What do you want to know, Gideon? I've still got business tonight."

"Yes, and that's why I'm here. I've never before had a guest—allow me to clarify that, a *female* guest at the Manor locked up for the night. And we haven't even been formally introduced."

"You make it sound as if we keep a dungeon." Max grabbed up his brushes and began working his way through his damp, faintly shaggy black hair that fell from a slight center part to below his ears, swearing under his breath as one of the brushes hit the now barely scabbed-over bump on the side of his head. "I told you her name. Zoé. Zoé Charbonneau."

He then headed for his bedchamber, knowing Gideon would follow him, which he did.

Gideon turned around a straight chair and straddled it as Max looked toward the door to the hallway. His brother was demonstrating how this was all just a friendly chat. That was one way of seeing the thing. But what the move really meant was *sit down, Max, because you're going nowhere until I know all I want to know. Sit down, now.* "Lovely name. French, although her English is perfect, not that you allowed for more than three words before having her sent off to the Manor. But that does nothing but spur more questions."

Max sat down. "She's just as proficient in Spanish, Italian, German—harsh language except when she speaks it—and with enough Russian and several other languages to get us by."

"*Us*. Impressive young lady. You never managed more than French, and when you speak it I'm afraid that melodious language turns *harsh*. So I take it from the little you've said thus far that you two once worked together on the Continent. And now you don't. Interesting."

"It was a long time ago."

"How long?

"Damn, you're like a terrier after a bone. I last saw her eight or nine months ago, all right, long before I last visited you in London. And since you aren't going to give up until I tell you more, allow me to get through this as quickly as possible. It's imperative I see her yet tonight."

"I don't know if that's wise. She's under my roof now."

"God's teeth but the Earl of Saltwood loves to give orders. If it eases your lordship's mind, I swear on Trixie's painted toenails I won't harm her, but I doubt Zoé believes that. She's probably already fashioning a rope out of the bed sheets and sharpening a letter opener into a knife she can then strap to her thigh with a bit of curtain cord. Unless nobody thought to relieve her of the sticker she carries in her boot. Perhaps she's managed to remove one of the bedposts and plans to use it as a jousting lance aimed at the first person to dare entering her room."

"Now you're exaggerating."

"Yes, of course. I'm exaggerating, but only that last bit about the bedpost," Max said, his tone more than a tad sarcastic. "All right, let's do this, as Trixie would just ferret it all out of me in any case. Zoé was born in France, where her father was fairly wealthy, thanks to the reputation of the knives, swords and other blades produced in his foundries. Many of the royal family and peers were his loyal clients. During the Revolution his foundries were taken over, and her family escaped to Austria. He had managed to take some money with him, but not enough to establish another foundry, so he played himself off as a *comte* until their luck ran out or, since he took power, Bonaparte's army could be seen on the horizon, and they were off again. Finally, he and Zoé—the mother had died somewhere along the way—ended up here in England."

"That explains her ability with languages, if not her father's insistence on being tied to the French noble class."

"They existed on that lie, Gideon. Lies and sympathy and quiet loans to the dear *comte* who would repay them threefold when the Bourbons were back on the throne. You know how mad our society matrons are for *émigrés*. He was invited to social events, even week-long parties in some of the best country houses—Zoé always invited along to be with the other children in attendance. When particularly pressed for funds, a few jewels found their way into the man's pocket after some of those parties, sometimes with her help."

"Wonderful. I've installed a thief in my household."

"Not the least of her talents. At any rate, the ploy worked well enough until another *émigré* recognized him for who he was. He then fixed his mind on returning to France and retaking possession of his various business enterprises. In order to do that, the French royalty had to be reinstalled on the throne. Zoé decided to help him by volunteering to work for the Crown."

"A woman? And so young? That's insane."

Max crossed one long leg over his knee. "Yes, thank you. I totally agree. Except for one thing—she's damn good at what she does, especially with languages, which was how she managed to be taken on in the first place. But they soon knew the treasure they had. She'd already been active for over a year before I was paired with her, very much against my wishes I might add, as I was considered to be the student, and her the mentor."

"I can see the reasoning, however," Gideon interrupted. "A man and woman, traveling together, don't raise as much suspicion as a man, or men, traveling together."

Max nodded his agreement. "She's a piece of work, brother, and raised to the blade, I suppose you'd say. Fences, shoots better than most men, the way she handles a knife should make any prudent man nervous and she's killed more than once when the situation called for violence. She can play the lady with the best of them, probably ten times better than Kate, but she's solid steel beneath that fetching exterior. Cold, hard steel. And she's deadly smart."

"With all these unique, commendable charms to

lure you, there was no question you'd become lovers," Gideon said flatly, ignoring the rest.

"Good on you, as Valentine would say. Yes, we became lovers. Together day and night. She's beautiful, I'm a man. We were in a dangerous business, never knowing if we'd live another day. It was inevitable." Max took a deep breath. "And then she decided working with the French was more profitable than a pittance from the Crown and the chance to save the world, one might say."

Gideon frowned. "Let me make an assumption here. The father died."

"Even with the return of the monarchy, Zoé could never lay claim to her father's possessions and property, not as a female. Did I mention she's also practical?"

"You knew about the father's death?"

Max avoided his brother's gaze, instead watching his own movements as he turned back his unbuttoned cuffs. That had always bothered him, that she hadn't told him. Damn, he could do with a drink. "Only afterwards."

"After what, Max?" Gideon asked quietly.

"After three agents she betrayed had been lined up outside the cottage where we'd occasionally rendezvous, trussed up like animals bound for market and shot in the head. Two Englishmen, the third French. All good men. I could have been lying there with them, but I'd spent the night meeting with a courier bound for London after gathering information from the other agents I'd summoned to the cottage, and didn't return until the next morning to find— I told you what I found."

"You won't mind if I say I prefer you alive."

"Thank you. Before you ask, yes, Zoé had been at the cottage when I left, but she was gone. The only one still alive was another late arrival, Anton Boucher, one of our French agents. He handed me the letter Zoé left behind."

"Not surprising. Women always feel this overweening need to *explain,* especially when their hearts are involved," Gideon said, nodding. "What did she write?"

"What I've already told you. Her father was dead and she'd sold her talents to the French. She would be miles away before I returned in the morning, and it would please her if I didn't follow her, hoping to change her mind."

'Did she admit to killing the other agents?"

"She never mentioned them, but what better way to prove herself to the French than to turn over names and locations to them? Was she there when it happened, or already on her way to Paris? I don't know. But one way or another, those deaths are on her head. Oh, there was something else in her note about how, as much as she'd cared for me, the time had come for her to take care of herself, as being a country wife would never suit her."

"Cared for you? Jesus, that's cold. No wonder you've been such a bear these past months, so much so that Val supposed you'd sworn off women or some such thing. Quite a blow to your pride, amid everything else, being *cared for* by the woman you love. My sympathies, brother, on the whole of it."

"Again, thank you," Max said shortly, feeling his

cheeks go hot. "Look, I don't want to go over this and over this. Boucher and I buried the bodies to hide them before both of us raced off to warn our other agents for fear Zoé had exposed them, as well, traded names I may have inadvertently told her for whatever the French had promised her. I had no secrets from her—as you pointed out, I loved her. I trusted her with my life. And before you ask, of the two dozen or so agents we had in place, five more died before we could successfully locate and warn them."

"Eight agents suddenly out of the field. That must have been quite the blow to Perceval. And to you, of course."

"None of this is about me, Gideon, and clearly never was. As for Zoé, she'd miscalculated, badly. It would appear the French weren't about to trust her to be loyal to them any more than she had been to England, something she might have learned from England's own Benedict Arnold. The last I'd heard, she'd been locked up in some Paris prison. *Now* may I be excused, your lordship?"

"I don't think so, no," Gideon said. "You can be a bit of a hothead, Max, much as I love you, not to mention having more than your fair share of pride. Dead agents, spurned by your lover—hoodwinked by your lover? I can understand your reaction, but do you still feel the same way eight months later? How do you know she wasn't forced to write that letter? How do you know she wasn't betrayed by someone, as well, even this other supposed late arrival, this Boucher fellow?"

"You should pen novels. To be truthful, I'd been concerned about him for some time—we'd been having a few too many more failures than successes, I thought—although I had no real facts. Just my suspicions, which I'd included with my other intelligence sent off with the courier. He would have been the first I'd suspected, save for one thing, one indisputable fact."

"I'd be interested in hearing that one fact, if you could indulge me."

We'd laughed together, cried together... "Anton's nephew Georges was one of the executed agents. The boy was barely eighteen, his dead sister's only child and the apple of Anton's eye. That left only Zoé, for nobody else knew of our rendezvous spot. Nobody. Boucher didn't betray us. It was all on Zoé. The only reason I can think of that she's still alive is that people like us are commodities, often to be traded, exploited, which makes me doubly curious about how and why she was released."

"Or escaped." Gideon got to his feet, turning the chair around, placing it carefully. "You're in a dirty business, brother, and I can't say I'm pleased with the Max standing before me now. It may be time you left his majesty's service. It may have been time eight months ago."

Max bristled. "We were suddenly rather short on agents, and then you came to me about the Society and we decided it would be best if I worked the thread from the Continent."

"And God forbid you could have told me the truth, or

I never would have asked that of you." Gideon looked at him for long moments and then nodded his head almost imperceptibly. "Water already passed beneath the bridge, leaving us with that creature upstairs. I know you're full of questions, as I am myself. If she was offered her freedom in exchange for selling her talents to someone—well, let's just say it and have it out in the open, shall we? Is it too large a leap of conjecture to believe she's now found employment with the Society?"

Max didn't bother to deny he'd already wondered the same thing. "Very good, brother. I told you, she has talents, and who else would have her? She's burned her bridges with both us and the French, and treachery would seem to be her only salable talent."

Gideon pinched thumb and forefinger to the bridge of his nose. "So many questions present themselves. You'd spoken to her of Redgrave Manor, of course. She'd be at least loosely familiar with the estate?"

"As I'd waxed poetical about the place, and the family, innumerable times, you can assume so." And then, because things had already gone too far to keep secrets from his brother, he said, "I sailed tonight with the person who led me to Gravelines and the Society-hired smugglers."

Gideon looked at him, then frowned. "Allow me to hazard yet another guess. This Boucher person?"

With his hand now on the doorknob, Max turned and asked his brother, "One and the same, yes. So here we are again, the three of us. Do you believe in coincidences, Gideon, because I damned well don't, and I'm beginning to wonder if I'm the greatest fool in nature, hoodwinked by the pair of them. According to Richard, it was Anton who hit me with the belaying pin."

"Go on."

"Yes. Maybe that bump on my head loosened something brilliant, or maybe I'm delirious, but think about this a moment, Gideon. What if they'd been working together all along? What if I was only allowed to live because they knew our reaction would be to pull all of our agents from the Continent in order to protect them, taking us months to reestablish ourselves there, while more and more French troops were secretly marched to the Peninsula? What if there never was a French prison? It's possible. If it weren't for Georges…"

"More and more I'm learning the most impossible things are possible. It will be interesting to hear what your Monsieur Boucher has to say. Did you see him with the other prisoners before they were led away? We've got them all locked up in various outbuildings until we can sort them out in the morning."

"I don't know. He's with them, already dead, or if he believes me still alive and now suspicious of him, or saw Zoé on the beach, has escaped somehow. The answer will have to wait until morning. Right now I need to see Zoé, before I confront him. She said something earlier that— No, that's enough. You, Valentine, Simon and I can talk more tomorrow over breakfast, before you and Jessica leave for London. Since you sent Richard after me, I imagine something important has been learned."

"Bad news can always wait. No later than nine, if you

please. There's a lot you don't know, little of it good, all of it shocking."

Max was more than simply curious. "Does any of it concern the fact that in a house literally overrun with staff, I found myself having to light my own fire in the grate and bathe in only a few inches of tepid water?"

"Yes, it does. Max? We men make most of our mistakes with women. I know it's not in your nature...but if we're to learn anything more of the Society from this Zoé of yours, you might want to consider treading softly concerning the past."

"I suppose you think I should visit the conservatory and pluck a few posies for her, as well? Clearly marriage has softened your head. Let me handle this, Gideon. I know the woman, you don't."

"The way you knew her eight months ago? Or the way you *think* you knew her eight months ago? Love can make fools of us all."

Max opened his mouth to say something, realized he had nothing to say, yet had more questions than made him feel comfortable, so he let the door he slammed behind him speak for him.

CHAPTER THREE

SHE RECOGNIZED MAX'S distinctive footfalls, could picture him advancing beyond the patchwork of carpets scattered over the thick wood plank floor of her attic cell. There was a near arrogance in his walk, a confidence that had others instinctively stepping aside to give him room to pass.

She'd teasingly termed it his "I am *so* much more than you could ever aspire to be" walk, as opposed to his equally brilliant old-man's shuffle, his wounded-soldier limp, his prim and proper vicar's modest gait, his prancing nincompoop's mincing step or his drunk-as-a-lord laughable stagger.

He was adept at all of them, but what came most naturally to him was that sure-footed stride that said: I am Maximillien Redgrave; take heed, ignore me at your own peril.

And he was heading straight toward her.

Not that she hadn't left the mullioned window open, with the light muslin draperies blowing in the breeze.

"Zoé?"

She lay back against the fairly steeply-pitched slate roof, her bare feet firmly braced against one of the ornate iron cleats that lined the edge, and looked up at the moon as the clouds slowly rolled by, revealing its grinning face.

"Look, you've either jumped, which you'd never do, or you've escaped, which is next to impossible. Which leaves you hiding out there somewhere like a sulky child. Never your best look, by the way. In any event, I'm coming out. I'd appreciate it if you didn't attempt to push me over the edge."

She'd known he was her man, her equal, the first time she'd seen him walking toward her, his handsome face a thundercloud as he realized he'd been put under the command of a woman. But that anger hadn't lasted much more than a sennight before he ceased resisting their undeniable attraction for each other.

She wondered now, as she had then, if he could hear her heart pounding in her chest.

Now, as then, she believed he was about to offer a limited, reluctant truce. As she was currently out of options, she decided to agree with him.

"You always did talk too much," she said, turning her head to watch as Max gracefully eased his way over the sill of the dormer window, found purchase for one bare foot, and then maneuvered himself onto his back not three feet away from her.

"That's because you usually devised interesting ways of shutting me up, as I recall."

Only his tone warned that he wasn't being teasingly reminiscent.

"You have no fear of me believing seduction would

work on you, Max. Not anymore. What do you want? It's late, and I'm tired."

"I also wouldn't suggest falling asleep in your current precarious position. Think of the mess one of the servants might trip over in the morning."

This time he did sound genuinely amused. Zoé rolled her eyes. "I was about to go in when you barged out here to harass me."

His gaze met hers in the moonlight. "So this isn't some sort of attempt at escape?"

Don't look at me, don't look at me. You make me want so much more...

"But of course it is. I plan to crawl to the very tip of the roof in this borrowed dressing gown and then flap my arms as hard as I can and fly away. That blow to your hard skull must have done more damage than I thought. Just remember, if you become dizzy and fall to the courtyard below, I take no responsibility."

"Yes, the consequence would be on my own head, wouldn't it? Probably literally. Now tell me why you climbed out here."

She turned away from him, looking into the seemingly infinite distance of moonlight and shadows. "I dislike closed doors, especially locked doors. After months in a dank cell with little light and constantly foul air, simply standing at the window wasn't enough to keep me from—but that was never your problem, was it?"

"If I'd found you and dragged you back to London, you would have been hanged for the murder of English agents. I chose the lesser of two evils, and let you go."

"For you, Max. The lesser of two evils for *you*. Admit it, I made a fool of you in front of your superiors, your message to them concerning your worry that Anton might be working for the French, while all the time being hoodwinked by your French lover. You washed your hands of me."

"If it's any help, you were already gone, and I didn't really have time to think at all beyond getting our other agents out of harm's way."

She knew the answer to her next question before she asked it. "And then you came chasing hotfoot to Paris, looking for me."

With the moon full above them, she could see a faint flicker of pain cross his features. "My superiors—*our* superiors—moved all of the surviving agents out of France entirely. I was assigned to the Home Office for a month—"

"Your punishment."

"Yes, my punishment for all but indicting innocent, bereaved Anton as a traitor while allowing myself to be, as you so incisively said, hoodwinked by my lover, thus losing us eight good agents. Then I was reassigned to the Peninsula with Wellington. And then...and then something else demanded my attention. I did eventually hear that you weren't on the loose, but in prison."

"I see. In that case, no, your explanation means nothing to me."

He nodded. "Understood. Why were you released?"

How she wanted to tell the truth, about everything.

But it had been too late for that eight months ago. So she'd keep him concentrated on the present.

"There was an arrangement. Nothing that concerns you." She pushed herself up on her elbows. "I want to go back inside now. Kindly take yourself out of my way and spare me the indignity of having to crawl over you."

Max didn't move, except to turn on his side so he could face her. "Not yet. You traded names to show your new loyalty. You as good as murdered those men, Zoé. What else did you expect from me?"

Don't, Zoé. Don't feel sorry for him, or for yourself. You only did what you had to do. You wanted him to believe you, remember? But now it's over, with events moved long past any hope of salvaging what we'd once had, because what we'd once had clearly hadn't been enough. The truth will aid nothing, and perhaps make things even worse. Just let it go... Let him go the same way he let you go. He was never really *yours.*

"Nothing else. I expected exactly what you did. I even prayed for it, something I hadn't done in a long time."

"But now you're claiming innocence? That is what you're doing, isn't it, Zoé?"

Too late. Too late for questions, too late for answers.

"I'm claiming nothing. Why I'm here has nothing to do with you. As far as I knew, you died months ago. I told you that on the beach. As far as I'm concerned, you're a walking, talking ghost from the past. Now move out of my way. If I'm to plead my case to be allowed to leave, it will be with your grandmother. Richard tells me she has great good sense."

"And I don't. I suppose you're right, because I'll be damned if I can't still imagine you in my arms, your legs wrapped high about my back as we drive each other out of our minds. My superiors were right to punish me. I never thought I was the sort of fool who, against all common sense, could be led about by his—"

"Oh, Max, just shut up. Please, shut up."

Without another word, he at last turned away from her and carefully made his way back to the opened casement, neatly easing himself over the windowsill. She followed a moment later, the skirt of the dressing gown and the night rail beneath it carefully tucked about her body.

"Give me your hand."

"I can manage on my own," she shot back, but the slates were becoming slippery with dew, so she only issued the complaint before tucking her hand in his. His touch devastated her, and for the first time she could see herself losing her balance and sliding off the edge of the roof.

"Steady, woman." In a moment he had both her hands safely within his grip, and she was half lifted, half dragged over the windowsill, to end with her bare feet on the floor, the length of her body pressed up against Max's lean strength.

She could see his dark features in the light from the fire and lit candles, just as she knew he could see hers.

How badly had the time in prison aged her? It had

taken her months to fully regain her strength, the weight she'd lost. But even now she knew she would never be the same Zoé Charbonneau who'd been all but flung into that dank cell, the sound of a heavy key turning in the lock presumably sealing her fate. No matter if she bathed in milk and rose petals every day for the remainder of her life. If she had been able to lose the stink of prison that had clung to her, she could never be rid of the new shadows in her brown eyes or the nightmares that still plagued her.

"You look just the same," Max said, raising his hand to run a fingertip down her cheek. "Life just doesn't seem to touch you, Zoé."

She turned her head away. "Now who's the liar? You look like hell, Max. You probably need some sleep." She disengaged herself and took several steps away from him, hanging on with her last fraying thread of resolve. "And a shave wouldn't come amiss, although I'd admit the earring is rather interesting."

Max touched his ear, and the diamond that winked there. "I don't know why you women suffer these things. It hurt like hell for three days, having that hole punched in me."

She sat in the only chair in the small servant's room. She wanted him to leave, but at the same time she wanted him to stay, so she asked him: "It's quite the stone. Is it real or glass?"

He stayed where he stood, the sloped ceiling of the room fairly well hindering him from moving too far in any but the direction of the door or single window.

"You'd have to ask the man I cut it from about that. No self-respecting wharf rat is without one, I discovered, and relieving the fellow of his earring after I'd milled him down for looking at me too long established me in certain quarters."

Zoé nodded. "It isn't enough to dress the part, is it? You have to knock down at least one man before the others learn to mind their own business. Did you have to slice his ear?"

"I wasn't going to kneel over him until he woke up, fiddling with the damn thing to figure out how to remove it. Besides, I'd already poked the hole in my own ear. Should I keep it, do you think?"

His rakish yet boyish smile curled her toes.

Suddenly the months disappeared as if they'd never happened. This feeling wouldn't last, she knew, but the moment was too precious to waste. "I'd say no. It makes you much too memorable. If you haven't had it stuck there too long, the hole should close up in a few weeks. After the swelling goes down, that is. I wouldn't have made such a botch of the job if I'd done it for—"

The moment was over. There'd probably never be a time when they wouldn't stumble over their past history within minutes of calling a temporary truce.

"Why were you following Anton?"

Very clearly over.

Zoé shrugged, as if the answer was obvious. "To see where he went, of course. Why did he try to knock you unconscious?"

"He didn't tell you why he was going to do that?"

Max said as he touched a hand rather gingerly to the side of his head.

"He didn't know I was aboard. I didn't know you were going to be aboard. If you can get anything into that thick head of yours, understand this—I do not work for or with Anton Boucher. I act on my own now. Trusting others is for simpletons."

"So it was all one grand coincidence, the three of us crossing the Channel tonight in the same ship."

Zoé pushed herself up and out of the chair. "You and Anton clearly were traveling together. You were the only coincidence. Taking Anton to meet your family, were you? That doesn't seem like anything you'd do, especially considering it was your family that very nearly blew us out of the water. See, Max? You have questions, but so do I. My solution is for you to let me go, putting an end to those questions. It would seem you and your family have enough on your plates without attempting to wedge me into whatever is going on."

He stared at her yet again, as if he could somehow bore a hole into her head and examine her brain for answers. "How do you survive? How do you live? How do you eat? You can't work for the French or the English. Who benefits from your talents now, Zoé? You were always amazingly inventive, but you couldn't have survived without some sort of help. Tell me about this *arrangement*."

So much for bravado, for lies. Sometimes the only ploy that works is to tell the truth. "I already was half-way toward convincing the night guard I would make him a rich man if he let me go, when I had a visitor from a very unexpected corner. Bonaparte has as many enemies inside France as he does without. If I would work for this person, I would be released. I agreed."

"Damn, we were right." Max was suddenly leaning forward, as if he could somehow physically drag the words from her. "Who? An Englishman? Give me his name."

"An Englishman? In Paris? Walking freely in and *out* of that terrible prison? The man introduced himself as Monsieur Périgord, but I believe that was only to test my intelligence."

Max straightened, nearly hitting his head on the pitched ceiling. "Charles Talleyrand? No, that's impossible."

"But true, although he was careful to keep his face hidden beneath the hood of his voluminous cloak. *Le grand négociateur,* who's turned his loyalties more than a poor man turns his shirt cuffs. Were I Bonaparte, Talleyrand's head would be stuck on a pike at the city gates. The day will come when the new emperor regrets not ordering the execution."

"Men like Talleyrand always land on their feet, one way or another."

"I suppose so. In any event, he'd somehow learned of my skill with languages, and entrusted me to carry a verbal message to Austria for him. I didn't ask how he knew. I was much more intent on his offer to free me. I traveled to Salzburg for him, paid well before I left because I was then to continue straight on to my second mission, which would take me to London."

"But with money now in your pocket, you went hunting Anton instead?" Max shook his head as if attempting to shake some bit of knowledge loose. "Not me. Anton. Just as you said."

"And so we've come full circle, only this time it would seem you believe me. Very good, Max. Now if you'd be so kind as to leave the door unlocked as you leave, by morning I'll no longer be your problem."

"I can't do that. How long have you been following Anton?"

That question surprised her. "You'd trust any answer I'd give you?"

"I'll *measure* any answer you give me, let's settle on that compromise. If your answers prove helpful, I might allow you the freedom of the house, but not the grounds. With any key to your chamber in your own possession so that you don't feel constrained to climb out on any more roofs."

Zoé sat down once more, her mind busy. This was her chance to prove herself, and she knew it. What had mostly amused her at the time could be just what Max might want to know. "A rather one-sided bargain, but I suppose I have no choice. Anton is a creature of habit, as you already know, or you wouldn't have found him— unless he found you?"

"No, I found him."

"Because you're so all-powerful, or because he let you?" Zoé asked, only because she couldn't help herself. There had always been this competition between them, once a friendly sparring, but now she realized the game had lost all its humor. "But no matter," she added quickly. "I haunted his favorite hotel in Ostend until he showed his face."

"You were taking quite a chance, confronting him."

"The opportunity never presented itself." Zoé's quick mind knew what was important and what was not, so she left any further telling of how she'd found Anton and told Max about the man's dining companions. "He was seated at a table in the open air outside the hotel, joined by a man and woman. The woman dark-haired and past her first youth, but rather beautiful still. And a man—tall, muscular—ten or fifteen years her senior. Blond, strikingly so, and blue-eyed. He seemed...agitated. The woman had her hand laid on Anton's forearm, while beneath the table she had slid off her slipper and was running her bare toes up and down his stockinged leg. Quite the coquette."

"And you recognized neither of them?"

Ah, she'd said something important. Zoé shook her head. "I was most concentrated on Anton. He seemed to be in charge of the conversation, at times appearing angry, until the blond man pushed back his chair so that it tumbled to the flagstones and he stomped off, leaving the woman to make amends."

She smiled. "After I'd cooled my heels for a good hour outside the hotel while Anton and the woman played upstairs, sipping some rather pleasant Bordeaux beneath my wide-brimmed bonnet and fairly hideous red wig, they reappeared, as did the blond man some moments later. He'd been propping up a lamppost directly across the street—clearly aware of what was transpiring inside the hotel. The woman teased him, kissed him, and then discreetly cupped his genitals as she flicked her tongue across her upper lip. Straight from one man's bed and already seducing another. You can see why I haven't forgotten her."

"And the blond man?"

"Imbecilic over the woman. He raised both her hands to his mouth, kissing her overturned palms while, if I heard correctly, apologizing for his behavior. Anton laughed—we both know how indiscriminate he is about who he ruts or where—and within moments the three had entered a coach and been driven off toward the waterfront. I admit to being intrigued. I followed them. Once I was certain Anton was in his hotel for the night, I returned to the small warehouse they'd visited and took a look inside."

"A dangerous move." Max held up a hand. "Wait. The man and woman. Could you overhear anything they'd said? Were they speaking French, or English? Did they *look* French to you?"

"The woman spoke French in the way of a proper English schoolgirl, and the man didn't speak at all until the end, and then spoke English. He had some sort of accent, a country-born accent, I'd say, definitely lacking in formal education. You know how I delight in languages."

"Do you remember anything else?"

She wished to heaven she did, because Max's interest was with the couple and she longed to know why. "No. Clearly they had business with Anton. That's all. And, although you may not be interested, it would appear Anton has been dabbling in opium trading. At first glance it seemed to be the usual contraband bound for England, but when I opened one of the brandy kegs it was solidly packed with oilskin-wrapped opium. Our mutual friend is quite the enterprising fellow, doubtless a fervent admirer of my most recent employer, and willing to serve any number of different masters, as long as it's personally profitable."

"I can't believe this," Max said, looking pale in the candlelight. "Anton and the Society?"

Zoé didn't understand what Max meant, but if she told him what she knew, gained at least a modicum of his trust, eventually he'd tell her the rest.

"It was time for my visit to Anton. Unfortunately, he'd already slipped away—a drawback to working alone—so that I spent that night watching for him only to realize he'd escaped me. It took nearly another month to track him down again, looking first in Dunkirk, and then in Gravelines, because of the opium, you understand. It would do Anton no good if it remained in France, and Ostend's harbor has lately come under English scrutiny. Two days later, and here we are, aren't we? I imagine if your family managed to rescue any of the kegs I saw onboard tonight, they're not filled with brandy."

"And the man and woman?"

Zoé sighed. Again, the man and woman. He'd already known about the opium, she could see it in his eyes. What in the devil was going on here? Why would Boucher have chosen Redgrave land to be his rendezvous point with his smuggling partners? Why had he brought Max with him on the crossing, and then tried to either knock him unconscious or kill him? And all this obviously of strong interest to the Redgraves. Walk away? She wouldn't leave Redgrave Manor now unless bound to the back of a cart and *dragged*.

Zoé believed she'd just seen the door to at least a conditional acceptance opening a crack in her favor, and she grabbed at it. "Are these questions in aid of something in particular? The trouble it would seem you Redgraves have found yourselves in, if I understood correctly earlier? Perhaps I can help, as it would appear I'm once again without financial prospects. For one, I'd definitely recognize the man and woman if I ever saw them again."

"You'd sell your services to the devil himself, wouldn't you?" Max asked, heading for the door. "Remember, I've seen your handiwork when you believe it time to change employers. Only a fool would trust you."

So much for conciliatory gestures.

"And you're certainly no fool, are you, Max?" she called after him as he turned his back on her.

She watched as his shoulders stiffened, as they rose up and down with his sudden deep breathing.

"I'm more the fool than you know," he said, his back

still turned. "If I'm beginning to believe you're innocent, what in God's name does that say about me?"

*Poor Max. She longed to shake him. She longed to
comfort him.*

"What does it say about both of us, Max. Other than
that we neither of us were so brilliant as we'd believed.
Anton duped us both."

He at last turned to look at her, but made no move
toward her. "He should be locked up with the others in
one of the outbuildings. I think it's time all three of us
had a small chat," he said quietly. "I'll ask Gideon and
Richard to join us, as I no longer trust my ability to
know who is lying and who's telling the truth."

"No, not yet," Zoé warned him, for she'd spent several hours out on the roof, thinking how best to handle
Boucher. "In your heart you know I'm telling the truth. I
don't think he saw me tonight, so perhaps you can continue as you were, pretending to still trust him. I don't
know what you mean when you speak about this Society, but I truly think that's best, and I know you can
do it. Think of your family, Max. Expose him at some
point, yes, but not yet, not when he might still prove
useful to you. Then give him to me. That's all I ask in
return for helping you, and I'll be on my way. I owe you
that much, and you owe me that much."

At last Max understood; she could see it in his eyes,
his expression suddenly bleak and defeated. "You were
following Anton to kill him. For no other reason than
to kill him. Not only that, or he'd be dead by now. You
wanted him to *see* who was about to kill him." Max

took a single step toward her, with her involuntarily moving forward at the same time. "Tell me what happened. Please, Zoé. What happened after I left to meet with the courier?"

"There's no point in that now, other than that you know your true enemy and can protect yourself. Otherwise it all would have been for nothing."

"All what would have been for nothing?" Max took another step and laid his hands on her shoulders. "Tell me. Please."

She bent her knees and ducked out from beneath his light grasp, returning to the window to look out into the night sky. She'd believed him dead, had resigned herself to never being able to tell him what she longed for him to know. Still, the story flattered neither of them, and she wanted to get over this rough ground as quickly as possible.

"I was asleep in the loft with the others napping downstairs when Anton rode in with three men. Before I could fully rouse myself and get into my boots, they'd dragged Ralph and Howard and Georges outside and were tying them up on the ground. Ralph and Howard were dispatched at once, bullets to their heads." She closed her eyes, seeing everything as if it was happening again. "And then…"

"Look at me, Zoé. Don't look at the past, look at me."

She turned around, leaning back against the windowsill, the moonlight most probably turning her unbound hair to silvery gossamer—drawing Max toward her like a moth to the flames. But now was not the time for such thoughts. She felt so incredibly sad. "Don't you understand, Max? You *are* the past, and so am I. It's too late to change that."

He looked at her for a long time. "I suppose you're right. Tell me about Georges."

"He was so sweet, wasn't he, and so young," Zoé said at last, a single tear escaping down her cheek. "Anton went down on his knees beside him as the boy sobbed, pleaded, saying he didn't want to die. Anton…Anton sat him up and hugged him close, kissed his cheeks, and told him no, his men had been overzealous in tying him up in the first place. Georges laughed and cried in relief, holding out his bound hands behind him so that his uncle could slice the ropes around his wrists. He was still smiling when Anton put a small pistol to his ear and shot him. Then he kissed him again as he gently laid the body back on the ground, thanking the boy for his sacrifice."

"Sweet Jesus."

"That boy's face still haunts my nightmares." Zoé scrubbed at the tears that flowed freely now. "I was too stunned to move, even knowing I was as good as dead if I didn't escape at once. Neither of those two things happened. I was dragged back into the cottage, where Anton was *kind* enough to explain what came next. It was up to me whether you and I died or lived, he told me. I could pen the letter you saw and we'd both live… or you would ride into the cottage yard all unsuspecting, and be shot only after he put a bullet in my stomach and you were forced to watch as it took me hours to die in agony. I'd just seen the man cold-bloodedly execute his own nephew. I wasn't about to hazard the odds on whether or not he might be bluffing."

"You wrote the letter. That *bastard*."

"Our friend Anton's an insult to bastards." Her upper lip curled in remembered frustration. "You'd grown suspicious of him, and he somehow knew it. Rather than simply dispose of you, he went to a lot of trouble, murdering Georges to prove his own innocence, and placing the blame on me. I didn't know why, but I felt I had to believe he still needed you aboveground. You might have lived in any case, but if I didn't say I'd co-operate, I knew I was as good as dead." She felt shame wash over her. "I wasn't ready to be dead."

"Sacrificing his own nephew to protect himself. God, Zoé, how he wept as we dug those graves…"

"Yes, but move beyond that now, Max. I wrote the letter, was tied to my saddle, and taken off by Anton's companions, not knowing whether or not Anton would keep his side of the bargain. He visited me a month later in my prison cell and told me you'd been killed, but not on his order. He went so far as to curse you for being so foolish as to get yourself shot, that you'd made a mess of his plans. I flew at him in a rage, intent on scratching out his eyes, but his companion threw me against the stone wall and I fell unconscious. I never saw Anton again until Ostend."

"He wanted you completely broken, didn't he? So when he came to you with whatever reason he had, you'd do most anything to be free of prison."

Finally, Zoé smiled, although it was a sad, rueful smile. "If so, he very nearly succeeded. But Talleyrand ruined his plans. I don't blame you, Max, you know that, I hope. I had a choice to make and I made it, knowing you couldn't help but believe I'd turned traitor if I could be convincing enough, all while praying you'd see through Anton's lies in time to save yourself—but not immediately, or else he'd have no choice but to dispose of you. He didn't dictate my closing lines, scoff at the idea of being a country wife. Those were my own invention. I needed you wild with anger, not questioning."

"And I reacted just as you thought I would, curse me." He placed his hands on her shoulders once more. "You saved me, and I've spent these last long months hating you, and hating myself for being so besotted as to think you ever loved me."

She refused to look at him. "Yes, you made that clear, earlier. I believed you'd gone to your grave hating me. I would have done anything to be free of that cell after that, wanting nothing but to find Anton."

She sensed he was barely listening anymore.

"I didn't question. I didn't trust you or your love enough. If anyone should be shot, Zoé, it's me. I should have done *something*. Anything. I'm so, so sorry."

She put her palms against his cheeks and looked at him intently. "We both are, Max. But we're no longer the same two people we were. I can thank you for believing me now, but there's no going back. We've already lost whatever it was we thought we had. There's no room in my heart now for anything but hate. My business was and is with Anton. I want to help you, Max, in whatever Anton is involved with that concerns your family, but then the man is mine."

Max rubbed at his forehead, his lips pinched tightly together, avoiding Zoé's gaze.

"I already understand that. You want to kill him."

"I'm *going* to kill him."

"And now I know why. Because of Georges."

"Because of so many things."

"All right, we're agreed." But then he hedged, just as she knew he would. "If you still feel the same way when this is over, Anton's all yours. Otherwise, he belongs to both of us," Max said at last, and turned toward the door. He had his hand on the handle before abruptly stopping, his shoulders rising and lowering on a sigh. "Zoé?"

"Just go, Max. Please."

But he was already on his way back to her and she was in his arms, their mouths crushed almost painfully together, his fingers knifing through her still damp hair. Her mouth opened on a quick, involuntary sob, and he was inside her, his tongue searching, dueling with hers, his body pressed closely against her softness even as she clung to him with all of her strength.

The fire she couldn't douse threatened to become a conflagration.

He kissed her face, her hair, her tear-wet cheeks… and then he let her go.

Had he felt the same fire? Recognized the same pitfalls, the same danger? Fire hadn't helped them in the past, had it?

"I'm sorry. I'm so damned sorry."

"I know," she said quietly. "So am I. *Telle est la vie.*"

"Yes, such is life. But does it really have to be that way? We still feel something for each other, you have to admit that at least. I realize it won't be easy, but if we can't change the past, there's always the future. You have every right to hate me. I couldn't have loved you enough, known you well enough, or I wouldn't have believed Anton's lies, even with Georges lying dead on the ground in front of me. You suffered, and that's my fault. You suffered to save *me*."

"I'm no martyr, Max. Remember, I was also saving myself, or at least believed so at the time. Anton proved one thing, though, didn't he? What we had, what we thought we had, wasn't enough, and shattered into pieces at the first hammer strike. Both of us are too familiar with distrust to even believe in ourselves. As long as we were dancing on the edge of the knife, we could tell ourselves what we felt for each other was a true, lasting love."

"But neither of us knows what the word means. You said something like that earlier."

"Some things break too badly to be mended, no matter how desperately we want to fix them, and that includes the past. Eight months ago was another lifetime for both of us. We've both changed, for the better or the worse, who knows? I don't know you anymore and you don't know me. Take care of the family you love so much, Max. That's what's important now. And, yes, if you're so certain Anton is somehow involved in your troubles, I'd like to help. But then we part ways."

She shook for a full five minutes after Max closed the door behind him, leaving it unlocked, leaving her alone once more. She didn't know which hurt worse, believing him dead, or knowing he was alive, yet out of her life.

He understood. Together, they were a bad opera. Whatever they'd had together, be it lust, the thrill of living in the moment, or true love, was over, and impossible to reclaim. They couldn't even be friends, but at least they were no longer enemies. That was the best either of them could hope for.

And he'd left the door unlocked.

So why am I still standing here?

She pulled the scrap of vellum from her pocket and unfolded it, to read the lines for at least the tenth time since the note had been pushed under her door. They still had the ability to make her shake her head at her own stupidity:

Foolish girl. You could have avoided all this inconvenience if you'd simply followed my dubious friend's order to bring a message to London. You will be escorted to my rooms at the ungodly hour of eight o'clock tomorrow morning. I greatly dislike tardiness, and our meeting is already more than a month overdue.

Zoé walked to the small fireplace and tossed the note into the flames. Richard Borders was right; she'd have to live at least another forty years to be so much as a patch on Trixie Redgrave.

VALENTINE AND THREE of the dogs were waiting for Max at the bottom of the main staircase, as if they knew he'd be coming that way. The large hallway clock was just striking out the hour of one, and the mansion was otherwise quiet.

His brother was dressed casually, but a dozen times more carefully than Max, his dark hair artfully tousled, his amber eyes twinkling, his mouth curved in a typically younger-brother mischievous smile. "Heading for the drinks table in the drawing room, aren't you? So glad I chose correctly. I always wondered what a thundercloud looked like, up close. I also wanted to get a better look at that diamond in your ear. I've still to decide if it's clever and dashing, or ludicrous and overdone. I think the latter, although I believe I could carry it off with aplomb. Just not you."

"Not now, damn it," Max warned as he opened the carved wooden dog gate and latched it behind him.

The dogs instantly dropped to their bellies at his tone, one of them whimpering quietly.

"Oh, now look what you've done. Up, boys," Val said, snapping his fingers. "He didn't mean you. Did you, Max? Did you leave Mademoiselle Charbonneau cowering under her cot? I know that's where I'd be,

were it not that I know you better. That black scowl is
only part of your charm. Perhaps all of it."

Max smiled, in spite of himself. "Gideon already
welcomed me home, you're too late. So is that it? Are
you finished now?"

"Yes, now that you're no longer in danger of the
top of your head blowing off—you aren't, are you?
Gideon told me about the lady. Yours couldn't have
been a happy reunion."

"Wonderful. Who else did he tell?"

Valentine frowned as he leaned against the newel
post, as if considering the question. "Well, let's see.
Jessica was in the room, Kate and Simon. Daisy—not
Kate's mare, my affianced bride. You'll adore her, as
she keeps me in line. I've been quite busy while you
were gone. Now, where was I? Ah, Trixie and Richard. I can't be positive, but I wouldn't be surprised if
Dearborn weren't listening at the keyhole. I suppose
you'd say everybody. A dangerous lady. We needed to
be warned."

Max briefly considered the logistics of booting himself in his own backside. What the hell was the matter
with him? He'd never been *chatty*. Why had he picked
tonight of all times to lay bare his chest to Gideon in
what had turned out to be the worst of misconceptions?

"Forget what you heard. I was wrong, completely
wrong. Val, you're looking at the greatest fool in nature and a man who deserved to lose exactly what he
lost, and more. Tell them, tell them all, and don't let it
wait until morning. Especially Dearborn. Knock on

every door, wake up anyone who's sleeping, until everyone knows. Zoé's completely innocent of everything I believed her to have done. And while you're at it, inform Mrs. Justis that our guest is to have one of our best bedchambers, although she's not to leave it until I say she may."

"Can't do that last bit, brother. Didn't Gideon tell you? Mrs. Justis is no longer with us."

Max raised his eyebrows. "I knew she was getting on in years. Damn."

"She's not dead, she's no longer with us. She's a Cooper, remember."

"I suppose you think that should explain things to me, but it doesn't. What does being a Cooper have to do with anything?" And then he remembered the lack of a fire, the very few buckets carried upstairs for his bath. Max didn't employ a valet, who would only be sitting about gathering dust on his head during his long absences. Instead, he used Douglas when he visited the Manor. Douglas Cooper. "I wondered where he was," he said quietly. "Are they all gone, all the Coopers? Why? No, don't answer that."

"I wasn't about to, as it's late and the story is not only long but would only lead to other questions, while you already look half-dead on your feet. I did point that out, didn't I? We can leave the Coopers and the rest to the morning. But don't worry about our straitened circumstances. My Daisy has taken over like the champion she is, and it's as if Mrs. Justis was never here. I already told you I'm in love, didn't I? Madly and deeply."

"I'm sorry, Val. My belated congratulations," Max said, wondering if he could go any lower without crashing through the tiles to the cellars. His brother was in love, and he'd barely reacted. "You must tell me all about her."

"We'll leave that for another time, as well. Was that the end of my instructions?"

Max cudgeled his brain to remember where he'd left off. "Please ask your Daisy to install Zoé in one of the best chambers—one of the largest—and to make certain it has lots of windows, but no balcony. She isn't to be locked in, but she also is not to leave the chamber until and unless I give the word. Tell Kate and Jessica to please assist her with a suitable wardrobe, and—and anything else you can think of, all right? You're better at these things than I am. Oh, and most important of all, nobody is to mention her name. I think that's it. I'll see you at the breakfast table at nine."

"And while I'm playing your messenger—not to mention incurring the wrath best directed at you—what will you be doing?"

He couldn't wait until morning. He had to know. Now.

"If I'm lucky, inviting the devil into the Manor."

'Well, that should be interesting. And it wouldn't be the first time, would it?"

Max headed for the front door, rousing a sleepy footman who rummaged in his pocket for the key, before the sound of whimpering behind him caught his attention, and delivered a fresh wave of guilt. Especially when he spotted good old Tubby looking up at him in happy anticipation. "Oh, all right, you bunch. Come along."

The dogs followed him as he made the rounds of the outbuildings, guided by the many burning lanterns employed by the guards, using a lantern of his own to examine the faces of each and every prisoner as he was ordered lined up for Max's inspection.

There were the Spaniards, still plying their beads. But only two Dutchmen. He'd stopped counting by the time he headed for the third and last outbuilding, having been told only the injured and dead were inside.

Anton wasn't among the wounded.

Nor was his body lying beneath the rude blankets that covered two forms laid out in a dark corner, the dogs hanging back, clearly smelling death.

"Is this all of them?" he asked one of the guards, a man he didn't recognize.

"Aye, mate, that's the lot. Have to be pretty slippery to escape the cap'n."

Ah, so he was addressing one of Simon Ravenhill's friends of the skull and crossbones persuasion.

"None drowned?"

"These two. Tide comin' in as it was, they washed ashore straightaway and we scooped 'em up."

"Very good." Max gave the man a lazy salute. "Smooth sailing to you, sailor."

"Sir," the man said, swiftly coming to attention, returning the salute.

"And my compliments to your captain," Max said, smiling. "Carry on."

But Max's smile faded as he retraced his steps to the Manor. *Slippery.* As good a description of Anton as any other. *And I brought him, and the Society, straight to our front door. How have I become so accomplished in attracting bad luck?*

Zoé had been wrong, and Anton had seen her. Or he'd assumed his *bon ami* was still alive and someone had told him who'd hit him. Either way, he hadn't been busy declaring himself Max Redgrave's bosom chum so he could be brought to the Manor and made comfortable.

So where was he, where had he gone? Was he even now in the company of the Society? Was he already miles away, plotting a new strategy? Max had always known Anton for the dangerous man he was, but learning about Georges had taken the man leagues beyond merely dangerous. Anton Boucher had sold heart and soul to the devil. *To the Society. Why?*

Max thought again of his remark to Gideon about the lack of servants, and his brother's response that bad news could always wait. He attempted to get his head around the idea that all the Coopers had deserted the Manor just as they were needed most. He remembered Richard's words to him on the beach.

So many questions. So few answers.

He looked up at the Manor, seeing the faint light of one small candle still burning on the servant floor. She'd probably keep it lit all night, and the window open, as well. He remembered her as fearless, and couldn't imagine her as she was now. He wanted to go to her, hold her, comfort her, keep her safe from whatever she feared from the darkness. But that was impossible.

Some things break too badly to be mended, no matter how desperately we want to fix them, and that includes the past.

Weariness finally claimed him and he stopped walking, unable to do more than simply stand there, wondering not how things would get worse, but when.

"Welcome home, Max," he said quietly as Tubby began pushing his cold wet nose against his hand, almost as if he might be offering comfort. "Welcome home...."

CHAPTER FOUR

AS HER LEATHERS had somehow disappeared the night before, while she had shivered in a cold bath, Zoé had no choice but to don the rig-out delivered to her by one of the maids—a grinning, red-cheeked barge of a woman who was remarkable for the hairs on her chin and her rolling gait. Not the sort of servant she would have expected in a grand house like Redgrave Manor.

At what she assumed was precisely two minutes before eight, she answered the knock on the door wearing a simple light blue muslin morning gown that served her proportions well save for its rather tight bosom, and its length, that left her ankles and borrowed, ill-fitting slippers exposed.

As she opened the door, it was to be confronted by an almost painfully thin young man most prodigiously yawning into a scented, lace-edged handkerchief, his eyes squeezed shut and his nose pinched. His features were well enough—or would be sans the wide-open mouth and his incredible clothing. He was wearing breeches, at least, and wildly clocked hose. His shoes were red, with heels that had his entire body pitched slightly forward while his bony backside jutted out, most probably for balance.

The rest of him was covered in a black satin banyan that fell past his knees, and a cravat tied with all the expertise of a five-thumbed orangutan. And then there was his hair, which apparently had been combed up and over a curling stick, the single fat ringlet stuck in place with heavily scented pomade.

Servant, or member of the household—the eccentric sort many families hid in the attics? Zoé couldn't be sure who or *what* he was.

"When you've recovered…?" she offered tentatively, as the youth was still yawning wide enough for anyone sufficiently interested to examine his tonsils.

"What? Oh—ohmigod, you're her?" He immediately put his spread hands to his thin chest and began patting at himself as if to be certain he was decent…which he then assumed he was.

He wasn't. He was a caricature of every silly young fop on either side of the Channel. And clearly not a blood relation, or else Max would have taken him in hand long ago, or at least relieved him of what must be a flagon of *parfum*.

Zoé knew she could have him on the floor and unconscious in less than a second, and be on her way. But she didn't do it.

"Yes, I am Mademoiselle Zoé Charbonneau. And you are—?"

The boy went into his quite singular version of sweeping her an elegant leg. "Mademoiselle, I am flabbergasted. I am all but overcome by your beauty. I am completely and eternally in love. I am—"

"You're making me late for my meeting with the dowager countess," Zoé interrupted when she realized the boy could probably go on for hours, as if he'd practiced, which he most probably had. "Do you think that's a good idea?"

"Oh, criminy-cripe!" He was upright in an instant and attempting to keep his feet under him. "My name is Adam Collier and I'm Jessica's brother and Gideon's brother-in-law and a dead man if you don't follow me now," he said, his words nearly tumbling over themselves. He turned toward the servant staircase and started off, only to look back at her and plead, "Come on, come on. Trixie may have taken me under her wing, dear lady, believing me salvageable, she says, but she can be terribly *amusing* when I've disappointed her."

With that as her only warning (other than the note she'd burnt), Zoé squared her shoulders and followed Adam Collier down two flights of twisting stairs and allowed him to lead her to a set of double doors he then flung open with a flourish.

"Trix—um, my lady?" Adam said, bowing with more alacrity than grace. "Please allow me to introduce you to Mademoiselle Zoé Charbonneau."

"You've got it turned around, pet. I hold the higher rank, therefore you beg my permission to introduce her to me." The woman, still not visible to Zoé, sighed audibly. "And another avenue closes. Adam, strike butler from your list of possible occupations."

"Butler? Trixie, don't fun with me. You know I'm to have all my father's immense wealth the moment I reach my majority, although you will persist in saying I'll run through every last groat in less than a year. Butler? I should think not!" He paused for a moment, obviously thinking, then added, "At the very least, majordomo."

Zoé laughed, and was immediately called upon to leave the curtained foyer and step farther into the enormous room decorated in delicate French furniture the color of cream and edged in gold, the predominate color everywhere else a grayish shade of pink. There were at least a half-dozen windows, but only one set of draperies had been tucked back to allow in the morning light. That window was nowhere near the immense fourposter bed draped in pink and holding, at its center, one petite blonde woman of indeterminate years.

"Tariq, you failed to mention her beauty," the dowager countess scolded, and the tall man from the beach stepped out of the shadows, his hands crossed in front of him as he rather regally inclined his head. He looked magnificent, dressed in a high-necked black jacket reaching past his knees and wide, full-length trousers. His head and shoulders were covered in a multipatterned black and tan square scarf that accented the deep tan of his skin and the desert-sand shade of his eyes.

"My most abject apologies to you both. May I only say, my lady, that you are correct, as beauty recognizes beauty. I am humbled in the presence of such."

"He—you're the man on the beach. You look so very different dressed that way, in *shalwar kameez* and *kef-*

fiyeh," Zoé said, if only for her own clarification. "You were *with* Max?"

"I have been looking after Mr. Redgrave these past several months."

"But…but Max has always been able to elude his grandmother's ridiculous guardians." Zoé looked to the countess, and curtsied. Her concern for Max's seeming lack of perception since last she'd seen him had caused her to commit an embarrassing *faux pas*. "Begging your pardon, ma'am."

"No offense taken," Trixie said, giving a dismissing wave of her hand even as she picked up a china cup thin enough to see through, and put it to her lips. "But to be clear, Tariq here only steps in when those *ridiculous guardians* manage to get themselves turned around, leaving my elusive grandson on his own, confident he is no longer being followed."

"Brilliant," Zoé said in admiration. "Your secret is safe with me." She stepped closer to the bed even as Adam pushed himself up on the edge of the mattress and Trixie tossed him a small sprig of red grapes from her lap tray.

He missed, and the grapes sailed past his head and onto the floor.

"Drat! I'll catch them one of these days. You only need to warn me."

"The lack of warning is the point of the exercise, pet. There are still moments I despair of you, but it's early days yet. Now take yourself off to locate clothing more appropriate to a young looby with pretenses to fashion.

And find someone else to tie your cravat. I suggest anyone you can find who sports no more than two thumbs."

"Yes, Trixie…ma'am," Adam said, jumping down from the high mattress. But first he leaned across the space and placed a gentle kiss on the woman's offered cheek. He then scooped up the grapes, popped one into his mouth, and pointed across the bed to Tariq with the rest of the bunch. "What about him? The heathen?"

"Heathen? Young man, his people were studying the stars and creating alphabets while yours and mine were still speaking in grunts and wiping their backsides with leaves."

It seemed to be Tariq's turn to stifle his amusement (while Zoé attempted to hide her shock and admiration), before he bowed to both women and followed Adam out of the bedchamber, pausing near Zoé only to whisper a few words in Arabic.

Listen and learn. She nodded her agreement.

"Warned you, didn't he?" Trixie said from the bed. "I suppose that's fair enough. His father was one of my lovers, eons ago. Looking at Tariq, I'm sure you could see my attraction. He was educated as a physician in Beirut, and has only lent his assistance these last months out of respect for his father, and perhaps some small affection for me." She patted the mattress. "Sit here, so I can embarrass you by inspecting you more closely with these old eyes of mine."

"I don't embarrass all that easily, ma'am," Zoé responded, but then did as instructed. She'd wanted a closer look at the woman in any case. What she saw was a woman who looked perhaps two dozen years younger than the few spots on the backs of her hands would indicate; a woman who would not flee her burning house before she'd been painted and her blond curls coiffed. *Quite an astonishing bit of iron-backed fluff was Lady Beatrice Redgrave.* "I believe it unnecessary to ask questions such as how you know about me at all. Why did you bring me here?"

There was another small sprig of red grapes from the tray suddenly moving in Zoé's direction. She plucked it out of the air without actually appearing to move. She could do the same with a thrown knife, but didn't believe she needed to share that information.

"Brava! Would you have done so well if you hadn't seen me toss that other bunch at my student?"

"You even ask?" Zoé shot back at her. "Although perhaps slightly out of practice, I'm nobody's student, ma'am, and not for quite some time."

"Trixie, pet, call me Trixie, all my friends and enemies do. And, yes, I can see the age and experience in your eyes. Just as certainly as a discerning young woman like you sees much the same in mine in my rare unguarded moments. You'll learn to hide better as you age. How did that devious friend of mine use you before directing you to Cavendish Square?"

"An important question, or merely conversational?"

"That would depend on your answer." Trixie smiled, and her eyes twinkled. "I suggest we go with the gloves off from here. You answer my questions and I'll answer yours…or we can continue this dance until Max is told where you are and comes charging in here like an enraged bull."

Zoé considered the suggestion—was it merely a suggestion?—and then nodded her agreement.

"Splendid. I'll go first."

Zoé couldn't resist. "Age precedes beauty, Trixie?"

"My congratulations. It's a rare person who dares speak to me so frankly—or to so clearly enjoy doing so. But you're incorrect. I go first because I *say* I go first. You agree, albeit not without comment, because you clearly weren't raised by wolves. I've come a long way capitalizing on society's finer sensibilities and good manners."

Zoé glanced at a gold and crystal clock on the table by the bed. Trixie was right; Max wouldn't wait much longer before going on the hunt for her. "I was dispatched to a particular inn located just outside Salzburg, to a particular room at said inn. After cooling my heels there for three days, a note was slipped beneath my door, directing me to a rendezvous at a fairly remote spot at midnight. When prompted from the shadows, I repeated the message I was charged with delivering, in German, as also so ordered, and then immediately dropped to the ground, rolling to one side even as a pistol ball sang over my head. Midnight meetings are never without their perils."

"Slimy toad. Our parting in Paris years ago wasn't quite amicable, although he accepted the mission quickly enough. He never planned to send you to me, but just to take my money. And use you to his own ends while he was at it. What was the message?"

"I won't bore you with its length. The kernel that might interest you pertained to carrying out an assassination of Josephine, with the blame clearly left at Bonaparte's doorstep. For a price, of course."

Trixie lifted one well-sculpted eyebrow. "Interesting. Many French remain enraged over the divorce of their beloved Josephine and the speedy marriage to Austria's Marie Louise. Our Talleyrand does love to stir pots, laboring for whichever faction appears to be on the winning side at any given time. I'll have to arrange a whisper in the ear of a Bonapartist friend in Paris, but only after warning Talleyrand. I, too, enjoy stirring pots, and England can only benefit if Boney is distracted."

Zoé smiled in admiration. "If the world only knew how wars truly are won and lost."

"Yes, by cowards or power-mad men, most of them who would faint at the thought of stepping foot on a real battlefield. There's much to applaud in Bonaparte's courage, but more to be feared in his ambition. You dispatched the recipient of the message?"

Trixie's mind moved at a pace that kept Zoé on her toes.

"He left me no choice. I had the payment the man was clearly sent to retrieve, as I'd already been told to go directly from Salzburg to London."

"Which you didn't do, were never meant to do."

"Which I didn't do, wasn't supposed to be alive to

do, no. I'd even debated about traveling to Salzburg at all, but couldn't be certain I wasn't being watched." Zoé hopped down from the high bed even as she popped a grape into her mouth. She felt completely comfortable with this woman, something she hadn't felt in a long time. "My turn. What's going on here? What is the Society? Is the family in danger? Are you all expecting Max to get you out of it? Why did you go to all the trouble to attempt to bring me here?"

"That's five questions, four of which I don't care to answer at the moment. I arranged to bring you here because I was curious. I refer you to Max on the others, as I'm certain his brothers and sister are currently bringing him up to date over eggs and good country ham. My turn. You and Max were lovers. Have you had others?"

Zoé looked Trixie squarely in the eyes. "Before or since your grandson?"

"I have no interest in the time before you came into Max's life."

"Has anyone mentioned the name Anton Boucher to you?"

"I've been brought up to date on the man, yes."

"By the inestimable Tariq." Zoé nodded. "In any case, Anton's orders kept me from rape, although I had nearly seduced the head guard, acknowledging it as my only way out, before Talleyrand arrived. Since then, I've been rather busy for romantic dalliance."

"Now you're angry. I apologize. Beauty opens many doors, especially with stupid men, but you couldn't bring yourself to the point of giving over your body to the guard, even believing Max dead. You love my grandson. Which more completely answers your fifth question. He's been a near madman since what we'll henceforth only refer to as the incident. He takes chances he shouldn't take, almost as if he has no regard for his life. I had to put a stop to it, and deduced that a meeting between the two of you was the only obvious answer."

"I should find this impossible to believe, except for the fact I'm here."

"By a roundabout way, yes, you are. Tariq made some inquiries, sent me his conclusions, and I was assured of your innocence and this Anton Boucher's guilt. He's fled, by the way, and I expect Max will soon be in hot pursuit. Now, my dear, I'll leave you and Max to for God's sake *talk* to each other so this old woman isn't forced to have one of her grandchildren underground before her."

Tears pricked at the back of Zoé's eyes. Beatrice Redgrave, this woman who knew everything, believed her, believed *in* her. Richard Borders believed in her. She owed so much to so many.

"We have spoken," she said, hating the slight catch in her voice. "Max…understands everything now."

"Oh, dear, I don't like the sound of that. Pride is rearing its ugly head, isn't it, along with unhealthy measures of guilt and regrets on both sides, I'd imagine? Love is frustratingly complicated, which is why I've always striven to avoid it, until Richard, bless him." Trixie raised her hands in surrender. "But I'm no ro-

mantical Cupid, pet, and I'm done interfering. It's up
to the two of you now."

"Yes, ma'am, it is," Zoé said, dropping into a curtsy.
"I understand now why Max so adores you."

"Bah! They're all terrified of me, how next I am to
embarrass them. Now go on, leave this old woman to
the necessary trials of hiding the ravages of time before
we're called to luncheon."

"I DON'T SEE why I can't meet her, at least," Lady Katherine Redgrave complained, pouting as she directed her
maid to lay the last pile of clothing on the narrow attic
cot. "Gideon says she's beautiful, and with the most
fascinating blond hair shot through with sunlight. Have
you noticed how poetical Giddy's gotten since Jessica?
What an adventure you two must have lived on the Continent. I envy you so much. Not that Simon would have
approved, but I believe the two of us well-suited to spying and skullduggery, and all that sort of thing. Max? I
would be ever so much more comfortable if you'd stop
shooting daggers at me with your eyes."

"And nicer still if you'd shut up and leave," he responded still attempting to convince his brain that his
baby sister was now, seemingly within a heartbeat, a
woman. "Kate? You're happy?"

Her smile was near beatific. "I still pinch myself
every morning, unable to believe such happiness. Simon
is—"

Remembering Gideon's warning, Max got to his feet,
dropping a kiss on his sister's cheek even as he grabbed

hold of her shoulders and directed her toward the door. "I promise to arm myself with a strong drink and hear all about you and your impossibly wonderful Simon the instant this mess is over. Zoé will be back here at any moment, and I've already ordered our mounts saddled."

"You'll be careful, won't you? This Boucher, he's a part of the Society, that's what Gideon told us. It's not as if he's stumbling around somewhere out there, lost and without resources. Simon and Valentine want to go with you, or at least send along a few of our new friends. We all feel much safer with the men watching over us, and some of their wives have helped bolster the number of servants. One of them is quite the cook—one of the men, actually."

"Pirates. Yes, that's just what I need. And nobody knows who they are?"

"Simon does, but he won't tell us, not even me, and believe me, I've tried *everything* to get it out of him."

"I could have lived the remainder of my life without hearing that, and died a happy man," Max said, continuing to maneuver Kate toward the door. He gave her a playful slap on her behind. "Scoot."

Max left the door open even after he heard Kate's retreating steps on the stairs, and then walked to the window to look out on what would be a fine morning, other than for the fact there were people out there somewhere who wanted the Redgraves dead. People they'd always believed loyal friends, men they'd played with when they were all children, women who had taken care of their comforts, wiped their noses, and even given their bottoms a good swat when they misbehaved.

The Coopers were now enemies. After generations of serving the earls of Saltwood, they had joined with the Society. They'd sacrificed one of their own in an attempt to assassinate Trixie, for God's sake. Redgrave Manor had gone, seemingly overnight, from a refuge and home to an armed camp under attack. The knowledge was still difficult to swallow, let alone digest.

Now Gideon and Jessica had ridden off on a flying visit to London, to take control of the gossip there thanks to the unfortunately public attempt on Trixie's life, and to gather up another member of the Society's Devil's Thirteen named Axbridge, the man identified in the journals as Hammer. The man was head of a private bank, responsible for turning opium into gold. He'd been left where he was for a time, but now he'd be reunited with his friend Burn, and questioned about the Society. They'd wanted to turn him over to Perceval as more proof of their theory of treason and invasion, but now they needed him more.

"Max?"

He turned around, to see Zoé standing in the doorway clad in a mostly flattering morning gown. Her gaze shifted to the piles on the cot. "Where am I going?"

"We're both going, if you agree. My brothers have things under control here, leaving me with an obvious mission."

"Anton." She was already examining the clothing, holding a dark blue jacket to one of Kate's riding habits against her, checking its size. "I'll need my own boots and leathers. Where do we start?"

"I have your boots here, but your leathers are still being repaired after your dunk into the Channel. But no questions? You've been with Trixie this past half hour or more. You have to have questions."

She put down the blue jacket and picked up a forest-green one with discreet golden epaulettes and frog closings. "At least a dozen. You'll answer them if and when you want to once we're on our way. He's already gotten quite a head start on us. Where are my knives? Or does your trust go only so far?"

Max reached behind him and produced the knives, a stiletto she kept in a specially made sheath in her right boot and the two smaller throwing knives she secreted around her body. "The horses are waiting."

She looked at him and obviously made up her mind, her fingers going to the front buttons of the morning gown.

He held his breath as the gown slid to the floor, leaving her in a chemise made for a less generously endowed woman, her long straight legs now bare as she kicked off the too-large silken slippers.

"Hand me one of those," she said, pointing to a stack of white shirts before grabbing her hair in both hands and quickly twisting the long locks into a knot at her nape.

She was thinner than he remembered, her collarbones more prominent. The scar on her left forearm, a protective wound courtesy of a French soldier who had been fatally introduced to her knife a moment later, didn't look as red and angry as it had the last time he'd seen it, when he'd sewed up the wound after getting her drunk enough to be singing naughty ditties with him while he stitched.

His gut clenched. If there was one thing he never would have questioned about Zoé, it was her courage.

He held out the shirt and she pushed her arms into it, dealing swiftly with the buttons before tucking the ends into the divided skirt she'd pulled on while he'd been staring at her like a simpleton.

She sat on the edge of the cot and held up one slim bare foot. "The horses are waiting, Max."

"Enjoying yourself?" he asked her as he helped her on with her boots. A simple, almost domesticated exercise, although he much preferred removing her boots as he straddled her legs and she provocatively traced her fingertips over his bare back...

She stood up, stamping her feet, and slid the knife into the right boot. "I think I might be," she said as she reached for the jacket. "It's not as if you've never helped me dress."

Or undress, Max pointed out silently, picking up a saddlebag from the chair and tossing it onto the cot. "We may return today, or be gone for two. Take only whatever else you absolutely need, and we'll be on our way."

"Could you possibly be more vague?" Still, she did as he said before balancing the saddlebag over her shoulder. "Would it be too much if I were to ask for an apple or something else to break my fast?"

"Some grinning hulk who calls himself Jacko promised a basket of food waiting for us with the horses. We're leaving via the kitchens. Otherwise, we'd have to pass through the gauntlet my family is probably organizing right now. Don't forget your hat."

She looked down at the dark green shako hat with its military gold braid. "Heaven save me, I should have chosen the blue," she grumbled, pulling the thing down on her head in a jaunty angle.

Max tried not to register the way a few curving strands of hair framed Zoé's perfect face, or the way the jacket of the riding habit nipped in at her slim waist, or how the intoxicating memory of the taste of her had come slamming into his head when she'd allowed the morning gown to slide down over her artfully flared hips.

They'd been lovers. Never really friends. Lovers, intimate in every way possible. Now they were neither. What joined them now was one man, Anton Boucher, and their pursuit of him, the destruction of the evil who had destroyed them and planned the destruction of the Redgraves, Redgrave Manor, perhaps all of England itself.

"Max? The horses, remember? We have to go."

Her voice seemed to come to him from a long way off. A lifetime ago. It was sweet, and gentle, and almost loving. Or he simply wanted that to be the case.

"This isn't going to work, you know," he told her, believing it only right to warn her. "Whatever else we've lost, given or thrown away or never had, we'll never be free of each other. Not in some ways. I'm not that civilized. I'll always want you, never stop desiring you. Are you still willing to go with me?"

She adjusted the saddlebag on her shoulder and headed for the door.

Max followed, his heart both light and heavy, as he and Zoé set off to dance together on the edge of the knife for what might be the last time.

CHAPTER FIVE

ANTON BOUCHER CURSED under his breath. "Damn her eyes. I was right, it is her. I wanted to take them on one at a time, not together."

The blond man *harrumphed* from his spot behind a concealing bush. "That's the woman you thought you saw on the beach? A pretty piece. Certainly doesn't look dangerous."

Anton kept his eyes on Max and Zoé as they turned their mounts toward a dirt path leading into an enormous stand of trees. "Keep thinking that way when you encounter her, *vous hulk sans cervelle,* and it will be your last earthly thought, I guarantee it."

"Yet you caught her," the woman beside him pointed out. "It sounds to me as if caging the pretty bird rather than slitting its throat and drinking its blood was your mistake. Or do you covet her?"

"He covets anything in skirts, and maybe more," spat the man Boucher had just called a brainless hulk. "Why do you think he chose to ride a mare?"

The woman laughed, a rather tinkling sound eerily edged with what could only be termed pure meanness. "Do you want her, Anton? It can be arranged."

The Frenchman licked his suddenly dry lips. "Spread before me on the altar? Her face gone flat with terror as I approach in my mask and cloak."

"Perhaps carrying a lit black candle, to drip wax on her body, to mark all the places you will later worship with your mouth, with the tip of your knife. Because I know you, Anton," the woman purred in clear delight, putting a hand to his crotch. "Nothing arouses you like someone else's pain. Even the mere thought of it wakes your flaccid manhood. I still carry fading bruises from our last encounter, don't I, Niall? Tell him how much you hate him for that."

The blond man repeated dully, "I hate him for that."

Anton laughed. "But you'll do nothing about it, because she won't let you. You haven't guessed why? It's because you worship her as some sort of goddess to be worshipped, while your *exalted leader* has a taste for—"

"Shut up, Boucher," the woman commanded. "You're not indispensable, not now, while you're on this side of the Channel, your enormous failure no more than twelve hours old. I should be enjoying the company of my pawn, rather than watching him ride into the trees with the blonde bitch."

Anton felt the same frisson of fear he'd experienced last night, when he'd broken into the clear after climbing up a steep incline to escape the shore, and run straight into the woman now expressing her displeasure once again. She was brilliant, but also fatally twisted somewhere deep in her black soul. He had to dispatch her at some point, but for now, his hands were figuratively tied. He needed her, and he needed the handsome blond baboon, as well. For just a little while longer. For that, for the future he saw for himself, he would allow her to believe, just this little while longer, that she was in charge.

"There are other Redgraves," he pointed out quickly. "It didn't have to be him. I would think any of them would do. Most especially the old lady. Max used to speak about her as if she was dipped in gold. I imagine they'd do most anything to have her back in one piece."

And then he dared stick his neck out over the chopping block. Ah, pride. If he didn't watch himself, he'd pay for that pride with his life. "Not that you've had many blazing successes here. Our meeting place at Fernwood destroyed. Redgrave's own supposedly exquisite vault of pleasure burnt to the ground, the ceremonial *heart* of the Society reduced to ashes. And how many of your precious Thirteen deserted, dead, or otherwise lost to us? Damn, woman, you've begun killing your own. I arrived to a debacle."

"The Redgraves have proved more inventive than we supposed."

"The Redgraves. A handful of pampered Englishmen, defeating your self-declared brilliance at every turn? How much are we staking our claim to Redgrave Manor rather than having been backed into the place as our last remaining refuge? Yet another full load of opium never to reach the city, leaving us powerless to convert it to the gold the emperor so desperately needs.

He's already losing patience with us as he begins to consider Russia, leaving England to its own destiny. We have to draw him back into believing he can safely trust us. More immediately, I have suppliers in Ostend awaiting my return and their share of that gold. You've compromised my safety, not to mention broken the rules as laid down by your own Society."

"I care nothing for your safety, and leagues less for the *rules*. With me, there are no rules save those that suit me. The Redgraves have proved more troublesome than we'd hoped, that's all," the woman declared as fire flashed in her eyes. "You forget our successes. The sabotaged foodstuffs meant for Wellington's troops. The diverted shipments of small arms and other supplies. The men in position all these months, prepared to seize the Martello towers once we've given the signal. The Society growing in spite of some small losses, our members neatly infiltrated into all areas of the government, the banks, the weaponry manufactories, primed to follow our commands. We safely landed and continue to successfully both hide and feed over one thousand Frenchmen. You call that failure? You were to bring us one man. *One man*. Again, dear Anton, you're on *my* side of the Channel now. You should be fearful of placing your head on your pillow at night until you redeem yourself, or you might wake to find your tongue on the floor, along with other pieces you'd surely miss."

The blond hulk smiled. "The Exalted Leader *is* the rules. She does not *follow* anyone."

And clearly she wasn't accustomed to being questioned. But Anton believed he had at last found her weak point—her own precious vanity. Anton leaned in front of the woman to smile at her companion. "Is she always like this? How long has it been since you last saw your testicles?"

"Ignore him, darling—I know just where they are, don't I?" She returned her glare to Anton. "Those two fools had a picnic basket tied to her saddle, as if they don't fear us. That in itself is an insult I can't abide." The woman got to her feet, slapping bits of grass from her deep brown leggings. "Are we going to follow them, or not?"

Anton rose, as well. "That depends. Do you want to do what they want you to do?"

She let out an exasperated sigh. "They expect us to follow them?"

"If they hadn't wanted somebody to see them, we wouldn't have seen them. I told you. You take care of keeping your pathetic Devil's Thirteen and the rest of your minions in check, and I'll handle the Redgraves. Five men, that's all I'll need. You'd need an army, madam, and that army can't be here until the Redgraves and the threat they hold for us are eliminated. Now, are you English entirely lacking in hospitality, or am I going to be offered something in the way of luncheon? Preferably something I don't need a chisel and hammer to cut through, yes?"

ZOÉ'S BAY MARE delicately followed the black stallion as Max led the way through the trees, leaving one narrow path only to pick up another heading in yet a third direction until she had to admit herself totally turned about, lost. The tall, leafy trees all but hid the sunlight, and it was nearly impossible to know if they were still moving to the west more than any other direction.

If anyone had been following them, either on horse-back or on foot, she was certain Max had managed to confuse and elude them a quarter hour ago.

At last they emerged into a clearing divided by hedgerows, a vast expanse of rolling farmland left fal-low. Crossing the field would leave them exposed for an uncomfortably long time, especially after the cover of the trees.

"Where are we? Surely not still on Redgrave land."

"Embarrassingly, yes. We call it the West Run. Our grandfather acquired it when the family living here died in a fire a long time ago." He stood in the stir-rups. "If you'll look to your right, you'll see a copse of trees grown up around the remains of the Manor house. Trixie decreed it and the graveyard remain, the graves kept in good repair. I suppose Gideon will have to as-sign someone else to tend to them, now that the Coo-pers are gone. Do you want to picnic there?"

"Thank you, but there must be more pleasant places. Such as right here, with our backs to the trees and able to see anyone who dares approach from the fields." She smiled at him. "Which is another way of saying my stomach has begun to believe my throat cut. I'm starving."

"Yes, you should eat."

"And what does that mean?" she asked, stung. Wasn't it enough she knew she was still too thin? Her leathers all but hung on her.

"Nothing. I meant nothing. Just that you should eat if that's what you want to do. Are you sure you don't want to visit the copse? There's a working well, and the stones are quite extraordinary. Trixie ordered them. And we'd have a better chance to see anyone approaching from any side."

"I don't want to visit a graveyard, Max."

"Very well." They dismounted, and Max tied the horses' leads to nearby branches while Zoé unrolled the wool blanket strapped behind Max's saddle and lifted down the straw picnic basket secured to her own.

Max smiled at her efficiency. "You're not worried Anton or some others will consider us vulnerable?"

"I thought we were rather hoping that's exactly what they'd think."

"Maybe some of them would hazard it, but not Anton, and we can rest assured he's told them just that. We're going to have to try something completely new, I'm afraid, to bring him out in the open. He's too familiar with the way we work." Max tossed a brace of pistols to the blanket before sprawling himself next to them, one bent arm used to prop up his head as he looked at the basket. "Is there chicken? I think I smell chicken."

Zoé rolled her eyes, then lifted open the split top of the basket, to begin laying out its contents. "Chicken," she said, tossing him a golden-skinned leg and thigh he snagged deftly as he sat up. "Cheese, a lovely fresh loaf, apples. Oh, strawberries! You have a succession house. I wonder if it stretches to a banana tree or two."

"Or more. Trixie brought back plants and trees from all her travels, to the point where Gideon had to order another greenhouse, and then a third. Careful there, madam. You'll probably want to retain all ten fingers."

Zoé had withdrawn a large knife from the basket, and was employing it to slice chunks from the half-round of fragrant cheese. "I know how to handle a knife," she said testily as she reached for the loaf and began slicing it, as well.

"Everywhere but in the kitchens," Max pointed out as he slipped a pair of blue-tinted spectacles from his pocket and slipped them on, only to lower them to peer at her overtop the glass. His accompanying grin did just what he'd probably wanted it to do.

Zoé felt herself melting. Then she felt the sickening, deep slide of the knife across the pad of her left thumb. "Damn you, Max Redgrave, you *wished* that on me!" she said, dropping the knife and sticking her injured thumb into her mouth to suck away the blood and the sting.

He had his hands on hers before she could insist he leave her alone, and a white linen square quickly wrapped around her thumb. "It's not too deep. We need to keep pressure on it for a few minutes, that's all."

He was close enough for her to smell the cologne he favored; it had always had the power to make her stomach clench in reaction, in anticipation. He measured her with his eyes. "You're not feeling faint, are you?

Of course you are, look how pale you've gone. Lack of food, most probably. Here, rest your head in my lap and keep pressure on the cut." His grin was devilish. "I'll feed you strawberries until you recover."

"Seduction, Max? You did warn me," she said, pulling her hand free, handkerchief and all. "But no. I won't say I'm not interested, because that would be a lie. My body recognizes you even when my mind reminds me no good can come from temporary physical pleasure. The past won't leave us alone, no matter how hard we try. So thank you, Max, but no."

"How very polite, and how very wrong. We'll both succumb at some point, Zoé, and sooner better than later. Otherwise, it will be impossible to devote our full concentration on finding Anton, and that could be more dangerous to us than daring to locate what you consider lost." His message delivered, he lifted her injured hand to his lips, pressed a kiss against her knuckles and let her go.

Maybe she was wrong. Maybe he was attempting to make up for abandoning her. Maybe she still hadn't forgiven him…even as she'd made certain he would abandon her. Maybe he felt pity for her. That would be the worst. Pity.

"Max?" He'd pushed the glasses slightly higher on his nose. She could still see his eyes, but she couldn't read them. "I'm sorry. It's simply too soon, too easy not to be a mistake."

"Wine?" he asked casually in return, as he lifted a bottle from the basket and showed it to her. "Gideon keeps an exemplary cellar. Although it would seem this Jacko fellow forgot glasses. Do you mind? We've shared the same bottle before. Remember that night in Madrid, when we—"

"Max, for God's sake, take those ridiculous spectacles off, shut up and look at me. If we're going to find Anton and this damned Society of yours, I agree. We have to settle this. I said something I thought important, and your only response was to offer me wine?"

"Settle this? And how do we do that, Zoé?" he asked as he removed the spectacles and slid them back into the inside pocket of his hacking jacket. "We never did love each other. Isn't that what you said? I want to prove you wrong, but I don't know how to do that, and I can't help thinking you may be right. I turned my back on you. I walked away. I did my best to chalk you up as a mistake, and move on."

Zoé nodded. "I deliberately hurt your pride, whether I meant well or not. There must have been another way to handle Anton than the one I chose. I've had months to consider them. A silent signal to you, one of those damn bird whistles you taught me—anything. Instead, I made you question your judgment, and every word you and I ever said to each other, every time we whispered love words while locked in each other's arms…"

She unwrapped her thumb and looked at the slice she'd inflicted on herself. Did Max realize what that slip with the knife meant? Of course he did. It meant she had lost her edge, her concentration. And that's the sort of lapse that got people killed; her, or someone else.

Like Max. She'd be no good to him, no good at all, if she couldn't pull herself together. What had seemed so reasonable last night didn't seem more than selfish nonsense to her today.

"Yes, my damnable pride. That about says it, thank you. In my defense, there were also the murdered agents. Georges. But I should have known you'd never trade their lives for your own benefit. Even if you say you forgive me, how do I forgive myself? *I should have known.*"

It was as if they were attempting to outdo each other, all but flogging themselves with guilt. But she couldn't seem to stop.

"I believed Anton when he said you were dead. That might have been easier to accept than the idea that you were still alive, and had simply abandoned me. But I still should have gone searching for you the moment I was freed. Knowing Anton's facile, lying tongue, I should have made certain."

She looked at him, attempting to read his mind, she supposed. "If I had come to you, told you what really happened, would you have believed me? Or did we need this time apart, need Anton's obvious betrayal last night, before you could ever begin to believe me? Please, Max, think about it for a moment, and answer honestly."

Max slid his gaze away from her and stood up, turned his back on her. "I hoped you wouldn't ask that question. Because I don't know, Zoé. How can I know? I only know what I believe now, what I feel now."

Zoé quietly got to her feet. That was the answer she'd

hoped for: the truth. Her heart was pounding. With fear, with trepidation. "And what is it you feel now, Max?"

"Shame," he said quietly. "Sorrow." He was quiet for a few moments, even as she stepped around the blanket, to stand behind him. "Against all reason, hope…"

Trixie had told her it was up to Max and herself to take the next step, to talk to each other. They'd done that now. Truthfully. Honestly. Now the time had passed for talking. Actions often spoke more clearly than words.

She slid her arms around his waist, laid her cheek against his back. She wanted so badly to give in; so badly. "Life is difficult enough, isn't it? To live it without hope makes life unbearable, nothing more than a dark, desperate existence. All that's moved me forward these last months has been my determination to be the instrument of Anton's destruction. I never thought beyond that moment. Yet I'll have nothing after that, Max. I'm afraid to have nothing, be left with a yawning void ahead of me and no reason to live."

He turned within the circle of her arms. "We could have each other. We could find a way. There has to be a way to begin again."

To begin again. She moistened her dry lips by pulling them in and licking them with her tongue. Yes, that was it. That's what she'd needed to hear, even if she hadn't realized it until he'd said the words. But still she couldn't trust her voice. She only nodded, her eyes speaking for her, his eyes speaking for him.

"A way to learn to love. Not again, because what we thought we had was clearly flawed, superficial, a passion of the moment or some such rot. But to really learn to love. I'm more than ready to do that. Am I worth the risk for you, Zoé?"

She raised her hands to wipe the tears from her cheeks. "I think you are, yes. I need to rid my heart of hate, which is all it has held these last long months. And…and when there's no reason left to hate, when I've had my rightful vengeance, and when you've made your family safe again, perhaps there will be more grown between us than simply hope."

She believed she might melt in the new light in Max's eyes as he cupped her face between his hands and lowered his mouth to hers. "To seal our bargain," he breathed, and she closed her eyes, waiting for his kiss. *Always the opportunist,* she thought. *Thank God…*

The pistol shot sounded like the thunderclap heralding the end of the world, and Zoé felt her breath half knocked out of her as Max threw her to the ground, covering her with his own body. He counted to ten beside her ear, and then rolled off her, toward the pistols lying on the blanket, even as she raised her right leg, bent at the knee, and slid the stiletto from her boot. Whoever was out there had destroyed what was going to be a new beginning for she and Max, and was going to damn well pay for the interruption!

"Anton?" she whispered as they took cover against the first row of trees, as the shot had come from behind them. And, she belatedly realized, had come nowhere near them.

"No. I think the shot was more of a signal that we have company. See anything?"

"Company? What the devil does that mean?" Looking into the trees after being in the bright sunlight wasn't easy. It was like looking from light into dark. To have any hope of seeing in the dark, one had to *be* in the dark.

"Sorry to interrupt a tender moment," came a voice from the trees. Max and Zoé both swung to their left, trying to locate the voice. But when the man spoke again, his voice seemed to be coming from their right. "I fired into the air, merely attempting to save any of us embarrassment. I'm Simon's friend, by the way. I believe you were told to expect me at the copse."

Zoé was caught somewhere between embarrassment and outrage. "What's he saying? This whole thing— suggesting the copse, the basket, *everything?* All so you could meet with some— Max, I could kill you right now."

"I rather sense that, yes." Max then put a finger to his lips, warning her to silence. "I'm sorry. I was going to tell you, but I was sidetracked. Pleasantly, but sidetracked. I'll explain later."

"You'll also apologize later, except that we're both idiots, and could be dead right now."

"*That* I'll ignore, even though you're right." He raised his voice. "Simon didn't give me a name, only where we should meet. I didn't want to insist on the copse when you said no to it, but you were willing to stop here."

The unseen man spoke again, with some humor in

his tone. "If you're through discussing our location? My name isn't important, only that I'm not an enemy. You met a few of my men last night."

"I thought it would be you. The pirate," Max said, discarding the pistols before he got to his feet. "Simon's helpful friend."

"He's a fine man, yes, but I first became acquainted with your grandmother several years ago. Now, young lady, if you'd kindly slip that stiletto back into your boot, I'll dare to step out of the shadows."

Zoé did as suggested—she refused to consider his words an order—and watched as a tall, well set-up man clad in superbly tailored but otherwise nondescript brown separated himself from the tree trunks. He wore a brown slouch hat pulled down over one eye, and a black silk handkerchief covered the lower half of his face.

"Pardon the dramatics, but I rather relish my anonymity," he said as he stopped just at the edge of the tree line, remaining in the shade. "You've got quite a lot on your plate, Mr. Redgrave, haven't you, even more than the rest of your family? What's his name?"

Max didn't hesitate. "Boucher. Anton Boucher. Do you have him?"

"No, more's the pity. Billy, one of my longtime associates, and more past it than he'd care to admit, nearly prevented this Boucher of yours from making it beyond the crest of the hill last night. But when two heavily armed riders appeared, leading a saddled mount between them, Billy prudently rethought his notion of heroism and hid in the bushes. Your man is gone, his companions one man, one woman. Or at least Billy believes one was male. Only the woman spoke, clearly unhappy with this fellow Boucher. Billy said he's heard fishwives with more civil tongues in their heads."

"The couple in Ostend," Zoé said unnecessarily. "Where does that leave us, Max?"

"If I may?" the stranger asked. "With the majority of your staff turned enemy, you are dangerously vulnerable, with all the Redgraves still in need of my assistance, which I freely grant. Some of my crew and their mates will continue their vigilance at Redgrave Manor, under direction of Jacko, my second in command. The rest will continue as they've been, systematically ridding the coastline of Bonaparte's smuggled troops. You are aware of the intention to capture the Martello Towers when the signal is given of an attack from the sea?"

"Max? That's impossible. Bonaparte doesn't have the ships to carry an army across the Channel. We haven't worried about a threat of invasion since Trafalgar."

"Mr. Redgrave? Would you be kind enough to inform Mademoiselle Charbonneau of the number of smuggling craft—from old tubs to the fastest sloops—routinely anchored in Gravelines on a prime smuggling night such as the one just passed?"

"Sweet Jesus," Max hissed, looking at Zoé. "He's right. Bonaparte has built hotels for the smugglers' convenience, not just in Gravelines but in Dunkirk, as well."

"And other places," the stranger added. "We've made

it our point to search them out. Quite the hospitable gentleman, don't you think? And more than happy to trade French silks and brandy for gold to pay his troops and wool for their uniforms. Not to mention smugglers being marvelous conduits for newspapers and other news, and for transporting spies."

"And troops. You're saying the emperor has been shoveling troops across the Channel, a few pebbles at a time, until he has built himself a mountain?" Zoé's mind was whirling, all thoughts of romance gone, her attention concentrated solely on solving the puzzle in front of her. That exercise didn't take long. "Positioning them to overtake the Martello Towers at his signal, silencing the guns aimed out to sea. For the invasion itself, he'd plan it for one of the nights the smugglers are most active, and simply commandeer their boats for his troops. All those boats, all at once. The Revenue cutters would be overwhelmed; not enough patrol ships, too many targets. With the towers already in French hands, the boats could land without much fuss." She turned to Max. "And Anton is a part of this?"

"It would appear so, yes. At the least, he works for the Society, while Redgrave Manor and its proximity to London is not only one of the landing points, but probably destined to become their headquarters. Granted, it's not a castle, with high stone walls and battlements, but it does have its subtle defensive qualities, not to mention ample land and resources to hide an army. My father and grandfather made sure of that, for their own treasonous purposes."

"Your grand— No, you can explain that another time. You can explain a *lot* another time. Continue."

"With your kind permission, yes, I believe I will."

The pirate chuckled. "Clearly you two aren't recent acquaintances, and have enjoyed sparring for a long time. This should prove entertaining."

"We have our moments, yes," Max said as Zoé averted her eyes. "But to continue? With the Towers' guns under French control, our English fighting ships wouldn't dare approach the coast, and by the time we could launch a land force of any size, it's possible the French would have already established themselves. With more troops to follow."

Zoé was still finding this information difficult to take in, until she realized what would be necessary for there to be any chance at success. "With our grand island a defense all on its own, Bonaparte needed co-operation from this side of the Channel. Rather an invasion from within. This Society of yours?"

"Treason, yes, but with the promise of a great reward. Trixie and the others believe they know what that is. As for Anton, he was either watching the Society for the French, or was recruited by the Society itself, and assigned, among other duties, to keep his eyes on me. *Use* me in some way, as they've used others. But then I got suspicious, and he had to make other plans. I was going to tell you, just as soon as I'd gotten it all sorted out in my mind."

"And how are you involved?" she asked, looking at the patiently waiting stranger once more. The pirate.

"You stumbled over this plan somehow, and notified Trixie? Or was it she who came to you?"

"I would say it was a smattering of both. Someone approached several of the entrepreneurs I lend my protection, offering them gold for their assistance, stirring my curiosity. Before you ask exactly who was approached, *mademoiselle*, yes, smugglers."

"You've traded piracy for smuggling? No wonder you don't want to show your face."

The stranger cocked his one visible eyebrow as he looked at Max. "Does she often speak before she thinks?"

"Not usually, no." Max grinned. "It was that kiss you interrupted," he returned easily. "Her mind is still muddled with moonbeams. Isn't it, darling?"

Unbelievably, Zoé found herself laughing. And apologizing. Oh, it was good to be back with Max again, on every level. Good to be back in the game. "Touché, Max. I apologize, sir. Please go on," she said, knowing her cheeks had turned a betraying pink.

"I will, thank you. Now, where was I? Oh, yes. The dowager countess supplied the information about the Society's existence, telling me only what I needed to know, that Redgrave land is possibly being used by them as some sort of safe haven. Over time, she has told me the rest. She's a very brave lady, and her secrets are safe with me. All Redgrave secrets are safe with me. I couldn't do less, as I have secrets of my own."

Zoé opened her mouth, to apologize again, but then prudently kept her silence.

"However, no matter who or what I was, I am an Englishman now, and loyal not only to my country but to those under my protection. I'm here to help, but I am not a Good Samaritan. I have my family, my loyal people, and I have my reasons to despise traitors. I want my corner of the world to return to what it was. When this is over we'll be gone, without thanks, which are not necessary, and without satisfying your curiosity. Simon understands that, but I've learned you Redgraves can be doggedly inquisitive." He looked deeply into Max's eyes. "That wouldn't be wise."

"Then I suppose I should thank you now, as we'd be in fairly dire straits if you and your crew hadn't stepped in when the Coopers showed their true colors."

Zoé was feeling neglected, left to do nothing but ask obvious questions. "You'll be in charge of those watching the Towers?"

"They're spread over too many miles of the coast for us to manage them all if the attack is scheduled for the next smuggler's moon, so we've already quietly removed thirty of them from Bonaparte's side of the ledger. There are no more than ten or twelve men needed for each Tower, and it's only a matter of identifying them and eliminating them."

"Capturing or killing them?" she asked, then wondered why she cared either way. She was getting soft, and that wasn't a good thing.

"We haven't yet thrown them a fete, no, but for the most part they're still breathing."

"But there are over one hundred Towers, aren't

there?" Zoé was mentally calculating how long it would take to secure the rest of them.

Max slammed his fist into his palm. "One hundred and eighteen, once those now under construction are finished, and to hear my brother Valentine tell it, they're being built only because the Society managed to hood-wink Perceval with false information. That means over one thousand men crossing the Channel in the past year or less, some of them landing on Redgrave land, un-doubtedly sheltered on Redgrave land by the Coopers. And all while we knew nothing—and while the prime minister dismisses us as hysterical old ladies. Or wor-ries we're traitors. If it all goes publicly sideways for Bonaparte and the Society, they'll all simply disappear, and it will be the Redgraves left to be tried for treason."

"That would about sum up your dilemma, yes," the stranger said, and Zoé was fairly certain he was smiling behind his handkerchief. "You might imagine my own frustration, as I lack even the opportunity to approach the government without possibly exposing my true iden-tity and putting my head into a noose. But such is life, as I've learned. What we do, we do swiftly, quietly, and bury the bodies, and the secrets, where they fall."

"That's succinct enough," Zoé muttered, scuffing her booted toe in the dirt. "We're fighting a secret war, and either we win, or we hang. Lovely."

"Quite. And now I'm off. If you need me at any time, put a word in Jacko's ear, but my hope is that we each solve this distasteful problem at our own ends. You to destroy this devil Society plaguing you, and me to prevent the possibility of invasion. I'd rather we weren't tripping over each other in the process. Agreed?"

"Agreed," Max said, holding out his hand. "Captain."

The man acknowledged the title with a handshake and a bow of his head. "One thing more. I already outstay my welcome, as my sons will begin to fuss if I tarry any longer. The Cooper children and women are scattered in small pocket villages along the Royal Military Canal, between Ruckinge and Warehorne, being watched over by a few old men. I don't think we need concern ourselves with them. Just the one, Billy's fishwife."

"And the men?"

"Nowhere to be found and, frankly, I've already spread my men more thinly than I care to do. I can only suggest you concentrate on the woman, her male companion and this former compatriot of yours. Cut off the head, and the rest of the fish dies. An old saying, I grant you, but still a true one. How clever is this Boucher of yours?"

Max and Zoé exchanged glances before she said with all the conviction she felt now that the two of them were working together again, "Very. But he has his weaknesses."

Another bow, this one to Zoé, and the pirate was gone, melted back into the trees. Moments later he appeared again on horseback, flanked by two other riders. They all crashed out of the woods and set the horses to a gallop across the wide expanse of fallow ground. She watched as a pair of horsemen rode out to meet them from the other side. They waited, their mounts dancing in an eagerness to be off, then turned and headed back into the trees, the pirate and his companions following, all four of the other men clearly keeping the pirate protectively in their midst. Were they the sons he spoke of?

"Damn it. Three. Not one voice, seemingly traveling, but three, thoroughly tricking us. And their horses with them? We can't forget the horses."

"And we heard nothing, not even a jingle of harness or a stray whinny. Not only are we out of practice, Max, but that pistol shot saved at least one of us some extreme personal embarrassment. We won't see him again? I can understand that. It would be he who saw us first. Do you wonder how much faith the pirate has in us now?"

Max took the blue-lensed spectacles from his pocket and slipped them on once more. "Do you think I could blame you for distracting me?"

"You might as well," she answered, rather inelegantly plopping herself down on the blanket. "After all, I was going to blame you. Or perhaps the fact that I still haven't had anything to eat."

CHAPTER SIX

MAX EXPLAINED THE rest to Zoé as they returned to their *picnic,* deftly slipping in apologies each time she frowned, letting him know there were things he could, should, have told her sooner. As in before they'd left Redgrave Manor.

She now knew the full history of the Society, going back to its inception with his grandfather, its resurrection via his father, and this third incarnation thanks to the Coopers, longtime loyal employees of the Redgrave family.

She'd asked no questions when he described what they knew of the Society: its rites, the perversions, the recruitment and then blackmail of members brought in by the inner circle, the Devil's Thirteen. In fact, she'd said nothing at all until he'd told her about the fires… the one Simon had set to obliterate the hidden chamber of treason and vice beneath the dower house, and his brother Valentine's destruction of a smaller such gathering place elsewhere.

It was only then that she said, "Anton must be distraught over their loss. If I were to attempt to *recruit* someone like Anton, I believe success would be a sim-

ple matter of indulging his tastes, just as you say the
Society has always done."

Max picked up the half-empty bottle of wine and
looked into its mouth, contemplating his chances of
asking the question that burned inside his head…and
the possible consequences. "Did he—"

"Never," Zoé answered before he could finish. "He
tried during his first visit to my cell, I'll give him that.
But by then I'd decided he needed me alive more than
he wanted his satisfaction, or else I'd already be dead.
I warned him I'd kill myself if he touched me, even if
I had to chew through my own veins."

"He believed you?"

Zoé shrugged. "He'd already told me you were dead.
I had nothing to live for, nowhere to go even if I somehow escaped my cell. Anton can be as practical as any
Frenchman. I believe he weighed the reason he was
keeping me alive against a *pleasure* he only need delay
until I was no longer necessary to some plan. He even
ordered my rations increased. But would I have done
it? Killed myself?" She shrugged again. "I wouldn't
know that until I was actually put to the test, would I?
I'd like to think I would."

"Well, don't," Max said, his temper rising. "Don't
think it, don't ever choose it, no matter how you're
forced or tempted. There's always a chance, Zoé, if we
just look for it. A chance to survive, another way out,
right up until our last breath. Don't ever give up on
yourself and, much as I don't deserve the right to say
this, don't ever give up on me."

"You'll never change, will you? Always believing you're the one in charge. So I say the same to you. Your grandmother told me you've become too reckless these last months. I believe our new pirate friend's surprise appearance proves her point. We both need to rein in our passionate natures."

"All of them?" he asked, feeling a different sort of recklessness within him.

"You already know the answer to that, Lord help us both. Now, tell me more about these Coopers."

He began with the recent attempt on Trixie's life by one of the younger Coopers, Liam, and her later conversation with the boy's grandfather. The Coopers had been with the estate even before his grandfather's time, and it was Trixie's conclusion that her husband had made promises to them in order to gain their help with his planned treason. Such help naturally included the initial construction and subsequent maintenance of the caves and the ceremonial rooms themselves.

"Of course. He would have needed help from somewhere, wouldn't he? And your father, as well, when he followed in his sire's footsteps? He would also have had to make promises. I imagine every hellfire club needs someone to dust and polish the sacrificial altar, empty the Exalted Leader's chamber pots."

"You're a cruel woman, Zoé Charbonneau," Max said, tossing her the last strawberry. "The only real wonder is that none of us had ever before thought of the logistics of constructing and maintaining a devil's pleasure den."

"Clearly somebody did. And that thought may have led that somebody to the Coopers, who would have known anything and everything about the workings of the Society. There can be no real secrets, not with servants in the house. I'd lay my money on the woman I saw in Ostend, were I you. Much as you won't want to hear this, it's women who consider the details while you men are more concerned with the larger picture, such as conquering the world. Naturally, those details would have led her straight to the Coopers."

"I agree. Highly sexed from your description of her, and hearing what the captain's man told him, clearly the one issuing orders."

"The man could be explained as the brawn behind her orders. Big, not too intelligent, but necessary to her in some way. Sex and power, power and sex. You men never get bored with either. It's the rare woman who turns the tables, seizes the power. Not that I applaud this particular woman, considering her treasonous goal. Remember, schoolgirl French. We're dealing with an Englishwoman. And with Anton involved, possibly at a direct order from Bonaparte, I imagine that at the end of the day these Coopers of yours are in for yet a third great disappointment. Kings and emperors aren't known for paying their bills."

Max had picked up the now reloaded basket and poured away the last of the wine before the two of them, together, folded the blanket. "Angus Cooper informed Trixie that Redgrave Manor belonged to the Coopers as much as it did to us. They'd built it, maintained it, and had been told it would all be theirs, the entire estate, if they did as they were told. After all, my mad-as-hatters ancestors truly believed they and their supposed Stuart blood would one day sit on the English throne."

"With help from the Louis, before the father died of his dissipations and the son lost his head to his. But now there's Bonaparte, and the Society has risen again. We can only hope the third time isn't the charm. So, enough talk. Where to now, Max?"

"We're all business again?" He watched as she deftly strapped the rolled blanket to the back of his saddle. He hadn't expected her to tug him down on the blanket so they could seal their tenuous new relationship in a more physical way. Not here. But he had considered moving the two of them to another spot on Redgrave land, a leafy bower he'd first been introduced to by, of all people, one of the Cooper women when he'd been no more than fifteen.

Zoé shot him a rather knowing look. "When were we ever all business?"

Laughing, he helped hoist her onto the sidesaddle, complete with a playful swipe to her rump as she lifted her foot into the stirrup.

They both had a long way to go, and he was certain she knew that, as well, but in time, two years of spending nearly every waking and sleeping moment together surely had the power to banish the last eight months from their memories. He knew he had a lot of making up to do, but they had the rest of their lives for that.

"The tide's out," he told her as he mounted his own

horse. "I'd like to see this man-made cave in the daylight. Gideon believes it once was farther inland, and built by the Romans as a sort of fort or outpost. Centuries of storms and a shifting coastline must have eventually chewed away at it, leaving behind only what we see now."

"You hope to find something, or is this simply curiosity?"

"Simply curiosity, I'd say," he admitted as he pointed toward the waters of the Channel, laid out below them. They rode in silence, each looking deceptively relaxed even as they were all vigilance, not about to be taken by surprise again. Redgrave Manor's grounds were vast, the West Run incredibly wide and long, leisurely leading down to the water, their progress broken up by strategically constructed hedgerows and stone walls.

The run ended at a wide but navigable cliff, the cottages below them and to the left of the stone jetty, the familiar jumble of huge boulders to the right of it. The receding tide had left behind bits of mast and curved boards ripped from the hull of the ship they'd traveled in last night. An old woman, probably one of the cottagers who had chosen to live out their retirement from service on this spit of Redgrave land, was busily loading wood into her apron, undoubtedly to dry out and use in her small fireplace. For cooking, to help tide her through the wintry days to come. The poor wasted nothing.

"Those four cottages?" he said to Zoé as they looked down at the scene. "Gideon leases them to the odd fisherman, or simply allows former Redgrave servants or laborers to live in them."

Zoé nodded, holding down the shako hat as the stiff breeze coming off the Channel threatened to dislodge it. "That's where we came ashore last night. Do you think the horses can manage this path?"

"They can. But before we do that, I want you to look at the stones and boulders to your right. What do you see?"

"I see stones and boulders, quite the opposite of the sand and shingle of the beach on the other side of our stone tunnel," she answered. "What am I supposed to see?"

"According to what Gideon and Simon told me this morning, we're to see what's left of a defensive maze carefully constructed by some ancient people—again, most likely Romans. Imagine the Channel at least seventy-five yards farther from the current shoreline, and the wall containing the pass-through cave, gone now, but if intact, curving around until it met the cliff."

"A fort. You're saying if we were to dig deeply enough, there'd be another stone wall just about here. Possibly once complete with parapets, the tops of the walls their first line of defense, their archers stationed there—and up here, right where we are." Zoé looked at the ground just ahead of them. "Yes, I can see it."

"Fascinating, isn't it? The Channel taking some of it, the rest covered up by those who cleared the West Run, disposing of hundreds, perhaps thousands of tree roots and boulders by dragging them down here and pushing them against and over the now actually man-made cliff, obscuring the original structure. The grassy mound to our left also probably covers a large section of stone wall. At one time, this seeming jumble was a complete square."

"An ancient Roman fort. To hear you tell it, Redgrave Manor already has everything…and now you can add a Roman fort to the list, as well. My congratulations. But what does any of this have to do with us now?"

"I'm not certain it has anything to do with us, unless we found ourselves facing a French landing party, as it's too treacherous to land anywhere but on the cottage side of the fort."

"Because the underwater walls succumbed to the battering of the tides, but parts of the maze remain intact just off the shore, ready to rip out the bellies of any vessel attempting to land? Amazing. I can almost see the sun shining off the polished armor of the soldiers."

She was standing in the saddle as her gaze traveled left to right, and then back again, her expression rather rapt. Max had always loved seeing the world through her eyes.

"Simon supposes the Romans used the cave as a stables or storehouse, but also as a convenient back door should the fort fall. That maze on the other side was built to slow attackers, protect Roman fighters as they retreated either to or from the fort, and to hide behind as their archers cut down pursuing enemies forced to come through the cave, setting themselves up as easy targets. You're right, Zoé, it had to be fairly amazing, in its day. That got me to wondering if we might use the cave in the same way."

"So all this is your way of saying the Romans built us an extremely clever mousetrap or hidey-hole, if we're ever caught out here in the open." Zoé smiled appreciatively. "One could even call it our rather singular Martello Tower. In that case, yes, we should go down there and figure out how Richard Borders managed to locate the cave entrance."

"And exit." Max led the way down the steep path before helping Zoé dismount. They waved to the old woman, who waved back before scurrying up the steep steps to her cottage. "Obviously not a Cooper," he remarked as they crossed the slippery shingle liberally mixed with the sand, looking for the place Richard had brought them to last night.

Zoé pointed to the ground. "See that? The shingle appears to have been scraped back over the sand a bit here. I imagine another few tides and we wouldn't be able to see that, but we can now. Oh, would you look at that. The poor old thing must have put some of that wet wood on her cooking fire."

Max turned about to see the thick grey smoke rising from the chimney of the woman's cottage, shook his head, and went to work on locating the correct stones, Zoé joining him.

They poked about in the same way Richard had done, and were soon rewarded. Max worked his fingers between the large stones and pulled. The door opened, not very far, but far enough. He stepped inside, leaving Zoé

behind to ask, "Can you feel anything, are there handholds on the other side? If closed, do you think it possible I could push the door open again from the inside?
There's several loose boulders out here. All it would
need is to roll one in front of the door, and—what do
you see, Max?"

Her recently acquired fear of being enclosed, locked
into the darkness. Damn. He'd forgotten about that.
He stepped back into the sunlight and told her he'd go
around the jetty at the shoreline, to open the other end
of the tunnel, as well. "Just stay here," he warned.

"You don't have to ask me a second time. Be careful.
Anyone could look down and see us here."

Max didn't know if the bell inside his head began
to clang at the same time as Zoé's did inside of hers—
the smoke, high, billowing smoke anyone could see a
mile away as it rose above the cliff—but before he got
to the end of the stone jetty he had whirled about and
was running toward her, just as she was flinging herself up onto the sidesaddle, his stallion's reins clamped
between her teeth.

He was in the saddle within a heartbeat and they
were both racing toward the end of the stone jetty,
around it to the other side, staying to the shoreline, their
mounts' hooves kicking up sprays of seawater as they
galloped on, until they'd gone well beyond the maze.

They both pulled up, looking around them. "Now
what?" Zoé asked.

Max had grown up around these stones, never understanding them, but definitely learning the area. "This

way," he said, even as he pressed his heels into the stallion's flanks.

And they were off again, pounding through the undergrowth of wind-stunted bushes and long, waving grasses that all but obscured the narrow path he remembered. Only turning inland again when they were a good half-mile from the stone jetty.

"We'll work our way back, but only halfway, and then we go on foot," he told her.

"On our bellies, if we have to. So much for the woman not being a Cooper. Not simply wet wood, but a signal, alerting somebody that someone was on the beach." She took off the green shako hat, now hanging by a single pin anyway, and angrily tossed it to the ground before twisting her long blond hair into at least the semblance of a knot after it had been blown about in the wind. "Poor doddering old thing? She's probably halfway to Dover by now, damn it."

"And with one side of the cave left standing open," Max reminded her. "There's not a whacking great lot of good luck between us at the moment, is there? But maybe that's about to change. Caught your breath?"

"I never lost it," she said, grinning in her old, mischievous way. "You? I suppose you need a moment?"

Max shook his head in dawning amazement. "God, I've missed this. The sparring, the way our brains seemed always to work together, almost as if we were the same person. But we're getting it back, aren't we, it's beginning to come back."

"It had *all* better come back very quickly, if we're to

keep our heads." Her smile faded only slightly. "We'll only know that answer once we've had a success. Lead the way, Max, before whoever's going to show up arrives, sees we're gone, and slips away."

Halfway back to the ruined fort, riding through the trees above the cliff edge, they dismounted, traveling the rest of the way on foot. Careful to stay hidden in the underbrush, they were both fairly well covered in burrs, their hands cut by more than a few thorns, by the time they were back in sight of the stone jetty, and the cottages they would not be able to see unless they left the cover of the greenery behind.

"Remember that old Irish song?" he asked quietly.

"You'll have to do better than that, I'm afraid," she answered, grimacing as she pulled burrs from her once-again tangled hair.

She cared about her comfort, but little about her appearance, which only made her more lovely in his eyes. Her beauty came to her naturally, dressed in silk gowns or covered in burrs.

"The sad one, about the doomed Irish soldier."

"And better than that. They're all sad, and half of them concern dead soldiers," she pointed out, still whispering, as they both knew the constantly shifting breeze could send their voices anywhere.

"True. How's this? 'You take the high road, and I'll take—'"

"'The low road,' and I'll be inside the old woman's cottage a'for ye manage that second opening through the rocks. Good enough."

"May I say again how good it is to be—"

But she was already moving, pausing only just before leaving the cover of the brush to listen for the sound of approaching hoof beats, then making a dash for the path leading down to the cottage...all while Max, using handholds remembered from his youth, navigated his way down the steep, rocky incline and jumped the last ten or so feet to the ground.

He didn't have the time to examine the standing stones to see evidence Simon had told him about, recent repairs made to some of them, probably by the Society. Instead, he went straight to the spot he hoped paralleled the opening on the other side of the man-made cave, to begin his search for the so-called door.

He'd been counting steadily inside his head since Zoé had left him, and was soon to approach three hundred, an uncomfortably high number considering their limit was five hundred, when his fingers at last located the concealed handholds. He knelt down and used his hands to push away much of the shingle so that the door would open more easily, pulled it free just far enough to slip inside, leaving behind an excavation hopefully barely noticeable from the outside.

His pistols were in his hands and cocked by the time he reached the other end of the tunnel and he could push that door open more fully, just enough to peek his head through it to see how Zoé was managing. And whether or not they had company.

He was in time to observe Zoé leaving the protection of the third cottage, quickly taking cover once more beneath the fourth and last, the one with heavy smoke still rising from its chimney, high into the sky. Because all the cottages had been built to sit on thick wooden stilts, he could see her boots as she left the third cottage and made her way around to the far side of the fourth, stopping only when she reached the end, and was able to peek around the corner to see the front steps. Now, other than avoiding being seen as she'd raced down the path to the cover of the first cottage, came the danger-ous part.

She was going to enter the cottage, confront the woman if she was still inside, threaten her into silence.

"Careful," he coached her quietly, having at last stopped his mental count. "I'm in place, you know I am. You trust me. You know I've got your ba— What in hell?"

He'd just seen the skirt of his sister's green riding habit fall to the ground.

Max only had time to think *God Almighty,* not say it, before Zoé was all but vaulting over the weathered wood railing of the step in her borrowed white linen panta-loons. She quickly regained her footing, and smashed one booted foot against the cottage door. "Smart door, it knew better than to put up a fight," he said, watching as Zoé, stiletto drawn, disappeared into the cottage. If the woman had remained inside, she wouldn't be scream-ing any warnings, not with Zoé in control.

Now, they'd wait. Five minutes, an hour, however long it took. Because that smoke had to have alerted someone, summoned someone.

As they waited, he noticed that the smoke leaving the chimney had changed color, was now mostly white, billows and billows of white smoke, and then slowed to little more than a few wisps. Zoé had put the fire out, and the smoke was more steam now, having had water dumped all over it.

Then he heard the sound of metal-rimmed wheels on the shingle, his position inside the cave confusing the sound, so that it could be coming from any direction. Yet there was only one logical one: the same way he and Zoé had taken the horses. Whoever was approaching was somehow driving through the maze and around the end of the jetty, an impossible feat at high tide, but reasonable now.

Signaling Zoé with the birdcall was out of the question; there was no way he could predict where the breeze would carry the sound, and next to no chance it would make it all the way to the cottage in any case. But she'd be watching, and would probably have their first clear look at whoever and whatever was coming.

Max dared to push the stone door wider and looked to his right, to see the head of an old mule in the traces of what was quickly evident was a farm wagon, a bent, cloaked figure on the bench seat.

Who attacks with a mule-drawn wagon?

"Nobody," Max said, answering his own question. He stepped out onto the shingle, uncocking the pistols and shoving them back into his waistband. Besides, he'd recognized the wagon, was certain he knew the man holding the traces.

"Angus!" He continued walking, completely leaving the handy retreat of the cave, waving toward the cottage to signal Zoé that everything was fine. "*Angus!* It's Max. I'm right here!"

Zoé exited the cottage, retrieved the riding skirt, and headed across the shingle beach at a near-trot, wearing nothing but the top half of the riding habit, his sister's white cotton knickers, and her own knee-high boots. He could smell the smoke on her by the time she was no less than fifty yards away, and read her expression, as well, the one that told him she wasn't a happy woman.

"Who's that in the wagon? Obviously you know him. That stupid old woman in the cottage was damn near dead when I arrived, with the smoke coming back down the chimney at her. She's fine, but I smell as if I've been turning on a spit the last quarter hour. I want my leathers back, Max, even if you insist I wear something over them. As it is, hopping over that railing, I must have a dozen splinters in my— Never mind. Let's go catch up with your friend, as he's clearly having second thoughts."

And that he was. Angus was frantically attempting to turn the mule, but the animal was having none of it.

"You probably frightened him. I know you scared the hell out of me. Put on your skirt," Max said as he took off toward the wagon.

"*You* try vaulting over a railing in a skirt," she called after him.

He didn't bother going to the mule's head, as the animal appeared half asleep, but went straight to Angus and reached up to set the wagon brake. "Angus. I thought you were gone. The last I heard, you were berating my grandmother at Liam's funeral. My condolences on your grandson's death, but no rational man would blame Trixie. Is that who I'm looking at now, Angus? A rational man?"

Angus Cooper was eighty if he was a day, and as Trixie had told them, grew up with their grandfather: laborer, employee, yet friend. A stonemason, as well—just the sort of occupation that would be called on to fashion pillars, simple statues...stone altars.

There was a time the man had used his skill to carve soapstone soldiers for the Redgrave boys to reenact ancient battles. Such as Culloden, where those loyal to the Royal Stuarts had fought for the last time. So many pieces, at last tumbling into place.

Angus looked down at Max with rheumy eyes, his nose oversize and red-tipped, quite nearly resembling the strawberries from the picnic basket. Max knew the man was old, but now he looked more dead than alive, a man with no expression, no heart left to him...only the remnants of a grieving soul.

"So you've heard. You know. They took Liam, Master Max," he said without preamble. "They took my grandson. They filled his sweet, simple head with lies and sent him off to die. I tried to tell myself he died for a reason. But there is no good reason. Just jealousy, and hate and greed. So much greed."

Max was struck by another wave of nostalgia, followed by one of pity. "We were always so complete here, all of us. Generation after generation, living and growing together, just as Redgrave Manor continued to grow. Until only a short while ago, my siblings and I had never heard of the Society. We never knew, Angus. We never suspected."

"Your grandmother knew." The old man blew his nose into an already-filthy red handkerchief. "It didn't take her long to figure out the rest, either, did it? Stood right up to me at Liam's grave, the way she's always done when she had something to say. I had to get away from her before I fell bawling at her feet, telling her everything."

"Angus, I'm sorry about Liam. So very sorry. But is he why you hoped to meet with one of us? To help us understand what's going on now?"

The old man didn't acknowledge the question. His mind was clearly somewhere else.

"You call this place Redgrave Manor, the seat of the earls of Saltwood, and nothing more. But there are many who believe all this is as much ours as yours, when you count in the blood spilled, the backs broken from years of labor. The babes put in our young girls' bellies. Redgrave? Cooper? How do they know the difference? How do you hold down the Redgrave blood so that the Cooper blood can muck out the stalls and harvest the crops and serve at table, blink in the sparkle of the diamonds around the old girl's neck, and then say thankee for a basket at Christmas or candle stubs and cast-off clothes? Tell me that, Master Max. Tell me how to explain that to the fierce Redgrave blood pumping hot in

Cooper veins. When we were promised so much, time and time again, and twice denied."

Zoé, who had crept up quietly, slipped her hand into Max's, and squeezed it. "Ah, Max, not only we French can mount a revolution."

Max shifted uncomfortably where he stood, thinking of the many bastards his grandfather and father must have sired on Cooper women—willing and unwilling Cooper women. "We always knew there'd been… incidents. With Charles, with Barry. But any of that stopped when our father died. Gideon told us our grandmother offered a handsome purse to those who might feel uncomfortable living on Red—remaining here— once Barry was dead, so that they could relocate elsewhere. I know not everyone chose to go, but how many did, Coopers, and others? God, Angus, how many were there? Is what's coming to be a fight between brothers, cousins?"

"Sisters?" Zoé offered quietly, and Max immediately thought of the woman.

Angus must have heard her question. "That one! She's the cause of it all. Stirring the witch's pot, saying what many wanted to hear. Her evil, filthy ways. She'll take us all to hell with her in the end, I know that now. Liam. My Liam…"

"You've met her? You know her?" Max put his hand on Angus's knee. "Tell us. Tell me, Angus. Who is she? Where do I find her? Where do I find the Frenchman? That's why you're here, isn't it? To tell us, to help us put a stop to whatever madness is going on before it's too late."

The old man looked down at the hand on his knee, and then straight at Max. Watching him, it was as if Angus was coming back to life, out of a dream. A nightmare. "What are you asking me, Master Max? I couldn't stay after Liam died. I couldn't go, where would I go? With the others, the ones who'd killed Liam? I brought my things and myself here, to live out my days in one of the cottages. I didn't think her ladyship would mind. We were friends once. Like she says, we have a *history* between us. There was a time we joined together to rid the…"

But Max had stopped listening. "Sonofabitch! Zoé, head for the cave. Now!" Max yelled, and she wheeled and ran off without questioning him. Then he reached up to grab Angus by the arm and haul him down from the wagon seat.

Only he was too late. The old man was staring dumbly at the arrow protruding from the center of his chest. A second later his eyes rolled back in his head and his body fell backward into the wagon.

Angus Cooper was gone, perhaps to be reunited with his beloved grandson, and Max was racing after Zoé, his eyes scanning the rocks and cliff above him.

"They're on top of the jetty. Two of them, both with bows. We go into the cave, and then out the other side, take cover in the maze. Zoé—go!"

She was standing in the narrow opening, but not moving, using the ancient door for cover. "No, the other side looks to be closed. It's a trap, Max. They know about the cave and they want us to go in there. I won't. I can't."

An arrow hit the ground, striking between Max and Zoé.

Max flattened himself against the stones. She could be right. The archers may have seen the opening and pushed it shut. He looked toward the nearest cottage, gauging the distance. He looked toward Angus's wagon, and the nearly somnolent mule, his mind whirling with possibilities. There weren't many, and Zoé wasn't going to like either one he settled on. But she could only berate him for what he was about to do if she lived that long.

He squinted up at the stacked boulders at least twenty-five feet above them and thought he could see a soft-soled leather boot tip protruding out over the edge. He had no clear shot with his pistols; he had to get them down, on a level with him. At least one of them.

"Do we have a choice? They still want us alive. Any of those arrows could have gotten me, but that doesn't mean they'll just let us simply walk away. I swear to you, Zoé, the other end of the tunnel is open. I opened it myself. Let's go."

Zoé turned to look behind her. Into the darkness, the damp, the memories of her Paris cell. "You'd damn well better be right," she told him, and stepped completely inside.

He deftly relieved her of one of the throwing knives tucked into the waistband of her skirt, and pushed closed the door behind her. Either the other end was still open, or after he disposed of their attackers, he was going to need to be rescued from her.

He began running, crouched down and zig-zagging his way until he could launch himself in the air, dive headfirst beneath the wagon. Laboring to catch his breath, he knew he'd just created a stalemate. He couldn't move from where he was, but nobody could get to him, also because of where he was.

Simple logistics.

Zoé might be trapped inside the cave, but she was armed. Anton would have warned anyone that the beautiful blonde Frenchwoman was never unarmed, that she was more deadly than any man with her knives. No, they'd leave her where she was for the moment, out of the game, and concentrate on capturing him.

This alone put their attackers at a disadvantage, the order to capture their quarry alive.

He'd give them five minutes to make up their minds, hoping they would be too embarrassed by the mess they'd made to summon reinforcements.

Now, what would he do if presented with the same situation? Discounting Zoé as his partner, because there was no one else like Zoé.

All right. He'd backtrack, leave the jetty entirely, and approach from another angle. Archers, not swordsmen, most probably not trusted with firearms because they were considered by someone as not bright enough to aim and fire, or too stupid not to panic and shoot. After all, if they'd been set to do nothing but cool their heels somewhere nearby while watching for smoke from one of the cottages, it wasn't as if they were the best men the Society had in their employ.

The smartest plan would be to have one of them going for help, the other left to guard the area. He'd already crossed that one off his mental list. The second best thing, if no help was close at hand, would be to separate, one to make his way to the Channel end of the ruined fort, remaining above the wagon, the other to scale down the cliff and make his way along the side, to come around the end of the jetty in an effort to surprise his quarry.

Stupid men would stay together, for comfort, and both attempt to attack via the end of the jetty.

Having convinced himself he was dealing with dunces, Max slipped Zoé's throwing knife into his boot, made sure his pistols remained secure in his waistband.

It was time.

The tide was beginning to come in, and the sound of the surf would block out any noise made by boots slipping on the shingle. Theirs, or his. Max took in three deep breaths, and pushed out from his hiding place to run toward the ruined wall of the Roman fort, hitting it at its lowest point, the wall no more than ten feet high.

No arrows hit the sand near him. The two were on the move, just as he'd hoped. How bloody cooperative of them.

Up he went, just as he had as a child: hand over hand, his boots occasionally slipping, but never losing his grip. He steadied himself once at the top, looked over the edge and smiled.

Seconds later, Zoé's knife between his teeth, a pistol in each hand, Max launched himself into the air.

His wasn't quite the landing he'd hoped for, as he lost his footing on the shingle and ended up on his rump a good ten yards in front of the approaching men. Even from this ignominious position, he knew himself to be in charge, although his teeth hurt after landing so heavily with the blade still between them. He dearly hoped he hadn't chipped a tooth, or else he'd never hear the end of it from Zoé.

He leaned to his left, opened his jaws so that the knife fell harmlessly to the ground. That left him with the pistols, which he had already cocked.

And yet one of the archers struggled, with shaking hands, to ready an arrow.

"You must be funning me, sir," Max said, getting to his feet even as he retrieved the knife and stuck it into his waistband. "Put that thing down, unless you think I can't aim accurately at this short distance. Both of you, toss away your bows, and then lock your fingers together behind your heads. Ah, that's better. Now, turn around, and move forward until I tell you to stop."

Once they were abreast of the ancient opening, he ordered them to sit down where they stood, keeping their hands crossed behind their heads. Damn if they hadn't pushed the stones back into place. With one pistol directed at them, he fumbled his way around edges and angles of rocks until he located the handholds.

"You. Yes, you, the one nearest to me. You shut it,

now pull it open again if you please. But then I'd step back, were I you, and quickly take a seat once more. She wouldn't kill an unarmed man."

CHAPTER SEVEN

"I'D INQUIRE as to the whereabouts of my hat, but since the rest of the outfit is already leagues past repair, I suppose it isn't necessary. I am curious, however, as to how you lost it."

Zoé, brushing her long, still-damp blond hair as she sat cross-legged in front of the fireplace, smiled at Lady Katherine Redgrave as the young woman took one last look at the jacket of the green riding habit, its golden-braid trimmings now sadly ripped or missing, before letting it drop to the floor. She looked just as Max had described her: always curious, definitely exotic and with lively eyes that spoke of a love for mischief. He hadn't mentioned how remarkably beautiful she was, but then brothers never notice the obvious.

"Didn't Max tell you, when he told everyone the rest?"

Kate sighed deeply. "The rest. Yes, he did. Poor Angus. Trixie was quite upset and has already ordered his body brought here, to be buried beside Liam. Liam was his grandson, you know. You do know, don't you?"

"I don't know that I know *everything,* but I believe

I'll catch up. Has anyone recognized the two we brought back with us?"

Kate shook her head, her loose dark waves catching any bit of sunlight coming in through the window beside her. "I'm rather glad we didn't."

Zoé thought she and Lady Katherine might be much alike in many ways, except that the younger woman, for all the Redgraves' current troubles, seemed to have a love of life surrounding her, a sort of innocent glow Zoé couldn't remember ever possessing on her own.

Except when she was with Max.

"I want to thank you for the loan of your clothing," she told Kate as she stroked a hand over the soft lawn of the dressing gown and matching night rail she'd donned after her bath. "Hopefully, nothing else will meet with disaster. Although I wouldn't count on that, if I don't get my leathers back," she ended, muttering under her breath.

Kate dismissed the thanks with a wave of her hand. "Don't worry about that, we've lots to give you. Since my shoes seem too large for you, I've had a few of Jessica's put in your dressing room. Daisy and her sister are still building their own wardrobes, as they both came to us rather— Well, Max will tell you about that, too, I'm sure. You'll see Daisy at dinner, but Rose still prefers to eat in her rooms most times. She's recovering from…from an illness." Then she leaned forward on the slipper chair she'd been occupying. "Are you and Max friends again? Trixie said it would be a world of help to all of us if you were."

"Out."

Both Zoé and Kate turned toward the sound of the voice coming from the now open doorway leading to the hall.

"Oh, Max," Kate complained, although she had gotten to her feet. "We were simply getting acquainted."

"By way of an interrogation, Kate? You may be all grown up, even betrothed—Simon a clear example of that business about love being blind—but you're still a pest. I repeat—*out*."

"Brothers." Kate rolled her eyes comically at Zoé, and then brushed past Max on her way out of the bedchamber. "You always were the bossiest one. Except for Gideon."

"Yes, and Val has always been soft clay in the palm of your hand. I know. Now go." Max followed her, turning the lock behind her before approaching Zoé.

He looked marvelous, as always, whether clad in his finery or dripping with mud. Although he could benefit from a shave. She wondered if he'd still trust her with a straight razor.

"Are you all right? We really didn't have a chance to talk while we were herding those men back here, or since."

"That would depend," she said, putting down the brushes. "The splinters are gone, the burrs, as well, and the scratches will heal in time. Then there are the small, itchy bumps, although the lotion Magret applied to them appears to be helping with the itch. That cave is filled with sand fleas, in case you're wondering. You saw Magret?"

"I suppose so, if you mean that woman I passed by in the hallway. Lovely creature."

"In her own way, yes. She hasn't had an easy life."

Ah, she seemed to have managed to pull his interest away from the opening of her borrowed dressing gown. "She's with the pirates? What did she tell you?"

"That she had a daughter, long ago, with hair the color of mine. But the child died, and then *everyone* left and sailed here, to England. Her man dug a grave and filled it with Dolly's clothes and toys, and fashioned a headstone with her name on it, just for his wife. She and the children they've had since still keep fresh flowers there. Many others did the same thing, just so they'd never forget, and the cap'n makes sure all those otherwise empty graves are well tended."

"Christ. I wonder what happened."

"As do I, but neither of us is going to ask."

"No. We're not. Do you forgive me for locking you in the dark?"

"Actually, Max, I should thank you. I panicked, I won't deny it. I couldn't breathe, not even to scream, I couldn't see my hand in front of my face. I thought about the tide coming in, what it would be like to drown. But then I thought of you, out there, with nobody to guard your back, and that made me angry enough with your recklessness to conquer my fear. I'd just located the interior handholds when the door was pulled open from the other side."

He approached her and sat down behind her, cross-legged, reaching around to lift the brushes from her lap. "Well, I'm gratified I proved useful, and possibly ecstatic that it was your concern for me that replaced your fears. No more being afraid of the dark?"

"I was never afraid of— Yes, and no more fear of locked doors. Although picturing seawater swirling around my legs, climbing to my chest, rolling into my mouth as I was at last forced to take a breath? That won't be so easily forgotten."

"But also forgiven?" he asked as he raised the brushes...which was just as she turned about and planted her fist in his belly.

That was better. "Oh, yes. Completely forgiven. *Now*."

Max dropped the brushes and clutched at his abdomen, desperately attempting to draw in air.

She grabbed at his shoulders. "Max? Max, are you all right? I know you weren't ready for it, but I certainly didn't punch you *that* hard. Did you sustain another injury when you went overboard? Why didn't you tell me? Max, for God's sake—breathe."

He was on her in a heartbeat, his injury clearly feigned. Together, they rolled away from the fireplace, onto a large plush carpet.

Still grasping each other, trying to get to each other with their mouths, their hands, their entwined legs.

"Let me," he gasped as she went for the buttons on his breeches.

"No, I can— Max! I promised your sister I wouldn't ruin any more of her— Oh…oh, yes."

He was ravaging her with his lips, his tongue, taking hungry nips of her even as she reached inside his now opened breeches, to be as ever amazed by the strength of him, the sheer heat of him.

He knew her every secret, and exploited several of them even as she managed the last button, released him to rear up, and then bring herself down on him, covering him, taking him in.

"Now," he said, rising to meet her, beginning the long, deep strokes that would bring them both to their goal, meld them, join them, satisfy their bodily hungers even as their wounded souls stood off, watchful, hopeful there someday could be so much more than this wild, excruciating pleasure. More than simply mating, like animals in the wild.

With one last long, low moan of pleasure, Zoé collapsed against him, her head in the crook of his shoulder, her breathing labored, her body still quivering.

Beneath her, Max was also attempting to recover his breath, lying nearly limp against the carpet, his manhood still inside her.

"Well…" he said finally. "Now that the inevitable is out of the way…"

"Wretch," she managed as she pulled back, looked down into his face, her long hair brushing against him. "But yes, now that that's out of the way—now what?"

"I hate to say it—loathe it, actually—but as it has been so many times, it's back to work. Unless you have nothing else to cover yourself with, which might delay that business for another few minutes."

"Methinks thou might overstate thy recuperative powers, good sir," she teased as she rolled off him, using the ruined dressing gown and its underlying night rail to tidy both of them. "Magret is a woman of the world, but we'll nevertheless burn these," she said as she stripped off her clothing and got to her feet. "Here, do the deed while I search for something else to wear. But first either stuff that thing back inside and button your breeches or prepare for attack."

Max laughed, ducked out of the way of the night-clothes, and propped himself up on one elbow, clearly intending to watch as she searched the wardrobe. "You've no shame, do you?"

She looked back at him over her shoulder. How little he knew. How she longed to return to his arms, rain kisses all over his face, rest her head on his chest just to listen to his heart's steady beat. She would happily lie like that for hours. "With you? No. Should I?"

"Never."

There was so much emotion in that single word, so much intensity in his gaze. She had to turn away, and busied herself locating a simple, modest night rail never meant to be seen by a lover or a husband. She doubted Lady Katherine had harbored any regrets in passing it along to her, now that she'd met her Simon.

She slipped the thing over her head and turned around in time to see Max slowly feeding strips of the ruined linen to the fire.

"You've questioned our two captives?" she asked, picking up what was left of the dressing gown.

"Here, give me that. I don't want to smother the fire by dumping everything in there at once. I think you've had enough smoke for one day. We'll just let that lot burn while I help you with those tangles. I love your hair as it is, but wish it longer, like before."

She went down on her knees on the hearth rug, her back to him once more. "Head lice," she said, wondering at the expression on his face now. "I refused to shave it, and rescued quite a bit, but ended in cutting much of it off. From prison lice to Redgrave sand fleas. Do you think that's progress?"

"Zoé, I—"

"No, don't apologize. Not ever again. I managed a return to my father's foundry before I left Paris for Salzburg. Bonaparte's crest hangs above the door, and the entire place, every last structure, was alight, even in the dead of night, with the forges burning hot, clearly to supply French troops. But I could still make out where the king's crest once had hung against the brick. Everything changes, everything remains the same."

He retrieved the brushes and set to work. "And the same poor sots who serve them generation after generation, all dying for an ambitious man's dream. How many times did we wonder why we do what we do, Zoé? Look what that brought us to. There'll never be an end to war, because there'll never be an end to man's selfish ambition."

"Never an end to the sort of man who seems to know

just what to say, just how to say it, to get others to blindly believe, blindly follow. Our pirate friend is right, as far as he went. Cut off the head, and the rest of the fish dies, true. But there will always be another ambitious fish rising to take over even the smallest pond."

"And to kill all the ambitious fish would give rise to nothing but anarchy, so we are left to choose between bad and worse. Were the Stuarts less of a hazard than the Hanovers? Is Bonaparte a better choice than bringing the Bourbons back to the throne? We can't know, can we?"

Zoé turned, took the brushes from him, put them down, and settled herself comfortably, her arms wrapped around her bent knees. "All we can do is our best, Max. Wasn't that always our conclusion?"

"It was. I just never thought there could be such evil ambition within my own family, this *poison* that corrupted those we believed our servants and friends."

"Promises of glory and money and rank, coupled with the irresistible lure of sexual pleasure. Looking back at history, hardly original. You have to know your grandfather wasn't the first to employ such methods. You and your family have a lot on your plates, I agree, but you all need to get past the shame of the thing before you can truly put a stop to a horror that clearly reaches beyond just you Redgraves. You, all of you, have to remain objective."

"We Redgraves," he said, sighing. "You asked about the two men we caught today. They told us *they're* Redgraves. Bought off or thrown off the estate by Trixie, of all people, when my grandfather died, and thus denied their rightful inheritance."

"Meaning?"

"Meaning, my dear, that their assertion is that Trixie was never legally my grandfather's wife. That he'd declared his love for one of the Coopers, and married her. Put more than one child in her belly, only to go to the altar with Trixie, ashamed of his first choice, who could never be considered royal enough to be queen of England. Meaning those banished Coopers of long ago have somehow convinced those who remained on the estate that what they've worked so hard to build and maintain is actually *theirs,* although some resisted joining them, Angus among them. To those two men, he was the enemy. The fact that he was seen speaking with me sealed his fate."

"My God," Zoé said quietly, even as her mind raced. But this was good, this was she and Max at their combined best. Between them, they'd always been able to solve any puzzle...save for Anton Boucher. But now they had a second chance. "The blond man. That's why he's tolerated. He must be the one carrying the most direct Redgrave blood. That's why she keeps him, that's why she needs him. Max, we've got to find the woman, the pair of them. Everything hinges on them."

"And Trixie? Do you think at least part of the story is true? Was our father a bastard? Is this blond imbecile you saw actually the true Earl of Saltwood? No wonder he took the code name Scarlet. Scarlet, for red. For Redgrave. Both Charles and Barry used the same name."

She could see the moral struggle in his expression. "Did anyone else hear their confession?"

"Only Simon. He advised me to consider it all moonshine, and both men are now locked up in the basement, our makeshift dungeon, as Val terms it."

"Good. And I agree with the marquis. I find it easier to believe the woman made up the story out of whole cloth, because it suited her. The question is, how did she manage to gather so much information in the first place, about the Redgraves, the Society, the plans your grandfather and father hatched?"

"By being there. That's the only possible answer." Max got to his feet, clearly feeling they'd stumbled on something important. "By being a part of the Society." He turned to look at Zoé. "You saw her. You said she was past her first blush of youth, or something like that. How old do you think she is?"

Zoé shrugged. "I know she was no debutante, but I'd have to say no more than five and thirty, or a few years beyond that. As your grandmother proves so well, there's magic in those pots and powders we women keep on our dressing tables."

Max was pacing now, rubbing at his beard. "According to Val and Simon, the Society had a penchant for relieving themselves of wives who grew either too fat or too long in the tooth to excite the other members, or too unwilling to cooperate in the ceremonies, then married younger women. Much younger. Look at Trixie, for God's sake, she was barely out of the nursery."

"They were in the habit of murdering their wives? Off with their heads? How terribly medieval."

Max stopped pacing and faced her. "Until their wives more recently began murdering them, yes, but let's keep to the point. I think we can safely assume this woman was brought into my father's re-creation of the Society."

"As the wife of one of the Devil's Thirteen, as Kate explained the hierarchy to me this morning, or else she wouldn't have been able to learn everything she learned. Do you know who the Thirteen were in your father's time?"

"Some of them. Definitely not all, but Trixie might agree to help us there. She only doles out information she deems necessary, and I can't blame her. I can give you one, and that would be Adam's mother. It turns out his father—Jessica's father—was my father's second-in-command, or some such rot. The Keeper. Keeper of the rules, for one, and keeper of the journals each member was required to turn over to him. He'd then condense everything into a yearly addition of the Society's bible. Everything's there, the code names they used, their rightful names, their assigned role within the Society."

"You're serious? Then we only need to find this bible, correct, and we're more than halfway there?"

"We did find it, along with the journals. Kate and Simon located them in a cave right here on the grounds. Society member names are all in code in the journals, unfortunately, and even worse, Turner Collier set fire to the bible before he—and Adam's mother—were similarly burnt to crisps in what we'll laughingly call a coach accident."

"I think my head's spinning. Your brother Gideon married Jessica—Jessica *Collier*—and Adam—that silly but rather adorable twit I met this morning—is her brother?"

"Half brother. Collier's first wife, Jessica's mother, died, and Mailer married—"

"A much younger woman. Of course he did. The aging wife conveniently deceased, to be replaced by that much younger woman, keeping to the pattern. But she's also dead."

"Very dead. Gideon made sure to see the bodies. That's what started this whole thing, you know. Collier's outdated will left Adam's future to the earl of Saltwood, Jessica wanted custody of her brother, and somehow the Society was mentioned. That's the first we ever heard of it, through Jessica. Our conclusion is that there was some sort of coup inside the Society, and the last of those remaining from my father's day were eliminated."

"To be replaced by one very enterprising woman who then assembled her own Devil's Thirteen, along with plotting with Bonaparte and, oh yes, somehow including Anton in there somewhere. You did say the wives had begun dispatching their husbands, correct?"

"Yes, that's true enough. Coaching accidents, tumbles down the stairs, eating spoiled food, fallen upon by footpads. The wives actually plotted together. We probably have at least three or four suspects to choose from. We've also got one of the new Thirteen tucked away upstairs," Max told her, actually smiling. "Valentine sent him to us, all but wrapped up with a bow around his neck. We have solid proof of another one, and Val was on the scene when a third was, shall we say, fatally punished for incompetence."

"And all to our benefit, Max. They're turning on themselves. The new order eliminating the old, the wives rising up against their husband tormentors. One faction of Coopers clearly mistrustful of the other branch of the family, those who'd stayed behind. Today, Coopers who'd remained here won't be pleased to hear that the returned Coopers murdered one of their own. Enter Anton, stir in Bonaparte, and we've got quite a stew bubbling on someone's hob."

"Please stop before you find yourself forced to say *woe, what a tangled web we weave.* But I have to agree. This Exalted Leader could be having considerable trouble at the moment. That's always helpful. How do you suggest we add to her problems?"

Zoé considered this for a moment. "I think the first thing we need to do is have a small chat with this captive your brother sent here. No. *I* have to have a small chat with him. He doesn't know me, doesn't know I exist, but he might know about Anton. Perhaps I can convince him I come as a friend."

"But you'll need some sort of story, some sort of disguise that gives you a reason to be in the house. I'm sure I can find a maid's uniform. A mobcap and apron. You'll look quite fetching. What else?"

"Clogs."

"Yes, and clogs. And the key might be helpful."

"Does your family keep country hours? Do we have time for this before we're called down to dinner? Oh, the devil with it, we'll make time."

She was already stripping off the night rail, and rummaging in the wardrobe for underpinnings. "Do you think he speaks French? That would be helpful, although just hearing French should be enough to convince him."

Max walked up behind her and slid his arms around her waist, pressed a kiss against her nape. "I was ready to sulk, and you knew it, and now we're leagues ahead of where we were, and I'm past feeling the least bit moral about trumped-up marriage lines or anything else. And you, my splendid partner, grow more beautiful by the moment. We might actually be happy. Do you think we're both insane?"

"Probably," she said, turning in his arms. "Or maybe we both like winning a bit too much."

He kissed both her cheeks, and then lingered over her mouth until she knew it would be dangerous to continue. Max seemed to know that, as well. They had work to do.

"Together, we can never lose," he said before letting her go.

"You never stop trying, do you? I think I'm beginning to like that."

His smile told her she'd said just what he'd wanted to hear. She probably needed to hear herself say the words, as well. Their sad past seemed to be melting away, fading into nothingness, as if they'd never been parted. She never would have believed that possible.

"Persistence has its own rewards. Shall we try it again?"

The first-warning dinner bell rang somewhere below them.

"Damn," he swore. "Civilization will get in our way, won't it?"

"Or we might have been rescued from something we'd just regret," she pointed out, hating herself. It was too soon, too soon. And Anton still stood between them. "At any rate, so much for your captive, and I have to wash again, and my hair is still damp. You should apologize for distracting us both from the business at hand."

"Never," he said, grinning.

She stepped out of his arms. "I'll see you at dinner."

He reached for her. "One last kiss? I may still be somewhat melancholy about this bastard business."

She gave him a playful shove in the chest. "Go! Come back when you hear the second gong."

ZOÉ ENTERED the main saloon of Redgrave Manor on Max's arm just as the enormous floor clock in the foyer struck the hour of six, aware that all eyes were on her as she cast a quick glance down at her bosom. Didn't any of the Redgrave women have more than ample chests? She felt as if hers might pop out of the pale blue gown at any moment. In a French ballroom, she'd hardly be out of place, but in an English country estate she could only be considered scandalous.

Max had been most appreciative of her appearance, but did ask if her borrowed wardrobe possibly included a shawl.

She curtsied to the room's occupants in general, and then allowed Max to tug her around like a puppy on a lead, introducing her to everyone. She'd seen some of the men that first night, but only barely, before she was ignominiously dragged away to her attic prison.

Lady Katherine—Kate—winked at her and smiled, and the handsome blond gentleman now bowing over Zoé's hand had to be no one else but Simon Ravenbill, Marquis of Singleton.

Adam Collier was next, his cheeks obviously rouged, his hair once again wet and slick with pomade and his rig-out beyond description. "My dear Mademoiselle Charbonneau," he said dramatically before kissing her hand. *"C'est mon honneur profonde pour laver vos chaussettes."*

Zoé managed to keep her composure, but Kate didn't hold back her laughter or her comment. "You birdbrain, you just said it was an honor to wash her socks."

Adam looked aghast, or perhaps bilious, beneath his rouge. "I did not! I studied all the afternoon, and I most certainly did not— Oh, crimey-cripes, I did, didn't I?"

Zoé nodded. "But I appreciate and applaud your effort, Mr. Collier."

"Adam. Everyone calls me Adam. Well, most everybody. Mostly, Trixie calls me the twit. Affectionately."

That comment sent Kate into peals of laughter again, until Simon whispered something in her ear that sobered her. "You're right, I'm being mean. I'm sorry, Adam. Kiss her hand, wash her socks? Hardly any difference at all." She then turned to her betrothed, her nose wrinkling delightfully. "That probably wasn't much better, was it? But you would make me do it."

"Not appreciably, no, but you did try. My apologies, my sweet," the marquis said, the look on his own face one of absolute adoration. Zoé could understand why. Lady Katherine Redgrave was a minx, but she was a thoroughly delightful one.

"All right, that's enough of that, Adam. You can perform again for us later when you tuck your serviette into your neck in order to slurp your soup."

"I only protect my neckcloth, Val," Adam protested to the handsome young man who'd just deserted the mantelpiece to stride toward Zoé. Another darkly handsome Redgrave. The place was littered with them. "I still say the soup spoons are defective. Now, if you'll all excuse me, I fear I must retire for a space, to collect myself."

"True enough. You are rather scattered," the man said, giving Adam a jovial clap on the back. *"Mademoiselle?"*

Zoé offered her hand, and he bowed over it, but did not kiss it. "Valentine Redgrave, *mademoiselle,* and delighted to make your acquaintance. Max has been a bear these past months, and now we know why. Please don't disappear again, or he'll doubtless go into a sad decline."

"Shut up, Val," Max said evenly.

The younger man smiled. "Do you know, for a few years, when I was still in the nursery, I actually thought that was my name? *Shut up, Val*. But now please allow me to introduce you to my affianced, Miss Daisy Marchant, and her delightful sister, Rose."

The young woman Zoé assumed was Daisy nearly rose from her seat, right hand extended, before Val's discreet clearing of his throat had her sitting down once more. "Delighted to make your acquaintance, *mademoiselle*. Please forgive me for not rising, but that rudely indiscreet man standing beside you has cast himself in the role of social tutor to this former governess. I humor him," she ended, and her smile transformed her rather ordinary face into a thing of beauty.

Zoé leaned closer. "Good for you. I'd kick him in the shins."

Beside Daisy, the petite blonde beauty with the eyes of a sorrowful saint looked up at her, slightly aghast.

"She didn't mean it, Rose," Daisy whispered. "Say your hello to Mademoiselle Charbonneau."

Hadn't Kate said something about the sister having recently been ill? She hadn't mentioned that the woman was also nervous as a butterfly in a windstorm. "Oh, please, I doubt this is the time for formality. Call me Zoé."

"Isn't that lovely, Rose?" Daisy said, lightly squeezing her sister's hand. "We're all going to be friends."

But Rose only smiled apprehensively and looked to Daisy.

"I'm delighted to make your acquaintance. What a

lovely gown. It makes your eyes look blue as corn-flowers."

Zoé hoped perhaps this time Rose would say something, but instead that cornflower-blue gaze shifted toward the entrance hall and grew to nearly twice their size. "Oh, *my*," she breathed, quickly getting to her feet, as did everyone else.

Zoé wasn't surprised to see the Dowager Countess Beatrice Redgrave Borders just entering the room, leaning delicately on the arm of her husband and looking positively regal, dressed as she was in black from head to toe.

"In mourning for Angus," Max whispered in her ear. "Until we plant him tomorrow."

Zoé nodded her understanding, smiled to Richard Borders as she rose from her curtsy and then saw what she should have seen the moment the man entered the room with Richard and Trixie. "Tariq," she whispered. "Your savior."

"Yes, we spoke earlier. What I don't understand is how I never saw him when he was trailing me around the Continent. It isn't as if he's easily overlooked."

"No, he isn't, is he? But, then again, you have been slipping of late," Zoé responded with a teasing smile, looking past Max to see Rose staring at Tariq and his magnificent attire in something close to rapture. He was probably unlike any man she'd ever seen.

"Good evening, my pets," Trixie said as Richard led her to an embroidered chaise and she collapsed gracefully onto it, her legs raised onto the cushions, arranging her satin and lace skirts around them. "Another long and sad day, I'm afraid. Max, you spoke with him last."

"I did. He'd found himself neither fish nor foul after Liam died, poor soul. Unable to return to his cottage at the Manor, unwilling to remain with the Coopers. Now he's with his grandson, and I don't think that's the worst that could have happened to him. Trixie, now that we're all here, Zoé and I have had an idea."

"Oh, here we go." Val drew up a straight-back chair and turned it about before straddling it. "Is this idea any better than the one that had you dragging yet another enemy across the Channel to us as if we didn't already have enough?"

Kate laughed.

So did Max.

Zoé hadn't had siblings. She'd always wondered what it would be like to have brothers, sisters, a large family around her. To love her, to love them…to have them tease her unmercifully? No, she hadn't considered that part. She had to decide if she liked it. So far, she thought she might.

"We've been considering the woman," she explained as Max led her to a chair and all the other men could finally sit down. Valentine Redgrave seemed to be a law unto himself, although Daisy had given him a shake of the head and an indulgent look that told Zoé the man was no fool; he just had his own way of living his life.

"The Exalted One, or Leader, or whatever she's called," Daisy said, nodding. "I've seen her." She looked to Val. "We've both seen her. Masked, unfortunately. She's evil. Sheer evil. A murderess."

The shy, lovely Rose moved closer to Daisy, and squeezed her hand until her knuckles whitened. Not in some offer of comfort, Zoé thought, but for protection. There was a story there with these two women, but she wouldn't ask. What she did notice was that Tariq had taken up a position behind their shared couch, both long, well-shaped hands grasping its back as he shot what seemed to be concerned looks at the fair-haired Rose.

"We think she's more than that. We think she's— Max?"

"We think she's a victim. Was one, that is. Possibly even one of the wives who turned the tables on their husbands. We believe she also may have acquired a— forgive me, ladies—acquired a taste for the ceremonies, along with a hunger for power."

Zoé lowered her eyelids and took a quick peep at Trixie, who'd gone pale beneath her subtly applied rouge.

The room went silent for a few moments, before Adam Collier entered once more, still looking into a small, hand-held gilt-edged mirror secured to a ribbon on his wrist. In his absence, he'd applied a black beauty patch in the shape of a star, Zoé noticed, and was looking at it worriedly, as if it might fall off, which could only be considered a blessing.

"Hi-ho again, everyone. Am I now unfashionably late? Not that it matters. I'm back, so let the festivities begin. Mademoiselle Charbonneau, I beg a second chance. I know I have it this time," he trilled as he ignored everyone else in the room in order to make a beeline straight at her, sweeping her an elegant leg that, remarkably, did not send him toppling over on his backside. *"J'ai passé cette journée nostalgie pour l'instant de notre élevage."*

"Indeed," Zoé returned, straight-faced, extricating her hand from his faintly damp grasp.

"You numbskull," Kate chortled. "You just said you spent the day longing for the moment of your and Zoé's *breeding.*"

The boy looked at Zoé, who nodded, and then staggered backward, clutching his hands to his ruffled chest. *"Sacré bleu!"*

"Adam, you're excused," Trixie said as the laughter died away.

He turned to the dowager countess and bowed. "Thank you, ma'am. I meant no harm."

"I know that. You don't have any harm in you, or much of anything else, more's the pity. However, what I meant was, you're excused. I'll be sure someone brings your dinner to your rooms. Daisy? If you'd be so kind as to escort Rose to her chambers?"

"There's no need. Miss Rose, it would be my honor," Tariq said, one palm to his chest as he stepped in front of the couch.

"You're very kind, sir," Daisy responded rather apprehensively, "but I don't think—"

But Rose was already on her feet. "I…I should like that above all things, sir."

"Well, if that don't beat the Dutch," Valentine said as all the gentlemen sat down once more after Rose had departed the room. "I suppose Piffkin will be all over the man tomorrow, vetting him, asking his intentions. But at least maybe I'll get him back. I rather miss the old rotter."

"Piffkin is Val's valet, just recently abandoning him in order to serve Daisy's sister. Rather as some sort of knight errant, or possibly *duenna*. Tariq will have to pass muster, I expect. I'll explain later," Max whispered. "Did you see Trixie's reaction to what you said? And now she's cleared the room of innocent ears."

"I suppose you're going to attempt to kick me out, as well," Kate said, sighing. "I'm not a child anymore, Trixie. I'm betrothed, for pity's sake."

"Yes, pet, I know. Simon is a saint. But I wouldn't wish to force you to listen at the keyhole. You may stay. There's little you don't know, in any event. So," the dowager countess went on, "now you want to know just who this woman might be, correct? And I have to tell you, sadly, I haven't the faintest idea. I need more information. You saw her, Valentine. Describe her, if you please."

Val shrugged. "It's as Daisy said. She was masked, and on horseback to boot. I'd say she's tall, though, well shaped, has no trouble riding astride. She speaks with command and has a…has a taste for deviant pleasures. She's violent, clearly favors the knife. We know she slit the throats of two women while we were there, and cheerfully—*cheerfully*—took a blade to one of her own Devil's Thirteen who had displeased her."

Favors the blade, does she? Zoé leaned closer to Max. "Mine," she breathed softly. "You're too polite, and might hesitate. I won't."

He answered her, also in a whisper. "That's two for you and none for me. We'll discuss the matter, later, and perhaps come to an obvious conclusion."

"No," she answered, realizing she'd just stepped into a trap of her own making. "They're both mine. You've plenty of others to choose from."

"We'll settle this later. In bed."

"You're insultingly confident."

"True. But I'm also right, aren't I?"

"And too cocky."

"I am? I don't believe I've ever heard that complaint from you before."

She felt her cheeks going hot. "Oh, shut up."

Trixie clapped her hands, calling everyone back to attention. "No more whispers. Valentine, do you have more for us? We need to know everything."

Valentine looked at his sister, clearly not wanting her to hear what came next, and then added quietly, his head down, "She had the man tied to their obscene altar and personally removed his manhood before setting the others to use their blades to put him out of his misery. I've never thought of the devil as a woman, but I now believe in at least the possibility."

"The blade is so much more…personal. One could even say intimate. Clearly she despises men, even as she uses them. And her fellow females, as well. If we now know what she hates—what does she love?"

"Nothing, Trixie," Zoé answered with renewed confidence, now able to use more bits and pieces to assist her in putting together the puzzle presented by this Exalted Leader she'd observed in Ostend. Trixie's conclusion about who might favor the knife she would ignore; she was brought up to it, and pistols made too much noise. "I suspect not even herself, not in the way others love, but in reality *admires* herself and her own extraordinary brilliance. She believes herself magnificent, unbeatable. Unstoppable. No, she may covet, but she doesn't love. Men, power, wealth. They're still all second to her hate for those she believes inferior. In other words, everyone but herself."

"Or in yet other words, my pets, she's mad. Insane. I have some familiarity with that condition."

Zoé knew she had the bit between her teeth now, but couldn't seem able to stop herself. This was why the Crown had at last agreed to take her on. For her knowledge of languages, for her brain. "Brilliantly so, Trixie. That makes her extremely dangerous, but also vulnerable. She'll take mad chances, believing herself the smartest, and always the inevitable winner. She'll make a mistake, if we push hard enough in the right places. Max and I believe she's already walking a fine edge. I only wonder what she wanted of you, Max, as clearly that was Anton's assignment, to watch you, to bring you to her when she decreed it. Because, considering how long Anton has been playing our friend, and then turning us against each other, whatever her plan is for you, it's of long-standing."

"Perhaps you're wrong, Zoé," Val said. "Perhaps she can love…or as you said, covet. She may have glimpsed my dear brother here across a ballroom floor, or while out riding that black savage of his, hell-bent for leather, and been instantly smitten. Remember, Max, we still all wonder at how well you and that scruffy beard attract the ladies."

"Coveted by a she-devil. Lovely," Max said sourly. "I'm flattered all hollow just at the thought."

Nobody laughed.

CHAPTER EIGHT

MAX LISTENED INTENTLY at the dinner table as Zoé told the story of seeing the Exalted Leader and her concubine, assistant, lover, sap-skulled devotee—whatever in Hades was the purpose of the man. He hoped she might say something, think of something she hadn't told him earlier, but he should have known better. Zoé knew how to observe, how to take in only important information and commit it to memory, and then relay it in a clear, concise manner.

Trixie spoke next. "Dark-haired, on her way to forty, definitely English. You two think probably no more than sixteen or eighteen when she was brought into the Society, perhaps even younger. That's more than possible. A second wife, or even a daughter, or else she'd be too old now to connect her with my son's Devil's Thirteen. Still, a long time ago, and I was not familiar with many of them. I have to take my mind back, concentrate."

"Please, before you do that, Trixie," Daisy said, "you did say daughter, didn't you? That's obscene."

Max turned to his grandmother, his expression one of *do we tell her?*

Trixie laid down her fork. "Jessica, Gideon's dear

wife, was very nearly just such a victim, and believed all these years that her father was responsible. Happily, his journals proved the case otherwise. And before you ask, Adam was also destined to join the Society, as sons were always encouraged, even *educated* to follow their fathers. Fortunately, some would say, my son died before any of his offspring were more than children."

Zoé reached over and squeezed Max's hand under the table. It was, he supposed, a lovely gesture, but he didn't want her feelings for him to be clouded by pity.

Soon after, none of the diners seeming to have much of an appetite, everyone adjourned, the men to linger over brandy and cigars, the women heading back to the drawing room.

Except that Max believed he and Zoé had learned enough about the Society for the day, and held her back when she moved to join Trixie and Kate. He grabbed up a cigar from Gideon's well-guarded supply, allowed Dearborn to light it for him, and led Zoé to the music room, and the French doors leading to the gardens.

"That may have been rude," she pointed out as they made their way along the path lit by well-spaced lanterns hanging from poles. "In fact, I know it was. I was going to ask Trixie more about your brother's wife."

"Yes, I know, but since the answers don't have anything to do with the point, we'll leave that to Jessica, if she so chooses to tell you. For now, I just want to enjoy the evening."

"And what smells like quite a lovely cigar. May I have a puff?"

Max handed it over and watched as she rolled the tip of the thing between her lips, and then drew in a breath, savored it, before blowing out a loud of blue smoke. Watching Zoé with a cigar was a most powerful aphrodisiac.

"A million times superior to those weeds we shared in Pamplona. But the wine was fairly memorable."

"We drank enough of it," Max said as they came out from the gardens and he could see the scars in the ground where once the dower house had been, hiding its macabre secrets in its basement ceremonial chamber. Supposedly, Gideon planned a croquet ground and tennis court in its place, with the new dower house to be build where Trixie wished—certainly not where the original had stood. "We were lucky to be alive after that near debacle, when the reed slipped sideways in my mouth and my lisp suddenly disappeared."

"Yeth, that'th thertainly tho." Zoé grinned and took another puff, then handed back the cigar.

"Amusing. You weren't the one trying to get the reed unstuck from his molars before the ambassador got too curious. I damn near choked on the thing."

"What're those ruins over there? The closer we get, the more I think I can smell burnt wood. It has to be the dower house you told me about. Is that why we're out here?"

"No, there's nothing left to see. Although it is amazing how its loss changes the landscape. It was once connected by underground tunnel to the foaling stable up on the hill. You can't see it in the dark. Anything of value is gone from both places, including some interesting framed communications to my grandfather and father concerning their cooperation in a French invasion. I don't suppose we'll hang them in the portrait gallery anytime soon. Would you like to see that? The portrait gallery, I mean, although I suppose we could consider at least part of it our own rogue's gallery."

"Another time." Zoé slipped her arm through his, leaned in closer to his body. "Besides, I'm sure that wasn't your original plan when you brought me out here."

"Really? What would make you think that?"

"I'm not sure. Perhaps it was somebody else, earlier, whispering in my ear. For God's sake, Max, are you going to make me beg?"

"It's a warm night," he said, taking her hand, rubbing his thumb against her palm. "There's a stream that runs near the greenhouses, and as I recall, the water pools in a deeper area somewhere in the trees before continuing on over the rocks. I haven't been there in a while, and Gideon's always making changes to the scenery, the course of the water. His last brilliant idea nearly collapsed one of the greenhouses. I think I can find it."

"But alas, not by standing here, running your mouth," Zoé pointed out facetiously.

They set off together, the dying light of dusk joined by what was left of the full moon that had already begun to reflect off the hundreds of small glass panes that made up the greenhouses.

Gideon had certainly been making a mess of things,

Max thought as he bent and lifted Zoé into his arms as he carefully stepped across areas of upturned soil still raw from having so recently served as a new route for the stream. And now, with the Coopers gone, he imaged the mess would remain until the Society was nothing more than a bad memory.

But, then, if the course hadn't been changed to make water more conveniently close to the greenhouses, then the disturbed groundwater wouldn't have collapsed the old tunnel inside one of them, and they might all still be in the dark as to what happened at Redgrave Manor all those years ago. Unaware they had enemies in their midst. Mortal enemies.

Zoé was laughing now, as she hung her arms around Max's neck. With the cigar still clamped between his teeth, and puffing to keep it lit, he'd begun breathing harder as, following alongside the stream, he climbed up the gradual slope that led into a purposely planted sweep of trees. There was nothing more natural-looking than one of Lancelot "Capability" Brown's designed landscapes. But did the man have to favor hills so much?

"Keep this up, and I'll have to do all the work when we get there," she told him, kissing the side of his neck. "Odd. You're not complaining."

"More like contemplating," he said, thanking the moonlight and his own sharp eyes as the deeper pool at last came into sight. "Besides, I don't want to give you time to change your mind."

He must have become lightheaded from the climb,

the smoke he'd inhaled, because he'd just said the dumb-est thing possible for a man with his intentions.

"You can put me down now. And you mean before I can remember that just because we are more than, well, companionable in some ways, that doesn't mean there's any reason to believe there will ever be more than that between us. That there ever was more than that between us, even if we thought differently at the time."

"Have you written all of that down somewhere, com-mitted it to memory?" Max asked, searching the bank for a grassy area wide enough for the both of them. "Perhaps you'll favor me with a copy, so we don't have to endure this discussion again."

"Now you're angry," she said, settling on the bank to remove her evening slippers, roll down her hose and toss it aside.

Max stripped off his evening jacket and waistcoat, kicked off his own shoes, and sat down beside her, his chin raised as he began work on ridding himself of his neck cloth. "Nonsense," he objected, rolling the cigar to the side of his mouth. "I'm never angry. Do you need help with those buttons?"

"No more than you require any with yours," she told him, reaching behind her for the few buttons neces-sary on her high-waist, otherwise loosely fitting gown. She lay on her back, using her bent knees to raise her enough to slide the gown down over her hips, then sat up to disentangle it from her legs. "Wrinkled Magret will understand. Even dirty. She's a common-sense, earthy woman. But I would rather not have to burn something again."

Max's hose was dispatched of, along with his knee breeches and underdrawers, leaving him to stand up once more, now wearing nothing but his long-tailed shirt. "As long as Magret's happy." He put his hands to the shirt buttons, attempted to control his breathing. "If I might point out something? You're lagging behind."

It was true; she was having some trouble with the thin satin ties and small buttons of her fitted shift and silly cotton drawers. "Begin without me," she gritted out, glaring up at him.

The cigar once again gripped between his teeth, he laughed at her frustration, then teased her by removing his shirt, giving her more than a hint of his arousal. "I believe I already have."

"Damn you, Max Redgrave."

"It's nice to know one is appreciated for his…finer attributes."

Zoé stood up, finally released from her silken confinement, and began pulling at the pins in her hair. "How deep is this pool, do you remember?"

He was already reaching for her. "Nearly as deep as you're tall, at least after a rain like we had the other night."

"Good enough." Without another word, she pushed both her palms hard against his chest, and he went into the pool on his back, arms whirling like paddle wheels as if that would help him keep his balance.

He surfaced, spat out the soggy cigar while shaking

his head like a doused puppy, to see Zoé's pale form coming toward him in a graceful, nearly flat dive, legs close together, her arms full out in front of her, her body only slightly arched.

She swam like a fish, had always delighted in the water, be it lake, pond or sea. She could have been a mermaid, for all her beauty of movement...but romantical as that thought was, it came with its impediments. He'd much rather she had legs.

As she wiped at her eyes, and tested the depth of the pool with her toes, Max swam behind her and slid beneath the surface, aiming straight for those wonderful, long, straight legs.

Even underwater, he believed he could hear her yelp of surprise when he grabbed her calves and pulled her legs apart, sliding between them to rise face-to-face, chest-to-chest with her, his arms tight around her waist. Her hair was wet and sleek around her perfectly molded head, and in the moonlight he could see her eyelashes clumping into long, curved spikes.

She was the most beautiful, sensual creature in the world, and he could barely contain his need to have her. There was a time when he'd laid her back in the warm, buoyant water of the sea, her legs scissored around his head, and come at her with his mouth and tongue until she'd screamed, and nearly drowned, or so she told him later. "Remember when we looked to cool ourselves that hot night in Cabreira?"

"Later," she whispered in his ear. "For now, I'd rather recall our midnight dip into the Seine."

"Oh, God," he said as she pressed her palms against his shoulders, partially rose up out of the water, drew in her breath, and then sank beneath the surface. "I'm a dead man…"

They *visited* the Seine, they *relived* that hot night in Cabreira, only leaving the water when, facing each other, Zoé said, "I never noticed before. With your hair all stuck to your head, your ears seem to stick out. Just a bit," she added hurriedly as he pulled a face at her. "Honestly, it's hardly noticeab— Max, put me down!"

He did as she ordered, but only to join her on the bank, his hands going to her waist because if she had one weakness, it was her taut, highly sensitive skin. She writhed beneath him, laughing, attempting to push his tickling fingers away, until he stopped, wanting nothing more than to look down in her beautiful suddenly carefree, laughing eyes.

"I've missed you," he said quietly, and her smile slowly faded.

"You missed *this*," she responded sadly. "I did, as well. There was a time I believed I could not live, not exist a moment more, unless I could believe we'd be together this way again. That isn't love, Max. I wish it were, but it isn't."

"I want to see our babies growing inside you. I want to see them suckle at your breast as I kiss their fair heads. I want to see your eyes in their eyes."

Zoé turned her head away from him. "Oh, Max… you hurt my heart. Our children? What would they be like with parents like us? I'd fear for their souls. I fear now for ours."

He held her more tightly, and at last she pushed her head into his shoulder, and cried. He'd known her so long, yet had never seen her cry, not until she'd told him about Georges. But she got herself under control quickly. Probably too quickly. He didn't want to believe that something, some vital part of who Zoé Charbonneau was had died in these past long months, never to be reborn.

What did he really know about her? She'd shared her early years with him, but hadn't told him about her father's death. How had she even heard of his passing, as they'd been constantly on the move? She certainly hadn't received more than a smattering of letters sent through dispatches. No, it made no sense. She would have told him.

Idiot! I'm an idiot!

His hand stiffened in the act of stroking her hair, as if the idea that had just struck him had turned him to stone. He looked up at the trees above them, then closed his eyes.

"Zoé? When...when did your father die?"

"Oh, sweet Christ, Max, not now. Let me up, I'm feeling a chill. I want to get dressed."

He rolled off her, reached for his smallclothes, using them to dry himself. "It was that day, wasn't it, that last day? Anton told you he'd had him killed, didn't he?" Picking up the rest of his clothing, he got to his feet even as she stood up, turned her back to him as she climbed into her undergarments. "Zoé? *Answer me*."

She whirled around to face him, her wet hair slapping against her cheeks. "Yes, yes. All right, Max. He told me that day. My father dead, Georges and the others lying in front of me, your life in my hands, safe only if I obeyed Anton, but forever lost to me. I had nothing left, do you understand that? *Nothing*. Anton took it all."

"I'm sorry, Zoé. I'm so damn sorry." Max wanted to throw something, break something, kill someone. Kill Anton Boucher. Kill him a thousand times over. His anger remained under control only because that sort of wild, unbridled fury would get him nowhere, wouldn't help Zoé.

"All because of the Society. All because of what my family began. Why did he involve you? Why was it you he picked to be punished for Redgrave sins?"

"Let it go, Max. I have. Otherwise I would have gone mad a long time ago. We can't change what we can't control." Zoé had finished dressing and used the hem of her skirt to wipe at her damp cheeks. "Besides, I was his instrument, never his real target. You were, from the beginning. You probably still are."

"But why not Gideon, the head of the family? Why not the others?"

"I don't know. It's only clear he wanted you alive until he and that damn Society needed you, and I could suppose, because he knew we were lovers, he planned to use me against you in some way. Perhaps to make you do something he wanted you to do. We've talked about this."

He bent down and helped her on with her slippers, attempting to wrap his mind around scattered pieces of fact and roll them together into some sort of understandable shape. "He knew I'd grown suspicious of him, and used you to show he was loyal. Poor Anton, losing his only nephew to a cold-blooded murderess. But to murder your *father?* He's gone to a lot of trouble, Zoé. He has to believe he's got one devil of a fine reward coming his way at the end of this."

"Not to mention indulging his penchant for cruelty in the interim. And his obsessive appetite for women. I think that becomes more important now that we know what else the Society does. Orgies, perversions of all kinds. And don't look at me like that—Kate brought me one of the journals when I was in my bath. She said she thought I should know. It was, uh, interesting reading."

"God's teeth. That child needs discipline."

"That *child* is as strong as any of you. Your grandmother did not raise any simpering fools."

"No, I suppose you're right. It's just damn difficult to accept she's grown up now and has had to face so many uncomfortable truths." He ran his spread fingers through his damp hair—to cover his ears? Certainly not! "You're ready to go back?"

"Only if we can enter through the kitchens and use the servant stairs."

"If you think that will keep Trixie from finding out, you've missed the mark by a long chalk."

"Yes, but at least she'll be made to work for it, or have to pay for it. I'm not going to simply walk in the front door and make it easy for her. She wouldn't like that."

Despite everything he'd learned again tonight, Max couldn't help but laugh as he slipped his hand into hers and they turned back toward the Manor. "You've barely met her, and yet you already know her so well. Are you quite sure I don't love you? Because I think you may be wrong."

Zoé rolled her eyes at him, but didn't smile. "You didn't ask me how I knew Anton was telling me the truth about my father, that he wasn't lying."

Max squeezed her hand. "I felt it best to take my cues from you. I know you'll tell me when and if you decide you want me to know."

'I…I want you to know. Anton produced my father's gold cross, the one he wore every day for as long as I can remember. The entire front was embedded with diamonds, and our names were engraved on the back. His, *Maman's,* mine. No matter how straitened our circumstances, he refused to sell it. Anton showed it to me that day, was careful to point out the dried blood embedded in the chain, and then smashed it under the heel his boot. Ground it into the dirt…"

Max had to struggle to find any words. He knew how to offer her passion, but not comfort. He felt a wave of shame crash down over his head. He knew so much about her, yet so little. Maybe she was right. *God, please don't let her be right.*

So he offered what he could.

"As you said, Zoé, he's yours. I didn't believe you should be so obsessed with his death, but I've changed my mind."

She stopped just as they'd made their way beyond the trees, out of the near-dark beneath them and back into the moonlight, and turned to face him. "Do you remember what I said at the dinner table? That you might hesitate if faced with the woman, *because* she's a woman?"

"I do. You're saying I was raised as a gentleman. I think you're forgetting that most of those lessons didn't exactly stick."

"But enough of them. You could hesitate, and that could mean the death of you. *I* could hesitate when faced with Anton, hating him so much, needing to know more about my father, not wanting to give him a quick, easy death. We both know that when it comes time to kill, you must strike at that moment, or the moment could be gone."

"And the tables reversed. We've been at this entirely too long. I don't think normal people calmly discuss who is going to dispatch whom to hell."

"Only one last mission, Max. Then I'm done. I hope you will be, too. We've given enough."

"One last dance with the devil, and with everyone I hold dear in jeopardy." He saw her shiver, and put his arm around her. "Are you cold? Do you want to go to your chamber now, or will you grant me yet another favor, and go with me?"

"You can't possibly still be—"

"Hardly. I need both of us thinking straight tomorrow."

"And walking straight," she responded, and her unholy grin was just what was needed. Or meant to divert the subject away from her father. How had they both grown so adept at avoiding uncomfortable subjects? "Yes, we need to concentrate on the Society."

"I'm glad you agree, because I've just had an idea. I don't know if it will confirm what we've been thinking, but we'll probably sleep better if we can be positive of our conclusions. Or perhaps you'll slumber, blissfully happy we were proved right, while I won't be able to sleep at all."

"That sounds ominous. Where are we going?"

"To the portrait gallery. It's mostly a long hall, wide enough for the ladies to manage their enormous skirts as they took their daily exercise there on inclement days. The portraits and busts and truly grotesque bits of art were put there to entertain them. Trixie always said it was a good place to avoid. I always thought she worried we might be frightened, but now, of course, I'm not so certain. If she was ever going to be haunted, that would most probably be the place."

"Wonderful. You certainly know how to pique my curiosity."

They entered the Manor via the kitchens, not even rousing the sleeping footman who had been left to mind the banked fire, and tiptoed to the library, where Max made short work of lighting one of the heavy silver candelabras, knowing the portrait gallery was never lit at night, for fear the ancient, dried-out canvasses could go up in flames.

"There's three steps leading up to the doors, so keep your attention on the floor," he told Zoé. "The doors themselves are solid copper, another of Gideon's ideas, and meant to keep any fire at bay until it can be extinguished from outside. But there are windows lining both sides, also to entertain the ladies with glimpses of the grounds. Connected to the rest of this pile only via that one set of doors, build atop massive arched pillars that allowed for a more open walkway below, using the floor of the gallery as a sort of roof."

"I'll want to look at it all again in the daylight. But why are you telling me all of this?"

Max held the candelabra lower, to better illuminate the stairs, and then pushed open one of the doors. "I don't know," he said, but then sighed. "Yes, I do. I want you to know the Redgraves weren't all monsters. My great-great-grandfather ordered the gallery built, designed it himself. Gideon favors him, I think. The plans he drew are framed and hung inside as a matter of fact. *His* son experimented with different breeds of cattle and sheep, as well as flowers and trees and seeds brought from America and the Caribbean, Africa, most of Europe. He tried his hand at tobacco, even wine—wine was the greater success. The only crime he committed was to smuggle tulip bulbs out of Holland, which in those days was actually a fairly serious offense."

Zoé placed her hand on his forearm. "Max, it's all right. You don't have anything to prove to me."

He put down the candelabra. "Maybe I'm trying to prove something to myself. Blood can't be denied, Zoé. Trixie always protected us, did her best to keep the taint away from us, but she also clearly believed I would be her greatest challenge. She recognized the...the *fire* in me and found a way to channel it, I suppose. She kept me on the Continent, always watching me, and I was the last to learn everything about the Society. Why? I don't delight in killing, but I do it, and I don't second-guess myself or lie awake trying to deal with regrets. Even now, you tell me what we have between us is some sort of lust, not love."

Max turned to look at her, intent on her reaction. "Are my siblings like our ancestors, their better half? Is there some dark animal inside me? Am I the one who is most my father's son?"

"Do you rape women?"

She persisted. "Do you enjoy inflicting pain? Have you dreams about power, and enormous wealth? Are you willing to do whatever it takes to get them? Did you ever—"

"All right, all right, I see your point. No, I don't crave any of those things. I'm more than adequately well-off, thanks to Trixie's careful management of some inheritances, but I'm rarely ever at my estate, and see no need of a residence in Mayfair as long as Gideon agrees to open the mansion to all of us. And only an idiot would want the crown. But—"

"Let it go, Max. You know you're not your father, or your grandfather. You fight to protect your country. You kill when necessary, but never when it's not. You'd probably hand Anton over to the hangman unless he left you no other choice. The only dark demons inside you are the ones you put there. You're an honorable man, and honorable men always act so brave and strong, while inside, you're all wasting your efforts questioning yourselves. I think that's called your conscience. Madmen don't possess a conscience, and they most certainly never question themselves. So I think you're safe."

When he told himself these things, he couldn't be sure. Hearing them from Zoé must have been all he needed. He pressed a kiss against her hair.

"The practical French. Thank you. But about this seemingly overwhelming lust I have for you...?"

"Yes, there is that. I think we may have to speak about that in more depth once we've saved the world, or at least this small part of it. I've been having questions myself."

Max felt something tight and painful at last uncoil within him. "We can be celibate until then, if that helps? I don't want to confuse you."

"I imagine it hurt to say that," she said, looking relieved now that he'd left off being so damnably maudlin...something he never thought he could be. "But, yes, that would be for the best. I broke my own rule."

"I helped you break it."

"Taking blame again now, Max, or credit?" she asked, picking up the candelabra, to begin looking at the portraits, slowly walking past one ornate frame after another. "Where are they? Your father and grandfather? I know they were English, and you all seem to favor your Spanish mother, but the dress in these portaits is all wrong. I should be looking for powdered wigs and satin coats."

"Barry refused to wear wigs or powder. He was too proud of his own hair." He relieved her of the heavy candelabra. "This way, down to the end. Gideon is soon going to have to enlarge the gallery, or else start packing some of the old boys and their wives away in the attics. There's really only room left for him and Jessica. All right, here we go. Charles always amazed me with his chosen pose. He appears in profile, as if he planned to have the image struck in gold coin…which perhaps he did, now that I know more about him. And this last one, of course, is my father. Gideon has yet to sit for his portrait."

He waited, holding up the candelabra, but Zoé only looked at Barry Redgrave's full-length pose, and said nothing. The longer he waited, the more he knew his worst fears had been realized. It had been one thing to discuss the possibility, make assumptions. But it was another thing entirely to *know*.

At last she spoke. "It's really rather remarkable. The same hair, the same eyes. They're even about the same age, about the same as your brother Gideon, I imagine. There's some resemblance you all carry of your father, mostly around the mouth and chin, but this? This is nearly an exact likeness. And there's your answer, Max. This consort, this man we're all looking for—

the man you all want to destroy, the man who clearly wants to destroy you all—is most probably your half-brother. That's really what you wanted to know when you brought me here. Well, there he is," she said, pointing to the portrait. "Not to be dramatic, but *there's* your real monster."

"Or the Exalted Leader's necessary dupe. She couldn't chance revealing herself and her plans to any of us, so it turned into choosing any Redgrave in a storm, so to speak?" Was he being too forgiving, was he hoping to avoid even the idea of fighting against his own blood? Yes, he was. This half-brother had poisoned the minds of Coopers, sent Angus's grandson out to be killed, then had Angus destroyed, as well.

"Whoever he is, he's firmly under the woman's control, to the point where he'd stand back and allow her to bed another while he waited on the street like some lost puppy. Can we leave here now? It's cold in here, and my hair is still wet. Oh, wait. Lift the candles again, please. I wanted to ask—what's that he's got pinned in his cravat?"

Max didn't bother to raise the candelabra. He didn't have to look. "A golden rose, depicted in full bloom, with a small diamond at its center. To hear Simon tell it, Barry had enough of them to fill a sash draped across his chest."

Zoé lowered her head, her voice dropped to a near whisper. "And what do they mean? Surely nothing good, not by your reaction to the question."

He worked his jaw back and forth, wishing he didn't

have to tell her. "The ceremonies. Most of them included wives and prostitutes brought in to play unwilling virgins. But from time to time, certain members were given true virgins, vestal virgins as they called them, presented to them on one of their sacrificial *altars*. Each man who then brought a bud into *full bloom,* was given one of those roses, and the poor woman was then handed over to the remainder of the Thirteen. As I said, Barry had at least two dozen of the things."

"Not just pinned to a sash," Zoé said, going down on her knees. "Look, there are more of them, worked into the tiles. Running down the center of the corridor. When did you say the portrait gallery was built?"

Max bent down, running his fingertips over the rose design, then moved along the corridor, the light from the candles illuminating another rose, and then another. "Much too long ago to believe them connected to my father, or my grandfather."

"But easily adopted by them as some sort of symbol?"

He raked his hands through his damp hair. "We'll probably never know."

"No, you won't. And it's getting late. We can't solve every puzzle, Max, much as we might want to."

CHAPTER NINE

NEITHER OF THEM spoke again until they had climbed the servant stairs and retired to Max's chamber…the one not containing a waiting servant charged with settling her mistress for the night.

Zoé grabbed up a cashmere throw left on a chair by the fireplace, and wrapped herself in it before taking a seat. Max simply sat cross-legged on the floor in front of the meager fire.

"There has to be a way to put an end to this without making widows and orphans of half the Coopers," he told her, rubbing at his forehead as if to summon an idea. "I wish Angus were still alive. He served as a patriarch of sorts to all of them."

"But they took his grandson. He couldn't stop them. Isn't that why he was living in that cottage? Unable to change what was happening, equally incapable of watching it happen?"

Zoé felt certain they had enough puzzle pieces to put at least half of the puzzle together. They just couldn't seem to align any of them in the right way.

Max resettled himself, putting his hands to the fire.

"Let's go over everything we know, starting at the beginning."

"Excellent suggestion. Let's begin at the beginning, and you're sure to come up with something brilliant. I've always loved watching your mind work," Zoé said, slipping onto the hearth rug, eager to listen. And watch. "Your eyes seem to light up when you've solved a problem, and you look very much like a pleased Jack Horner, who's just pulled a plum from his Christmas pie. You begin."

They knew about the Society, didn't need to discuss its origins, the reason behind Trixie's offer of money to any Coopers that would leave Redgrave Manor, and probably any of the other cottagers and house servants and laborers who could have been one of her husband's bastards. They knew some of the Coopers had gone and some had stayed.

They knew Barry had grown up to repeat his father's actions, from resurrecting the Society to impregnating what could have been a dozen or more Cooper women.

"Including, we can safely assume, the man you saw in Ostend, the hooded figure Val and Daisy saw with the woman during their adventure into the Society."

"Clearly she needs a Redgrave for at least part of her plan, just as she needed cooperation from the Coopers in order to be able to use Redgrave land for landing troops, for smuggling opium in and gold out. Are we decided yet on precisely why she needed you?"

"No, but I suppose I was chosen to be the earl, once Gideon was dispatched, as I'd remain next in line until

Gideon and Jessica had a son. Enter Anton, both to make certain I stayed alive, and to gain my trust, until the time came she felt ready to have him bring me to her. I also imagine, if I balked, they planned to use you to convince me to cooperate."

"Which would also mean, horribly, that none of your family would have survived whatever she planned, because that would have been too dangerous. She was relying on what Anton told her about you and me to ensure your cooperation, especially since she'd already figured out that, although she needed your half-brother, this *Scarlet,* to keep the Coopers content, his bastard status wouldn't help her reach her ultimate goal."

"But now it's all falling apart. You escaped from your cell. Richard and Tariq saved me from capture the other night. An overly zealous idiot murdered Angus. Gideon and the others not only exposed them for attempting to disrupt supply lines to the Peninsula, but have managed to intercept the Society's last two smuggling runs."

"Meaning no opium to sell, no gold flowing across the Channel to Bonaparte. She must find you Redgraves all thoroughly annoying. I can see the beginnings of a happy glimmer in your eyes. Go on."

"*Happily.* For all we know, they might be aware some of their carefully positioned French troops have begun to disappear, thanks to our pirate friend. Bonaparte's troops could be less than weeks from their covert invasion, or else the emperor is ready to discard the entire plan as a failure. The Exalted Leader's failure. Perhaps even Anton's failure."

"Even more delicious," Zoé purred. "Although trapped animals can be exceedingly dangerous. How can we make things the worse for them? All while avoiding as much Cooper bloodshed as possible, taking your sensibilities into account."

"We know where the women and children are. I'm certain I can get a message to Gideon before he leaves London. We're still avoiding Perceval, but Gideon should have no trouble finding other help. Quietly remove the wives and children, and the Coopers will lose half their heart for fighting. I know them, at least half of them. They're good men at heart, and losing Angus must have crushed them."

"And everyone here? What about their safety?"

"We've got our own pirate crew, we've got the gates, we've got the moat."

"I beg your pardon. The *moat?* I saw the gates as we rode out this morning, but I'd hardly call the ha-ha that joins gate to gate a moat. With the sun shining on it, it was actually rather pretty. Colorful."

"You must have been too dazzled to be with me again to not notice. The ha-ha, that sunken fence, does more than keep sheep from wandering loose. It's deeper than most, for one. The bottom of the thing might be lacking water, but the top of the stone wall that's level with the Manor lawns is embedded all over with broken glass, not pretty stones. It only looks innocent, and yes, colorful."

"But the Coopers know that. It wouldn't deter attackers for long."

"Some of them. I doubt they're all as committed as their leader would wish them to be. Once their families are gone, I think the Exalted Leader will have a desertion problem on her hands, if not an outright mutiny."

"And while she and Anton are struggling to control what they've built, you and I will destroy them. Have we figured the *how* of that yet?"

"I'm rather hopeful they'll be panicked enough to do that for us." Max helped Zoé to her feet. "Try to sleep. I'll go downstairs now to pen a letter to Gideon and hunt down Val and Simon. I think we can trust the defense of Redgrave Manor to them."

"And what are you and I going to do, other than hope?"

"We can't hide behind the safety of these walls, that's for certain. So we're going to do what we do best, go on the hunt. You and me, together. I'll locate your leathers. Be ready to leave before dawn."

"Finally!" she said, putting her hands on his shoulders and giving him a hard, bracing kiss. "We are who and what we are, Max, and it's time we came to peace with that."

ANTON BOUCHER and the woman reclined on a fairly tattered, deep red velvet chaise longue. Naked, finally sated, they passed the small ivory opium pipe back and forth between them. "I hate cellars. I can't believe you let that marvelous ceremonial chamber burn," he said. "I only saw it the one time, enjoyed it the one time, but the memory will never leave me. Money and unconventional appetites make for clever companions."

"We'll build another, even better than the first. Besides, you said you hate cellars."

"The lowest level of a magnificent dower house is hardly a cellar. *This*," he said, looking at his surroundings, "is a cellar. Dark, damp, smelling of candle smoke and sweated bodies. A sad imitation, madam, much worse than that idiot Mailer fellow's Fernwood and those bloody standing stones you all thought so perfect for your devil-laden gibberish."

"Yes, I think Post had second thoughts about constructing the circle and altar just before he died. Have you ever seen a man hanged, Anton? I've heard it said they often die appearing fully aroused, just as Post conveniently lifted himself to my knife. I know I was stirred to my depths just before I struck, but had his fear turned to anticipation?"

"We might want to give that possibility more study. I suggest your idiot as our first candidate."

She turned in his arms, handing him the pipe. "So jealous, Anton. You're rarely here. I have needs. Besides, once we have your lost sheep back in the pen, I'll take care of Niall. I think about it all the time, whenever I'm with him. So handsome, so well set up, yet still a bumbling ox, but necessary for now."

"I'll have the girl shortly. I wasn't so stupid as to leave myself without a trump card, and only had to wait until it was brought to me. It has to be now, as I know their habits. They believe the best way to victory is to move fast and make up their plan of attack along the way. Especially him. I don't think he understands fear. I had his only weakness in my hands, and I lost her, yes. I'll have her back."

"Because of this supposed trump card."

Anton put down the pipe and levered himself lower on the cushions, to begin lightly biting the woman's skin. Watching her nipples tauten as his bites came closer, closer. Draw it out. Make her squirm, begging for more. Then the pleasure. Then the pain. She asked too damn many questions. It was time to remind her yet again that he was the one in charge.

"Your last question, bitch. Yes, it's being delivered now."

He raised his head, smiled up at her unblinking, opium-befogged eyes. Then he lowered his head once more and moved on....

ZOÉ QUICKLY DROPPED her leathers to the floor and kicked them beneath the bed. "Oh, it's you, Magret," she said when she saw the maid. "Again, I apologize that Mr. Redgrave woke you and ordered you to bring my leathers to me at this ungodly hour." She bent down and retrieved them. "What has he bothered you with this time?"

Magret scratched at the hairs on her chin. Her rough-cotton dressing gown made her into a man-o-war in full sail, but then most anything would. Magret certainly didn't hide behind the door at mealtime. "Don't know as I can say for certain it came from him. One of the lads guarding one of the gates brought it to

me before he was off to bed, all sealed up everywhere
and everything. Think there's somethin' in it. Here you
go. I'm for m'bed myself, and this time to stay there.
Morning comes sooner now than it used to."

Taking the offered square-folded paper, Zoé thanked
the maid and then took herself over to the fire, breaking
the seal and unfolding the single sheet. Something fell
to the hearth. She only glanced at the letter as she went
down on her knees to locate whatever had dropped.

She located the golden object by its shine, thanks to
the fire, and held it in front of her for a long time. Her
mother's wedding ring. Her father had worn it on his
little finger ever since her death.

Another cruel stab at her heart, delivered by Anton
Boucher. He knew where she was, he knew how to reach
her, and most of all, he knew how to hurt her.

But that's all it did. The cross, now the ring? Both
were probably taken at the same time, with Anton holding on to the ring if he thought he ever needed it. In reality, it meant nothing.

Then she remembered the letter. And recognized her
father's bold, distinctive handwriting, and his use of her
favorite form of endearment, *my little jewel*.

Do not come, *ma petite bijou*. My fate is mine,
not yours. I implore you, do not believe anything
this heinous creature tells—

The rest was nothing but a trail of black ink, as if
the paper had been pulled away before her father could
finish.

Below these words, Anton's usual chicken-scratch slanted across the page.

I graciously allowed him to write whatever garbage he wished, Zoé, *ma cocette,* as long as he would write. As the clock strikes three, be at the gate you and your lover used this morning. Tell no one. You and I, we have matters to discuss, a bargain to be struck. Shall I be conspicuously dramatic, and say your dear papa's fate hangs in the balance?

Zoé's hands were shaking so badly that the ring dropped once more, and she jumped at the faint sound it made, clinking against the hearth, nearly rolling into the fire before she could retrieve it.

She read the single page one more time, and then yet another.

She knew what she should do. She should immediately go to Max, tell him. Show him the letter. Let him see that he was right to be hopeful.

The last thing she should do was anything Anton ordered her to do. The very last thing. She could be walking into a trap, a web of his making, and when Max found out he'd come searching her, all caution thrown to the wind. Because he believed he loved her, she would be risking his life, as well.

And her father? How could she disobey her father? But how could she obey him and live the remainder of her life knowing obeying him had meant his death?

He'd been lost to her. She'd finally begun to accept that.

But now…?

Zoé rubbed at the tears streaming down her cheeks, touched the ring to her lips and kissed it, telling herself the warmth she felt wasn't from the fire, but still held her father's body heat. She held the ring, and held her father.

The clock on the mantel struck out the hour of two. If she was to be at the gate in an hour, she had to make up her mind. If she was going to tell Max, argue with Max, even plan with Max, she would be late and, knowing Anton too well, her father would die.

The paper went into the fire, Zoé watching as it turned black and fell into ashes. When she explained, if she lived to explain, Max would understand.

"Perhaps," she told herself.

She had to get on the move, and quickly stripped off her dressing gown before climbing into her leathers. Her hands continued to shake as she wrapped the blade of the stiletto in a strip of white linen ripped from one of her borrowed petticoats, and slid it into her left boot, because Anton would expect it to be in the sleeve in her right boot. She didn't bother with her throwing knives at all, as she wasn't about to hand them over in any case. She didn't plan on leaving her side of the gates.

If he asked, she'd tell him that Max had taken her knives. That he'd believed the truth when she explained it, but still wasn't about to trust her with her weapons. Yes, that was plausible. Anton could believe that lie.

Besides, clearly tonight was for Anton to display his brilliance, to take a bow for producing her father…and then make his demands. He didn't want her dead, not yet. He wanted her at his mercy.

She looked at the mantel clock. Forty-five minutes left, and by her rough judgment, she had to cover nearly a quarter mile of scythed lawn to reach the gate. She had to get out of the house. She wanted time to better reconnoiter the grounds, and she may have to deal with any guards at the gate.

"Calm, what you most need is to be calm," she ordered as she sat at the dressing table and tied up her hair before pulling on the black knit toque. She'd be nearly undetectable in the darkness once she donned her thin, black kid gloves, if it weren't for her pale-as-death face, which looked as if all the blood had drained from it. Steadying breaths didn't help. Attempting to slow her pounding heart didn't help.

Her father was out there somewhere, with Anton. He'd been a prisoner of the Society, all these long months. They'd hurt him.

Her hands drew into tight fists. *They'd hurt him.*

And she had no plan except to show up at the appointed time, and listen. None. She'd have to take her cues from Anton.

She made it down the servant stairs without being detected, and the footman guarding the fire was still asleep. If the banked fire died, and it appeared close to doing just that, he'd be in considerable trouble when the cook discovered it—what was his name? Jacko? One of the pirates and probably the meanest in the bunch if her one glimpse of him meant anything. She needed to avoid him, at all costs.

Zoé crept to the door, balancing on her toes so that her boot heels wouldn't betray her, only to find it locked. *Idiot!* Of course it was locked! Every door and window in Redgrave Manor was locked or otherwise barred against the enemy. There might even be a pirate guard standing on the other side of the door, one who probably wouldn't care for her explanation of why she was sneaking about dressed all in black like a thief attempting to escape the house.

There had to be another way out. As it was, the West Gate was on the other side of the huge building. The moon would be of some help, but the ground was unfamiliar and she couldn't dare be late.

If only Anton had given her more time, but that would be the last thing he'd do. He wanted her reacting, not plotting some sort of strategy.

Think, Zoé! Think!

"Good evening, *mademoiselle*."

She froze where she stood.

The voice was almost directly behind her. Soft, cultured. "Leaving us, are you?"

"Tariq." Zoé turned about to face him, her mind racing once again. *Friend or foe, friend or foe?* She chose *friend.* "Goodness, you nearly frightened me to death."

"If I may be so bold, I believe someone had already accomplished that before I spied you in the upstairs hallway."

"What were you doing in the— Never mind that. Are you going to try to stop me? Because fair warning, Tariq, I won't be stopped."

"Yes, that is also obvious. Miss Rose suffers from cruel nightmares, and I offered to prepare a calming draught, as her sister didn't feel comfortable leaving her. Simply some warmed milk and a few drops of laudanum."

Zoé didn't believe him. "You've been assigned to watch me. Trixie's orders. Did you see who gave Magret the note earlier?"

"I'm sorry, but I did not. Miss Rose called out for me in her distress, and her sister sent Mr. Valentine Redgrave to summon me. I have trained as a physician in Beirut. Do you wish to question me further, or do you perhaps have more pressing matters to pursue?"

"You're not going to attempt to stop me? You'll notice I don't believe you'd succeed."

Tariq smiled, his even white teeth flashing against his honey-colored skin in the light from the fire. "I believe I was warned not to, quite sternly at that, by another determined lady."

"But…but you work for Trixie."

"I *oblige* the dowager countess to honor my father, and as a friend. Clearly you are set on whatever it is you need to do. How do you plan to circumvent the guards?"

"Guards," she repeated. "Are there many?"

"I believe it would be safe to assume that, yes. May I brook a suggestion?"

Time was running out. "I don't have much choice, do I? Nor do I have much time."

An uncomfortable minute later, with one of her boots only slightly singed, Zoé was free of the rear clean-out grate of the massive fireplace, somersaulting out onto the ground, covered head to foot in wood ash. At least she wouldn't have to worry anymore about her pale face betraying her.

She'd have to stir the fire when she returned, as well as remember to tell Max about this unconventional but effective way to avoid the guards.

She spared another moment to pray the posted guards were superstitious, because if any of them were to spy her out now, they might believe they'd just seen a ghost.

She crouched against the wall until her eyes became more adjusted to the faint moonlight, and then took off at a dead run. By the time anyone could believe what they were seeing, she'd be just a fading shadow, glimpsed, then gone from their sight.

At last, near-breathless from the run and the ashes that seemed to clog her throat, she could see the darker outline of the gates and their flanking stone guard-houses. She slowed, remembering the ha-ha. That's all she'd need to do, fall into the damn thing.

She saw no guards patrolling inside the gates, and quickly assumed the worst before nearly tripping over a pair of long legs splayed out on the gravel drive.

"Merely sleeping, the pair of them."

Zoé's every muscle tightened. *Anton.* Where was he, out there in the dark? Still on the other side of the gates, ignoring the fact that a tall ladder and a tough length of leather placed over the sharp glass were all it would take to conquer the ha-ha? But he didn't need to put himself to that trouble, did he? He'd known she'd come to him.

"Seems the earl's hired henchmen aren't averse to bribes, or to taking a sip or two from the bottles conveniently left inside their certainly uncomfortable posts. They'll wake, too ashamed to report their failing. In other words, my reluctant dupe, if you can manage not to be discovered, it will be as if you never left your room tonight. I had worried, knowing how you and Max loved to *rut*. How did you manage to slip away?"

She went to the gate, grabbing onto the wrought iron bars with both hands. "*Cochon*. Enough! Where's my father?"

"Why, right here. Standing just in front of me." A shuttered lantern was opened slightly, and her father's beloved face came into view. His silver hair was disheveled, his clothing nearly in tatters. He'd always been so proud of his appearance, so meticulous in his grooming. Having his daughter see him this way had to be worse than hell to him.

In his obvious agitation, Charbonneau abandoned his careful English for a rush of his native French. "Zoé. Is that you? Why do you dress like a lad? I can scarce recognize my sweet angel. Have you been playing in the ashes? Run away. Don't linger to hear this man's empty promises. He will kill me no matter what you do. Already his knife presses into my back. I welcome it, once I know you're safe with the people in this house.

Cling to them, and I die happy and go to be with your mother, having seen your face one last time."

He managed a small smile. "Although I will tell you I think a bath and a more suitable ensemble wouldn't come amiss for the daughter of a man of my stature. Now go, and may the saints go with you."

He was being so brave! Zoé could barely remain on her feet. *You know I can't simply turn my back and walk away, Papa. You're not going to die. I'm not going to lose you twice.* She wanted to scream, to cry, somehow open the gates and throw herself in her father's arms.

She wouldn't give Anton Boucher that satisfaction. Her father wouldn't approve.

The bastard was smiling, standing behind her father; hiding there, the coward. "Anton, enough of this farce—make me your offer."

"My *offer,* Zoé? There is no *offer.* Even a simple mind like yours surely can grasp that much. You do what I tell you to do or your father dies."

"No, no!" her father shouted, his spirit at last breaking, even as two large men in masks grabbed him by the arms and wrestled him away into the darkness. "Don't listen, don't listen—"

"I almost like him, you know, save for his foolishness in attempting to martyr himself to save his whore daughter. We've had to keep him bound and constantly watched since bringing him here, or else I do believe he might have found a way to take his own life. Again, to save you. Just as you threatened me in that Paris cell, if you'll recall. You should have stayed away from all of this, Zoé. I think you and Monsieur Charbonneau could have become disgustingly wealthy if you'd both just taken to the stage."

Where were they taking him? She hadn't even had the chance to tell him she loved him.

The stiletto was in her boot. She could have it out in an instant. Even through the bars of the gate, she knew her aim would be true. Anton knew it, as well, but also knew she couldn't chance such a move, not when her father would pay the penalty. "He's an old man, Anton. If he is not allowed to grow older yet, I will find you and slowly slice you into very small pieces."

He reacted to her words by stepping back a few paces, although he laughed as he did so. "As I said... the stage." Then his voice turned hard. "No woman is the equal of a man, let alone his better. You're inferior in both mind and spirit, meant only for pleasuring a man, attending to his needs and bearing his sons. Yet you all will insist upon believing that isn't true, that you are as brave and capable as any man. That you're here tonight, groveling, threatening, weeping like a puling infant, only proves the truth of what I say."

"While you know the true face of bravery. Does that include putting a pistol to your nephew's head even as he believed you were about to save him?"

"Georges made the necessary sacrifice and would have understood why what I did was necessary. He's a hero!"

Zoé could feel bile rising in her throat. "And what does that make you, Anton?"

He let out a long string of obscenities aimed at her, and she smiled, knowing she'd hit her target full-center. When he'd finished, he said, "It's as you yourself demanded, *enough*. I have some small chores for you."

As Anton began to speak, for the first time since Magret handed her the note, Zoé was certain she'd done the right thing.

Now all she had to do was avoid the guards once again, brave the fireplace, rouse Max, apologize, listen to him call her a fool, explain, listen to *him* apologize (in his own way, which some might defer from terming an apology at all) and then they'd figure out some way to take what she'd learned and turn it all to their advantage.

She'd begin slowly, with the fireplace....

CHAPTER TEN

"THIS HAD BLOODY well better be important, even earth-shaking," Valentine Redgrave complained as he made his way into Trixie's elaborate dressing room, followed by Simon Ravenbill and, because their love was still young, and Simon hadn't quite mastered saying *no* to her, Lady Katherine, as well. "And why is it so blasted dark in here?"

That was true enough, it was dark. The only two windows had been covered over in black velvet mourning draperies Dearborn had hastily unearthed from the attics at Max's request.

"Oh, sit down, Valentine," his grandmother implored, barely visible in the shadows. "All of you, sit down. Dearborn provided enough chairs. Obviously we've been reduced to holding clandestine meetings in our own house."

"So that's why we all had to stumble through the near dark? Because the house is being watched, even in the middle of the night? That's fairly disgusting, I must say," Val said. "Trixie, I'll sit next to you, if that's all right."

There was a slight rustling in Trixie's general direction. "As long as you promise to sit down and stop asking questions. I'll make room on the chaise. Max, scoot. And get on with it, please. As Valentine said, we're hoping for earthshaking."

"Then never mind. Earthshaking, I think, should be faced while standing. Where's your bridegroom?"

"You'd have to ask your brother, since he sent him off somewhere."

The door opened one last time and Zoé slipped in, shutting the door behind her and leaning against it. In her leathers and toque, she was nearly invisible, although the smell of smoke and ashes still somewhat clung to her.

Max was proud of her for being so brave, angry with her for being so foolish and madly in love with her because—well, because he was, damn it. Whether she believed that yet or not.

"Now that we're all here and the door is closed, I think we can light more candles," he said as he rose from the end of the chaise and stepped into the center of the room.

"Well, and would you look at you two, all dressed in black," Val said a few moments later, as he leaned against the dressing table and lifted the crystal stopper from one of Trixie's vials, sniffed at its contents. "Are you planning to be chief mourners at somebody's funeral? Not any of us, I hope. And may I say, Mademoiselle Charbonneau, my sister has been longing to have a rig-out similar to yours ever since I told her about it. Haven't you, Kate? Not Daisy, though. I'm hav-

228   WHAT A HERO DARES

ing enough trouble just convincing her to stop wearing *brown*. Oh, don't scowl, Max. I'm finished now. But you did wake me only minutes after I'd finally returned to bed after poor Rose's nightmare. Happily, Tariq seems to have a calming effect on her. Do you suppose—?"

"Yes," Trixie interrupted testily. "Anyone with eyes and half a brain would *suppose*. We can only keep our mouths shut and our fingers crossed, and in time we may be delighted. Lord knows the child deserves some happiness. A new country, a new life, a new love and her bad memories all left behind her. I vow, Valentine, you've been playing the fop in society too long. Thank God you had the good sense to convince Daisy you're salvageable. Max, remind me again why you wanted him here?"

"When I remember, yes," he said, standing in front of the mantel, where he could see everyone and everyone could see him. "We've had a development tonight. Zoé was approached by fellow agent and now known traitor, Anton Boucher, the man who sailed here with us the other night. It would appear he's got her father—yes, Zoé saw him—and is using him for leverage, commanding her to do what he wants or her father dies. And before anyone asks, again yes, we both believe he'd do just that."

"I didn't mean that sort of earthshaking," Val said quietly, all trace of the fop gone in an instant. "How do we help?"

The rest joined in immediately.

"You saw your father. That means you saw Boucher. Tonight?"

"Yes, of course tonight. And here, at the Manor."

"No, not in the Manor. Somewhere close to the Manor?"

"He couldn't have gotten far. In the dark, in unfamiliar countryside."

"Dragging an unwilling man along with him."

"The horses will have left tracks."

Max clapped his hands for silence. "Just wait before you all go running for the stables, because that's not the whole of it. Ah, Valentine, now I remember why you're here. Do you recall telling me what you'd concluded while infiltrating the Society? That, in the end, it would turn on itself, destroy itself? Congratulations, brother. You were right."

Valentine grinned. "You did hear that, Trixie, didn't you? But if your hearing is beginning to fail you, I can repeat it."

Kate giggled. "That's one for your side of the board, Val." The two were the closest in age, delighted in each other's company, and between them had been behind more mischief as they were growing up than a regiment of hooligans.

Max looked at Zoé, raising his upturned hands and shrugging, hopefully to remind her that Redgraves weren't your usual sort. They might appear frivolous, but the more Redgraves relaxed, the more dangerous they became.

Simon spoke for the first time. "Do we yet know

Boucher's part in all of this? Is he the Society's connection to Bonaparte, or Bonaparte's connection to the Society?"

"Not a simple question, and without a simple answer." Zoé stepped forward. One thing about Zoé, Max thought proudly, she wasn't shy. If she had what she believed to be a valid opinion, everyone was going to know it. "I believe the man must pin notes to his small-clothes each morning to remember who he's supposedly loyal to that day. Mostly, we believe Anton is loyal to Anton. He's cruel, ruthless, totally lacking in morals and conscience, and highly ambitious."

She moved her gaze around the small chamber, pausing for a moment as she looked at every occupant, to bring her point home. "And he's got my father, has been holding on to him for months, just as he hoped to do with me. Just in case he needed me. He wins, or I lose everything."

Yes, that was one reason he loved her. Although she had to be longing to scream out her frustrations to the heavens, Max knew she would stick to business. Sympathy, at this point, would probably destroy her, so she simply wouldn't allow it. She would keep her emotions in check, her mind clear, until she had succeeded or died. And for Zoé, just as it was with him, failure was not to be considered.

"Obviously we can't let either of those things happen." Max motioned for her to join him in front of the fire. Together. Whatever they were about to face, to dare, they'd do it together. "We've heard about your prisoner in the attics, Val, planned to see him, but haven't yet had a chance to talk to him. Tell us what you know about him."

"Harold Charfield? *Burn,* as he's known in the Society. He's one of Perceval's many undersecretaries. Captured and sent here—someday I'll tell you how I managed that—just in case we might need him. I suppose you'd say that, in some ways, the Frenchman and I think alike. But not to that degree, and that's not what you want to know in any case, is it? Thinks very highly of himself, old Burn does, but he's mostly bluster with a weak bladder. It wouldn't take much to break him. So far, however, he doesn't seem to know much. The Society is careful to limit information only to what each member must know to perform his assigned job. The Frenchman's interested in him? I don't know why. The only names he could tell us were ones we already knew. A prize of war, or some such thing and no longer able to make mischief in London, but as I said, so far, useless to us as a bag of warm spit."

"Not anymore, Val. He may have been feeling safe as long as the Coopers were here, probably passing him notes from the Exalted Leader promising him rescue was close at hand or some such rot, but now he has to be concerned for his safety."

"What are you supposed to do, Zoé?" Kate asked. "Kill him? He couldn't want you to— Oh, my God, he does, doesn't he? To save your father."

"No, he doesn't seem concerned about Charfield, and we're hoping he's made a mistake. It may be he doesn't even know we have the man. It certainly isn't a failure I'd share, were I the Exalted Leader." Max looked to Zoé, who only nodded, her eyes shining bright with unshed tears, allowing him to continue answering for her. "Whatever their plans in the past, and whatever they planned to do with me, it's now Zoé they want, and Anton convinced them he knew how to get her. After all, she'd already proved she'd do anything to save someone she—"

Max paused, to allow the pain that stabbed in his chest to pass as he remembered how much Zoé had sacrificed for him. "It's important to know this is a recent development, and that Anton hasn't shared the fact that he has Monsieur Charbonneau. He has him hidden somewhere."

"A man with that many balls in the air is bound to drop one of them, sooner or later," Val interjected. "Now, and only for a moment, Max, where do you fit in all of this? I seem to have lost my place."

"What the Society originally had planned for me, we might never know, although they may believe they still might need at least one legitimate Redgrave male alive after the French land in England."

"An intriguing thought, that last bit. Perhaps you were halfway on your way to a wedding as you crossed the Channel?" Simon was leaning forward now, his tone soft, concerned. "And now to the heart of this strange new development. What are you to do for the Society, Zoé?"

"Assassinate Lord Spencer Perceval," Zoé told him, sighing. "You tell them, Max."

"Let me preface this by saying the idea belongs to the Exalted Leader, not Boucher. A Frenchwoman, penetrating Perceval's inner sanctum, delivering the fatal blow. Successful or not, managing to escape or not, and already a known traitor, the result would be the same. The Exalted Leader—damn, how I hate saying that, over and over—believes Perceval's death would provide the killing stroke to England, perhaps even double her and France's chances of success. Zoé?"

"Anton was quite forthcoming about the remainder of the French plan, a sure sign he believes they still hold the winning hand. Yes, it's everything you all thought it was, and thank God for your pirates. Vain men brag when they think they're winning, long to explain their brilliance to the losers—always one of Anton's failings, and I admit to encouraging it tonight."

"Indeed, huzzah for the failings of men," Trixie said fervently, lifting a glass of wine in salute. "I've traded on them all my life. My apologies, pets, I certainly don't include my own family in that statement." She smiled reassuringly at Zoé. "Go on, dear."

"The Society is well aware of the broadsides in London, the newspaper articles, the essays, all condemning the monarchy and praising Bonaparte as a far-thinking man of the people. Hot-heads, scholars, wits—all of them stirring the pot. I've seen them, I imagine we've all seen them."

"I've read more than enough of them," Simon said.

"If any of those blowhards was ever called on for more than words, they'd run to cower beneath their beds."

"I agree," Max told them, "but think about the thing before shaking your heads in dismissal and consider the matter from the Society's perspective, the people most likely to agree with those broadsides. Perceval suddenly dead and Parliament thrown into disarray. King George mad as a hatter, his son and heir a wastrel and spendthrift, as unsuitable for the throne in his way as the king is in his. In many ways, just as Charles, and then Barry after him, designed for their own plans to fall out. The Society truly believes our countrymen will first panic, but then rise, turn on the monarchy, the greedy aristocrats who have kept their foot on the collective English neck for far too long. The French march in, to be met by showers of rose petals, and as their reward, the Coopers are awarded ownership of Redgrave Manor and all the considerable family wealth."

"And perhaps Max's hand in marriage for the ambitious Exalted Leader. Fools believe differently, but it remains the ambition of every Englishwoman to obtain a title, preferably with a male heir within the year and their husband in the ground shortly thereafter. Yes, it's all far-fetched, pets, but possible," Trixie told them. "These past years haven't been easy for the populace, always with the threat of war over their heads. Costs and taxes rising to pay for the wars, new laws passed to better control our citizens. Unhappy people look for a villain to blame, as well as a hero who might save them. Remember, the Society has worked its members into positions in several levels of the government, and they're presumably ready to act. How many times have you heard that England is ripe for a revolution of its own?"

"In recent years? Too many," Simon said, nodding. "But it sounds as if Boucher has grown disenchanted with this plan?"

"Not Anton, as I doubt he cares either way as long as he's well paid," Zoé corrected. "Your answer is Bonaparte. Which probably best answers your other question. Yes, while pretending to work for the Crown, Boucher in fact works for Bonaparte…or at least fears him more than he admires the Society. And if anyone needs another reason that he told me all of this, I believe he wanted me to know how desperate for success he is, how serious he is about killing my father. In any case, when the emperor was made aware of this new part of the Society's plan, he balked. A clever strategy, even if it failed, was to be commended, but he would not be remembered by history as a petty assassin. Anton came here, was ordered here, to deliver that message, and to… How do I best say this? *Nettoyer son gâchis?*"

Valentine smiled. "Clean up his mess? And how is he to do that?"

"It would seem he's been told to take charge, personal charge, of the Society," Max told them, taking Zoé's hand. "He doesn't want Zoé to go after Spencer, as the Society believes he came here tonight to order her to do, but only pretend to do so. In reality, he wants Zoé to kill the Exalted One, the leader. The woman."

"So it was *her* plan, this assassination of Perceval. All right, I've found my place again."

"Very good, Val. She's begun acting on her own. Supposedly this isn't the first alteration she's made to the agreement with France. She's become too enamored of her power, and too attached to the more tawdry *activities* of the Society."

"The same failings of my husband and son. A consequence for anyone of ambition to consider with care," Trixie said. "I believe I can tell you the rest. In short and in long, she's become an embarrassment as well as a danger, and clearly must be eliminated. I suppose, put in Bonaparte's position, I would have concluded the same thing."

"Gone rogue is how Boucher put it, Trixie," Max added, hoping it was only the flickering light from the candles that suddenly had his always indomitable grandmother looking so very sad and old. "On top of everything else, to my understanding, things haven't been going so brilliantly for her of late."

Val smiled at Simon and Kate, and then looked somewhat smugly to Max. "You're welcome. So, how can we help you now?"

Max reeled off what he needed. "I want this Charfield person brought to this room. Now, tonight. Richard is already doing that for us, after softening the man up a bit by rudely waking him, ordering him to dress, and plying him with wine, frightening him and reassuring him the entire time. With your help, Val, Zoé and I think we might have a way of loosening his tongue."

"A-hem."

"Yes, Trixie. You and Zoé and I believe we have a way to loosen his tongue. My apologies."

Good. She already seemed to have recovered from whatever had made her look so defeated. That was Trixie. Down, but never out.

"And one thing more." He looked at Simon. "Please allow me to finish before jumping up to break my nose, remember she is my sister, and that I love her dearly."

"Go on," Simon said, his jaw clenching.

"If Boucher no longer trusts the Society, I doubt the Society still trusts him. Kate, I need you to go upstairs now with Zoé, and put on her leathers. There's got to be someone in the Society's employ watching the primary gate, and I need that person to see Zoé ride out within the hour. Sooner, if possible. They'll be opened for her and she won't be questioned. If the woman is smarter than I begin to give her credit for, she'll otherwise conclude Anton has betrayed her, and I fear for Zoé's father if that happens."

"Now look here, Max…" Simon protested.

Max held up his hand. "You'll fit in the leathers, Kate, that's one thing, but not the most important. You ride better than any woman I've ever seen, even better than Zoé, ride astride when you think no one's looking. But for tonight, it's the sidesaddle. You know the grounds, all the twists and turns in the drive, and could probably find your way blindfolded, at a gallop. You're the obvious choice. God help us, the only choice. Simply move fast, and keep your face covered. The Society has to believe Zoé is on her way to London."

He looked at Simon, whose face most resembled a thundercloud. Kate, however, was all but dancing.

"Simon, you have to leave now, careful not to be seen. There's a mount already saddled and waiting at the foaling stable. A jumper, one the head groom assures me has routinely been able to clear the ha-ha from this side, so you can avoid the gates. But first, between you, pick a point of rendezvous no more than a mile from the Manor. Take a riding habit along for Kate to change into, stay at the ready until you're certain Kate hasn't been followed, which I highly doubt, as they'd be unable to keep up. Wait for dawn, and then proceed to the Eagle, to calmly order breakfast before returning to the Manor, making certain everyone knows you had taken your mounts out for an early morning run. Any doubt we've tried to fool them will be gone the minute they see her face. Are we agreed?"

Simon rubbed at his cheek. "Agreed. But, once this is over, be aware I've reserved the right to break your nose."

Kate threw her arms around his neck and hugged him.

WITH ZOÉ AND TRIXIE discreetly hiding behind the folding screen, Harold Charfield was ushered into the dressing room by Richard Borders. He was given a bracing clap on the back and a fairly menacing, "Well, boyo, here's luck to you."

When the door all but closed, with Richard now on the other side of it, Charfield was left to stand there in the near dark, his hands tied behind his back, a man clearly apprehensive about the future, and his place in it.

"Hel—um, *hello?* Is anyone here? I'm not frightened, you know."

Zoé and Trixie exchanged looks.

And said nothing.

"I'm serious. You can't frighten me. Lord Saltwood gave me his word. Civilized, he said. He's civilized. Are you there, my lord? If you were pleased to show yourself? Civilized, that was it. My lord? Anyone? *This isn't amusing.*"

If they kept quiet much longer, Zoé thought, the man was going to drop to his knees and burst into tears.

The same door opened again, and then closed. Val was in the room.

"Oh, I say, Burn, has your isolation caused you to become unhinged? I could hear you talking to yourself as I approached. Forgive me for forgetting your nervous nature. You haven't pissed my grandmother's carpet, I hope, as that would be a bloody shame."

"You." The man managed to turn that single word into an accusation, a curse and an admission of fear, all at the same time.

Zoé was rather impressed. It had already become apparent to her that there was more to Valentine Redgrave than he preferred the world to see, and now she definitely wanted to see what that was. She peeked out from behind the screen, to get her first look at Charfield, to watch Val at work…and wonder about the condition of Trixie's Aubusson carpet.…

"Yes, yes, congratulations on this talent for stating the obvious. It is I. So sorry I haven't stopped by to see you in a few days, but I've been otherwise occupied. Have any of the servants told you? We managed to intercept this enormous shipment of opium the other night. Our second success in that area, you know. Anyone would have thought the smugglers wouldn't use our beach again, but it's true, I suppose—dogs always return to their vomit."

"What do I care? I don't even know what you're babbling on about. Am I to stand here all night?"

"You don't care about the opium? Strange. You had quite the supply and quite the obscenely carved ivory pipe in your guest chamber at Fernwood. Nasty stuff, opium. Still, would you like some now? As I said, we've plenty."

Zoé watched as Charfield's shoulders stiffened. "Would you—*no*. No, I would not. I know what you're trying to do, Redgrave. First the wine, and now the opium. It's painfully obvious. You want me willing to talk to you. But that's impossible, because I have no answers for any of your questions."

"Splendid, Burn, perhaps you're not as stupid as you look. Still, I would like to chat. I must admit my curiosity is piqued about this Society of yours. How it works during those, you know, *ceremonies*. Do you really serve up virgin sacrifices?"

"Virgins?" Charfield snorted.

Val stayed silent, clearly waiting for that silence to become uncomfortable, a ploy that more often than not had someone in the room speak up, say the first thing that came into his mind, if only to break the growing tension.

Charfield wasn't an exception. "I've never had a virgin, not even my wife, curse her." And then: "She promised me one, you know, but it never happened."

Zoé held her breath. *Yes, you baboon, let's talk about the Exalted Leader, why don't we?*

"Never had one? Never got yourself a golden rose? Such a pity. We have a few dozen of them lying around here somewhere. Do you know what I think, Harold? I think the woman has been cheating you. Could we even stretch that to say *using* you? She's a bit of a bitch, I'd say. Oh, and did I tell you your friend Mailer is dead? He'd made one too many mistakes, some of them cleverly manufactured by me, by the way, and she had him stretched out on that stone altar he'd ordered built, and personally sliced off his— Well, you can imagine. This makes me wonder, Harold. If she were to succeed, if the Society were to succeed, and she came marching in here to take possession of the Manor…how would she deal with your mistakes?"

"You're lying. You would have said all of this before, if it were true. You're only trying to frighten me. That's all you had that day at Fernwood, much as you threatened and blustered, and that's all you have now."

"Yes, so you persist in saying. I can't decide if you're really that unimportant, or just too brick stupid to trust with more than your single job. Clearly the Society considers you expendable, or else one of the Coopers would have been ordered to poison your dinner. They're gone, you know. Run like rabbits. We'll have them, and all the Society by the end of the week. You can hang in London as a group. Won't that be cozy, one last reunion— and even with hoods over your faces as the hangman pulls the lever." Valentine pulled out one of the chairs, turned it and straddled it. Obviously his preferred way of seating himself. "Good fun, what?"

Zoé watched as Charfield, no longer asking permission, backed up until he could collapse into the chair Simon had been sitting in earlier.

Val rested his chin on his crossed arms. "Actually, I was trying to be kind. I also could have brought you evidence, I suppose, but I didn't wish to go scrounging around the perimeter of the altar at midnight. You know, *searching* for the thing."

All right, Zoé thought impatiently. *Now I know how you do it, you're just having fun now. Get on with it.*

"Say anything you want. I'm done listening to you," Charfield told him.

"My, you are the stubborn one, aren't you. Almost confident. Why is that, Harold?"

"Your brother the earl promised me no one would hurt me. His solemn word. As a gentleman. As a gentleman yourself, and his brother, you're bound to his promise."

And that's when Trixie began to chuckle softly, because Charfield had walked straight into the trap set for him.

"Is that so?" Val said, getting to his feet in order to light a few more candles. "And I suppose you're probably right about me. I'd much prefer you spoke freely with us simply because we asked so politely. But tell me, Harold, have you ever met my *other* brother? The one who *isn't* a gentleman?"

The door from the hallway opened one last time, and Maximillien Redgrave stepped into the room, powerfully striding straight up to stand a few feet in front of Charfield, his booted legs spread, his hands on his hips. Dressed all in black, his black locks hanging free and wild about his bearded face, those damn blue spectacles resting low on his aristocratic nose, even Zoé found him intimidating...although in her case, it was delightfully so.

Trixie had stepped out from behind the screen now, and was openly giggling. She might even have begun to applaud.

"You're going to answer *my* questions, you spineless pig," Max growled in a most menacing voice. Then he pulled a riding crop from behind his back and snapped it directly in front of Charfield's nose. *"Aren't you?"*

Moments later, Val was standing over Charfield, the man's body lying, unmoving, on the floor. "Well, ladies and not-quite-the-gentleman, that was a whacking great help, wasn't it? I believe the object of our little farce was for you to frighten him into talking, Max, not to death."

"Oh, shut up, Valentine," Trixie said. "I was beginning to think you were attempting to *talk* him to death. Zoé, pet, please bring me that vase."

Zoé did as she was asked, and watched as Trixie upended the vase to dump its contents, flowers and all, onto Charfield's face. He came up to a sitting position as if propelled by magic, sputtering and coughing and spitting out at least one leaf.

Max went down on his haunches beside the man, leaning close to his ear. "Now, shall we try again, *hmm?*"

For all his air of menace, to Zoé at least, Max looked like a handsome, even beautiful, happy, but naughty little boy enjoying himself to the top of his bent.

And for the first time since receiving the note from Anton, she actually smiled.

CHAPTER ELEVEN

"OH, NO, not on my chaise," Trixie declared as Val and Max helped Charfield to his feet, then looked around as they decided where to put him. "I'd have to have it burned, and it was fashioned for Versailles and given to me by a certain good friend who— Well, never mind about that. Those days are over, thank God, but that doesn't mean I wish to part with any of my treasures."

"You're all rather insane, you know," Zoé whispered in Max's ear once Charfield was seated, half propped up on two straight-back chairs hastily pushed together. "And I believe I agree with Val. I don't know what job that fool over there was assigned to by the Society, but I doubt he was very good at it. We may have just wasted an hour of precious time."

"You'd rather we simply blindly ride out, hoping for some sort of miracle? A star in the sky, perhaps, shining down on the Society's hiding place? Our best hopes lie with that wretch over there, and you agreed." Max closed his eyes for a moment, then pulled her rigid body against him. "I'm sorry, I shouldn't have said that. We're going to find them, I promise, and your father is going to be safe."

"I know," she said quietly as she stepped back, her eyes once again shining with tears. "Thank you. I'm just…"

"I understand. I don't remember either of my parents, but I'd be the same if Trixie was out there somewhere. Look, Zoé, you don't have to do this. Val and I can handle it. Maybe this is one mission you shouldn't—"

"No," she said, cutting him off, which was probably a good thing.

He'd insulted her, had questioned her abilities in the face of her fears for her father. But, damn it all to hell, this wasn't just another mission, and he had every right to worry. Didn't he?

"All right. Let's get on with this before Trixie decides to take over the questioning. I know she's dying to do something more than watch, but I'm not sure we'd like her questions. Besides, she's already managed to get hold of the riding crop."

Zoé gifted him with a small smile, and they took up chairs in front of Charfield.

"Feeling more the thing now, Mr. Charfield?" Max asked, as if he cared a bent farthing about the man's comfort. "Ready to answer a few questions?"

Charfield leaned slightly forward, his eyelids slitted, his chins, both of them, stuck forward defiantly. "You're a monster." But then he seemed to reconsider his bravado. "What do you want me to tell you?"

"I want to talk to you about the Society, of course. Oh, not the tawdry details, as I'm already disgusted enough, just having to speak with you, look at you. I want to know where it is."

Charfield's head came up. "Where what is? I don't understand."

Trixie pressed the flat of the whip against the man's chest. "Mr. Charfield, you don't want to make me angry," she warned tightly. "I have lived the majority of my life dealing with the Society in one form or another. The plots, the traitorous schemes—they all rest on the success of satisfying filthy little men like you, horrid little minds like yours. Greed, ambition, whatever the reason behind the Society's existence, the main attraction has always remained the same. *Sex,* Harold. Sex in all its most tawdry forms. And for that, you need places to meet. Tell me, Harold, or I'll show you what I learned about little toys like this. You know what I mean, don't you?"

Charfield looked down at his chest, and the riding crop, and then up into Trixie's face.

There was no question in Max's mind that she meant exactly what she said, and had said precisely what she meant. Even a fool would know that. Trixie Redgrave may have been a victim, but she wasn't a victim now, and hadn't been one for a long time.

"Fernwood. We meet at Fernwood."

"That's gone," Valentine said, looking at his grandmother a little sheepishly. "But I did hear the Exalted One complain about *this* sanctuary being lost to them before she and her consort rode off from the place in rather high dudgeon, actually. That means there are more, doesn't it, Burn?"

With a cautionary look to Trixie, Max took over the questioning. "One quite naturally being here, on or close to Redgrave Manor. That woman didn't recruit the Coopers with her charm and a polite tea party. She's trained them to want the masks, the women, the ridiculous hellfire rituals. The opium. That's why you're so enamored, isn't it? Prancing about naked in your capes and puppet heads, hiding your faces while rutting with anyone or anything that had no other choice. Come on, Harold. You know it and we know it. There's another sanctuary, and you're going to tell us where it is."

The man's eyes had gone rather wild. All these people, strong, dangerous people, hovering over him, knowing his deepest secrets, demanding answers from him. He began to struggle to free his hands.

Max was growing concerned. Had they gone too far? The fellow looked as if, next time he went down, it wouldn't be in a harmless faint.

"I can't. You know what she'll do to me. Don't think Mailer was the first. I can't. I can't!"

Max motioned for everyone to back away, and they gathered in a corner while Charfield sobbed.

"We were right," Trixie said. "There is something out there. Ceremonial meeting place, sanctuary, whatever they want to call it. The woman will be there. With all the trouble you children have caused her, she can't chance being anywhere else, demonstrating that she's still in charge."

"Knowing it and finding it are two different things. We've only had our suspicions confirmed," Zoé said. "That's a far distance from finding her or Anton. Or my father."

Max was in agreement. "I know. Let me try this again, on my own. Trixie, I love you past all bearing, but you've done enough. Please, go join Richard. I'm certain he's worried about you."

For a moment he thought she might fight him, but then she nodded and handed over the riding crop. "I'm too old for any more of this. All these years, over and over again. How I hate them for what they took from me. What they made me do, what they made me of. My husband, my own son... Yes, yes, I need Richard."

Zoé leaned down to kiss Trixie's powdered cheek, to give her a quick hug before the woman turned and slowly, almost painfully, headed in the direction of her bedchamber.

Max waited until she was gone before looking at Val. "We never heard anything she said tonight."

Val looked toward the floor, took a quick swipe at his eyes before nodding his agreement. "You don't... I mean, we really don't think she— My God, Max."

"First to protect her son, and then to protect us," Max said as Zoé slipped her arm around his waist. "No. That's impossible. And if it isn't, we have to pretend it is. For her sake. We can only be glad she has Richard. Oh, for love of heaven—where do you think you're going?"

He walked over to Charfield, who, on knees and

nose mostly, was attempting to crawl toward the door to the hallway.

The distraction was something all of them needed. "What do you say, Val, how far should we let him go?"

"That's probably far enough," his brother answered, leaning down to one-handedly pick up their prisoner by the waistband of his breeches and haul him to his feet. "Come along, old boy. We've all seen enough of this room."

"We'll take him down to the music room," Max told him. "Dearborn has covered those windows by now. I doubt anyone is still watching at this late hour, having seen Kate leave, but since Dearborn's already gone to the trouble, we might as well."

"Don't want the old boy to think he's been wasting his time," Val agreed. "Come on, Harold, you were just about to tell us something, remember?"

This time, before they pushed him down onto one of the striped-satin couches, they untied his hands, Val having suggested this might make him think better. Or at least think. "A man who'd believe he could *crawl* his way to— Where the devil were you going anyway, Harold?"

"Trapped animals," Zoé commented wryly, looking at the mantel clock. "He may have been heading to the attics."

Max glanced to the clock, as well. He calculated that it was nearly dawn on the other side of the carefully draped windows. Another night gone, and little accomplished. No, a lot accomplished. Just not enough.

But then the unexpected happened.

"You really believe you can...you can beat her?"

Zoé whispered something in French. Max was fairly certain it was a short prayer of thanks.

"Yes, it's only a matter of time," he told Charfield. He took a chance: "She won't be able to control you anymore."

Freeing Charfield's hands did seem to have freed his tongue.

"I didn't know. You have to understand that. I didn't know. It was a lark, that's all. A bit of fun, and that was the end of it. Except it wasn't. I went the first time, and mostly watched. I couldn't believe what was happening."

He took a long breath. "When I was asked again, I went back. By then...by then they knew my...my preferences. I couldn't believe my good luck. I'm the fifth of six sons, you know. Not a prospect in front of me, only my employment as one of dozens of undersecretaries. But all that changed. Suddenly I was elevated in position. There was money, all my debts were paid."

"How fortuitous for you," Max said, having difficulty hiding his disgust.

Charfield looked at him hopefully. "Yes, yes, that's it. Fortuitous. That's precisely how I saw it. And the Exalted Leader. She allowed me to service her." He shot a quick look toward Zoé. "It was a great honor," he said sheepishly.

Was there any other man so pathetic? Unfortunately, Max realized, there were many more. Had always been many more, and probably always would be, as long as cockroaches roamed the earth.

"But then I was given my first assignment. I would do as I was told or else everything would go away. The position, the money…the ceremonies. Do you understand now? Nothing was my fault. I was forced to do what I did."

"Yes," Val drawled, "I noticed that about you the moment I first met you, while you were out hunting up a young boy for that night's *ceremony*. Wretched, broken man, obviously a victim of the Society, even as you were raised up to the select Devil's Thirteen." He held out his leg toward Charfield. "Here, Burn, pull this one now, it's got bells on."

"You have to keep her away from me. I don't want to die that way."

"Few of us would," Max agreed, knowing they were finally going to hear something of importance.

"I don't want to be hanged, either."

"I can't prom—"

But Val cut him off. "That much is true. My brother can't help you there, but I can arrange that. I'm very close with Perceval. Why, I was just at his house not that long ago. Go on, tell us what you know. Where's this damn sanctuary?"

KATE'S MARE WAS tied to one of the spokes of a large, flat, wooden wheel in the stableyard, and being walked in wide circles to cool her. Max had pointed that out to Zoé with some pride—and probably more relief.

"She's very brave for a young lady of her, shall we say, pampered background. But your brother is incorrigible," she told him as they pulled away from the stables on the rough plank seat of a farm wagon, wearing homespun brown cloaks with the hoods turned up to hide their faces. And to protect their noses, as the bed of the wagon was heaped high with manure.

Not many would care to come within a hundred yards of them, and certainly wouldn't stop them.

"I don't see why," Max told her, as the mules drawing the wagon were urged toward the North Gate. "He promised the man he wouldn't be hanged, and Perceval is bound to agree."

"Yes, he'd agree to a firing squad. Very clever. Where is Val meeting us?"

"He's not. He feels this need to speak with Trixie the moment she's awake and ready to see visitors."

She wasn't sure that was wise. "He's not going to talk about last night, is he?"

"No. He's going to tell her he loves her. Val has the softest heart of any of us."

Zoé considered this for a while as they moved along the track, heading for a destination that couldn't be arrived at soon enough. "Are you angry with her?"

"I don't know how I feel. What she did cost us our mother, but Trixie may have had her reasons for that. Barry was dueling with his wife's French lover. But it's as you told me, we can't go back and change the past. I believe I argued that we could forget it, and look to what we have now, and to the future. How can I say any less about anything Trixie felt compelled to do?"

"She loves you all very much, and you've told me how she's always protected you. When she saw history repeating itself she had to make a choice. She chose her grandchildren, and has fought for you ever since. There's no dark animal inside you, Max. Trixie made certain of that."

He looked away, toward the trees. "I know. We make ourselves. Charfield tried to blame the Society for his failings, but by returning a second time, a third, he'd already chosen the Society. He made his own life."

"We either learn our lessons or learn to live with the same mistakes, over and over again. I've been a fool, haven't I? I'd convinced myself that once something is lost it can never be regained. Yet here you are, and here I am. I don't think I'll ever want to be anywhere else."

Max looked deeply into her eyes for a long, unblinking time. "After hoping with all my heart to hear you say those words, would it offend you if I suggest we discuss more about where we want to be forever only after we're free of this wagon?" he asked her just as his smile squeezed her heart.

They were met on the road barely twenty minutes later by Simon Ravenbill, who had a handkerchief tied around the bottom half of his face. "God's teeth, Max, I could smell you coming long before I saw the wagon come into view. There was nothing else?"

"It seemed a good choice at the time," Max told him, setting the brake once he'd directed the mules to the side of the dirt track they'd turned onto, leaving the gravel drive behind them. "The wagon leaves every morning around this same time for the last several months. I understand Gideon has ordered its contents raked out and dried on the North Fields, then plowed into the dirt before the next planting. Gideon's a fine custodian of Redgrave Manor. To the Manor born, some might say."

"That's all well and good," Simon said as Max helped Zoé down from the plank seat, and her borrowed cloak became caught on a large splinter. "But who's going to deliver this particular load to the fields, because it damn well isn't going to be me."

"All arranged," Max told him. "And the horses?"

"May I first admit it wasn't as easy sneaking out of the Manor a second time as it was the first?"

"No. We'll save that for another time, when both you and Val can regale me with your combined brilliance over these past weeks."

"I didn't think so. Would it be all right to tell you our watchers have been reduced by two? Not dispatched to their heavenly rewards, as Kate explained we aren't to just go killing off those who might be redeemable Coopers, but definitely out of the fray, neatly tied up with a bow wrapped around the base of a tree, and awaiting my return."

"You can, and just did. Thank you. Now where the hell are those horses?"

Simon inclined his head to the right. "Over there, behind those trees. Zoé, your leathers are rolled up in a small blanket tied behind the saddle. Same for you,

Max. Everything you asked for is there. My friend's man Jacko saw to it personally. He has also, as I understand it, had a stern talking-to with the men who guarded the West Gate yesterday. I don't think I'd want to be on the receiving end of that man's idea of a talking-to."

"Having seen the man, I concur," Max said. "Our thanks to both of you. I can't change into something fresh soon enough."

Zoé only nodded, and headed off into the trees.

"All business this morning, isn't she?" she heard Simon say as she hastily untied the cloak and tossed it into the bushes. "She looks pale, although that could be the effect of the manure."

"She'll be fine, we'll both be fine. We've made our way through more than one Paris sewer in our time together. This is what we do, Simon... What we did."

"But not with her father's life hanging in the balance."

Zoé felt her bottom lip begin to tremble, and pushed a hand against her mouth, willing the betraying trembling to stop, and then quickly lowered it again.

Max joined her a few moments later, even as she heard Simon's mount's hoof beats fading into the distance. He looked at her, as if inspecting her for some flaw. "You heard that, I suppose," he said gently. "Zoé, it's not too late for me to bring Val or Simon in on this. You don't have to go."

"We've had that discussion," she told him sharply, already half out of the plain brown gown "donated" to her rather happily by Valentine, accompanied by the request she forget to bring it back. "You promised a stream. I don't see one, and without one they'll smell us coming, and we might as well just approach openly, and surrender."

"I also promised soap. Other than the obvious, what's your rush? We're stuck here until it begins to grow dark in any case, but at least we're safely away from the possibility of spying eyes. Admit it, the plan was brilliant."

Zoé sniffed at the back of her hand and grimaced. "With one obvious major exception."

He laughed, trying to ease the tension between them, she supposed. "Come on," he said, untying the reins of the two waiting horses. "We're safe here, the north section of the estate is barely yet to be cultivated, and this particular area is only visited by our huntsmen. The stream is this way."

"And you're positive my father is where you say he is?"

"We've also had *that* discussion. Yes, I'm positive, and so is Val. But for now, since we can't do anything yet anyway, and Anton won't do anything unless you don't do as he said—and if the Society was watching, the Exalted Leader believes you're off doing what she had Anton order you to do. Other than pacing and second-guessing our plan, there's really nothing more we can do than relax, and let the time pass. Maybe we'll even sleep, since we didn't do that last night. Zoé, if you want to help your father, you've got to pretend this is no more than another mission. And that means we prepare, we consider alternatives, we decide how we'll go on, and then we remain calm, detached and we get the job done without getting caught, let alone killed. If you can't do that—"

"What if he's wrong? What if this she-bitch lied to him about where she and Scarlet were going to be tonight? What if Anton was lying and we're walking straight into a trap the two of them set up for us? What if we're all playing games, with nobody telling the truth?"

"Zoé, stop."

She knew she wasn't helping her case of being fine, calm and ready to proceed. But she couldn't help herself. "What if Papa is already dead, now that Anton believes he has me under his control? He has to know he can't keep me on a leash as his assassin. I agreed to do this one thing for him, and if I were to be successful, he wouldn't need me again, would he? There's simply no reason to keep my father alive."

They'd both stripped by now, and were standing waist-deep in the cool stream. Max was soaping his chest. "Is that it? Are you done now?"

"Yes." She took the soap from him and began working it into her wet hair. "Max? Do you remember the night we infiltrated the French lines just outside Wagram after the first day of fighting was over, sent there to gauge the strength of Bonaparte's remaining forces?"

"Père Francis et Sœur Marie Magdelene," he said, nodding, "come to pray over the wounded and dying. I remember. What of it?"

"I don't know," Zoé said just before bending her knees and sinking below the surface, coming up blowing air through her nose, her hair now free of soap and sleekly hugging her head. "It was terrible, it was frightening—it was most certainly a wildly dangerous thing to do. And it was all a game. I don't think we ever felt so alive as when we were a hair's breadth from dying. How…how did we ever consider any of it a game?"

He helped her back onto the bank and handed her a length of toweling. "I don't know. Youth? Blatant stupidity? I take it you don't feel that way anymore."

"No," she said softly. "Not anymore. And never again. I'm ashamed that I ever thought it was."

"We did a lot of good, between us. Saved many lives."

"And took a few."

She bent to one side and twisted her hair, squeezing water from it, and then handed him the damp toweling to dry himself while she slipped a soft white lace-edged chemise over her head, laced it shut and stepped into a matching undergarment. There was also a simple dark blue skirt and a white blouse for her. She ignored the blouse, and selected only the skirt. The blouse would only get wet when she combed out her hair.

Max also had finished dressing. He wore simple nankeen breeches without hose and a collarless white shirt with ridiculously wide sleeves, left open, even at the cuffs. He could have been one of the pirates she'd glimpsed that first night, although lacking a brace of pistols hanging around his neck from a length of rope or a cutlass stuck in a red sash.

"You don't mind if I want to be alone for a space, do

you? I'm going to try to find a place to sit in the sun, so that my hair dries," she told him, looking up through the trees. It wasn't even close to noon, and the day stretched before her as if it might prove to be endless.

"No, I don't mind," he told her. "I'll pack up things here. Too bad no one thought to include a shovel, or else I'd bury our clothes. Not to hide them, but to be rid of the stink. Never let it be said that all of nature is beautiful."

She smiled weakly, nodded and turned away, heading toward what looked to be a fair-size patch of sunlight off to her right.

What she had thought to be only a small clearing turned out to be a perfect, miniature-size meadow in the midst of a fairy forest. The tall, sweet grass waved gently in the breeze, and seemed to be dotted all over with wildflowers: blues and yellows and reds and pinks, their perfumes blending with the smells of sunshine and white clover. A soothing place to sit and reflect, she supposed, and decided that's just what she would do, sit cross-legged among the flowers, and listen to the birds sing, the bees buzz.

She'd pass the time, and the time eventually would pass, and clear her mind of her fears.

Otherwise, she might fall to pieces again, and Max would toss her over the front of his saddle and deposit her back at the Manor.

He was keeping his distance, and she was grateful for that, especially after she'd told him…well, what she'd told him. She hadn't said she loved him, and he hadn't pressed her to say the words.

What she knew, what she'd finally acknowledged, was that she'd lived life with him in it and without him, and the idea of living without him again was unthinkable.

Was that love?

She ran her fingers through her hair, holding it up to the sun, lifting the thick blond hair to the breeze.

She'd believed him dead, and remembered her rage, her sorrow, her bone-deep grief. She'd raged against him for dying, screamed out her anger until the guard warned her he'd throw a bucket of slops at her through the bars. She'd cried, she'd drowned herself in memories and regrets hour after hour; she'd curled up on the dirty, damp straw piled in one corner of the cell and stared at nothing until her eyes had burned themselves dry.

Was that love?

She was physically attracted to him from the first moment, certain from that first night together that there could be, would be no other who would satisfy her the way he did. The passion, the desire, the hunger that never seemed to be far from the surface whenever they were together, and even when they were apart.

Was that love?

Standing face-to-face in a stream, ridding themselves of the smell of manure, assisting each other, questioning each other: old friends, deeply caring friends, their nakedness simply a condition of the moment, and not a mandatory prelude to what might come next. Passions

laid aside, leaving them two people simply comfortable enough with each other to stand naked in front of
each other.

Was that love?

She sensed him behind her before she felt him carefully place something on her head. She lifted her hands
to lift it off, only to see he'd fashioned her a daisy chain
of pink and yellow flowers. It was the most beautiful
thing she'd ever seen.

She replaced it, allowing the ring to tip forward,
onto her forehead.

"Thank you." That's all she could say. *Thank you.*

He knelt behind her, laid his hands on her sun-
warmed shoulders.

She closed her eyes. "I don't think we should be—"

"It's not like that, Zoé," he told her, pressing warm
lips against the side of her throat. "Not anymore."

He slipped one lacy strap aside, and then the other,
before employing his thumbs and fingers to knead at
her taut muscles, relaxing them, her terrible tensions
seeming to melt away beneath his fingers.

"That…that feels wonderful." She probably hadn't
had to tell him. He only had to see how she'd dropped
her head forward so that he could continue his minis-
trations.

Human touch. Not invading, not requiring any response other than to accept what was offered. How did
anyone survive without it?

"Lean back against me, Zoé," he encouraged, sliding his hands halfway down her arms. "You can always lean on me and feel safe. I'd never let you fall."

"I never thought you would," she told him. "You never did. Max, I—"

"Shhh," he said as she did as he'd asked, and was now snugly held between his legs, the skin of her upper back in contact with the warm flesh of his muscled ribcage.

He put his arms around her, crossing them in front of her, his hands drifting up and down her upper arms. He was close beside her now, as well, his cheek pressed against hers. His skin warm with sunshine. She was cocooned, with growing hopes of one day becoming a butterfly.

"It's beautiful here, isn't it?"

"A small perfect world of its own," she agreed.

"Let's just look at it for a while, enjoy it, remember this moment. A time just for us."

She could stay like this into eternity. Safe, as he'd just promised. Protected, surrounded by Max's strength.

She'd never felt like this. Never.

Zoé realized she'd spent the majority of her life on the edge, always moving, always with one eye trained behind her, never feeling safe, secure. Life had taught her to rely on herself, and that everything good in that life sooner or later went away. People passed in and out of her life all the time, as she was shuffled here, taken there, told to wake up, gather what she could and follow where her father led. Leaving behind her home, her quiet life, her mother.

Maybe that's why her new life, working for the Crown, had come to her so naturally. She didn't know how to stay in one place. Or relax. Or become attached.

Until Max. She'd held him so fiercely, become so protective of him, needing him not to disappear. Even their lovemaking had been fierce, even greedy.

Just in case it went away, if he went away.

And when he did…ah, when he did, the heart she'd believed she'd learned to protect broke into little pieces. Impossible, she then believed, to ever be put back together again.

It was easier to believe you didn't care, that being on your own was the best way to be. And much less painful.

Zoé felt a tear run down her cheek, and looked down to see it had splashed on Max's arm, to be followed another.

"Don't cry, sweetheart," he whispered against her ear. "Don't cry. Another night, another day, and it will be over. You'll have your father, the Society will be in tatters and we'll all stand together at the Manor and raise our glasses to salute that we've accomplished what no one else but us would either believe or suspect— thank God. And then we'll get on with our lives, and forget any of this ever happened. Can you do that? Can you wait just one more day, can you believe in the future?"

"I believe in you," she said quietly.

He pressed another sweet kiss against her neck. "Thank you."

She disappeared into her own thoughts once again,

her mind floating, touching on so many things, then flying off again. Just like the colorful butterfly she watched flutter from flower to flower.

After a time, be it moments or minutes, she asked Max a question. "What's it like…having a home you always know will be there when you return, having a family?"

"You mean *my* family? I think you've pretty much seen what it's like. We're all so different, yet all so alike. We laugh, we argue, we tease. We can be apart for months, but when we see each other again it's— I don't think I can explain it, Zoé. But I want you to be a part of it."

She turned in his arms, to smile up at him. "I'd like that. I didn't know, I didn't realize, nearly up to this moment, but I'd like to…to *belong* somewhere."

"You belong with me, and I belong with you. I think we've earned that."

He lowered his mouth to hers, and kissed her. Softly. Gently.

And a sob hitched in her throat, and her body went warm with wonder.

She slid her arms up and around his neck, or else otherwise she might melt into nothingness and disappear, to float above the meadow. She was already halfway there, as if she was with Max and yet also above both of them, hovering, watching him as he lowered her to the ground among the tall grass and flowers, their mouths still fused together, and held her. Simply held her.

She barely noticed her laces opening, and could

only sigh when his hand reached inside the chemise and cupped her breast. She cradled his hand as he kissed her face, her eyelids, her hair, and then began a slow, leisurely descent along the side of her throat, to linger again at her chest, before moving on yet again.

She was crying again when he took her into his mouth, his tongue velvet against her nipple. She'd never felt this way, had never been loved this way, even by him.

There was no fire, no blaze. Just a slow, simmering heat that stirred her heart as much as it did her senses.

"Max..." But that was all she could say. His name.

Inch by inch, her clothing fell away, always to be followed by Max's touch, his kiss.

And still the tears fell, slipping silently away, into her hair.

She stroked his back. She listened to him breathe. She put a hand to his heart, and willed her own to beat with his.

When at last he came to her, hovered over her, looked down at her with his eyes dark with passion, she welcomed him, rejoiced in him, took him deep inside her and raised herself to him, met him halfway, to both give and receive the sweetest, most eloquent kiss two people had ever shared.

She was shattered, she was made whole again. New. Different. Complete.

Was this love?

Yes...this was love.

CHAPTER TWELVE

MAX LAY ON HIS SIDE, his head propped against his hand, and watched Zoé sleep.

He wanted to wake her, to hear her whisper again as she'd done earlier, *"Je t'aime, Max. Je t'aime."*

I love you, Zoé, with all my heart.

The breeze played with her hair, brushing wisps of airy blond waves against her slightly flushed cheek. She looked so young, her slightly open mouth accentuating her bee-stung bottom lip. She'd laid her head on her hands, pressed together as if in prayer, and he believed she looked more like an angel than any portrait he'd ever seen in his travels across Europe.

Although he doubted any angel had such a wondrous body. Long, and slim, with an enticing dip at her waist as she lay on her side, an entrancing flare to her hip. Still, she was, to him, innocent perfection. And her new vulnerability tugged at his heart in a way he'd never felt until these past strange days.

She'd never left him. Even after she'd gone, as he tried to hate her, forget her…she'd always been there. She'd always be with him, even if they were never together again.

He'd be forced to go on, to walk the world only half a man, all the better parts of him gone. That didn't bear thinking about...

"Max?"

"Zoé," he responded, smiling. "You're awake."

She boosted herself into a sitting position and pushed at her hair, frowning as she encountered tangles. "How long have I been sleeping? I never thought I'd sleep. Is it soon time to go? I have to get out of these clothes and into my leathers." She pulled a thick lock of hair forward and gave it a disgusted look. "And do something with *this*."

"Papa wouldn't approve?"

"Papa wouldn't approve, no. But at least I'm clean today. Last night I made for a fine chimney sweep. Are you nervous? I can't say I'm not."

"I'm rather glad of that," Max said, helping her to her feet. "It shows your intelligence."

He leaned in and kissed her, and she kissed him back, and then they just stared at each other for a time, the pair of them grinning like idiots.

"*Je t'aime,* Max. I love you. I don't believe I'll ever tire of saying those words."

"Good, because I know I'll never tired of hearing them. *Je t'aime,* my darling, always and forever. Now get up and get moving. You've been waiting all day for this, remember?"

"But no longer fearful."

They walked back to the stream arm-in-arm, her long legs matching him stride for stride. In tune with each other, the way they'd always believed they were, but now knew they hadn't been, not in the ways that really mattered.

Silently, and with occasional pauses to down bites of ham from the basket Jacko had provided, they went about the job of turning themselves into what neither of them wanted to be ever again. Hunters. Possibly killers.

He'd wanted her to sleep as long as possible, but he might have sliced it a bit too thin if they were to be in place before dusk had turned to dark beneath a moon that wouldn't be as helpfully bright tonight.

"Do I get to ask one more time?" Zoé was sitting on the ground, tugging on her right boot, pulling it up and over her leathers.

Max had already finished dressing, his clothing as black and close-fitting as hers. "Charfield's description of the private dining room at the Golden Goose was too precise for their meeting place to be anywhere else. They met, they dined, they proceeded to the ceremonial chamber, or whatever the hell he called it."

"The Chamber of Celebration," she corrected, "but I suppose you were close enough. Stuffed boar heads? *How* many did you say are mounted on the walls?"

"I never counted, but at least a dozen, on every wall, and all with brass rings through their snouts." Max took the last slice of ham and stuffed it into his mouth, then spoke around it. "At Christmastime, our worthy innkeeper strings lengths of holly through them, like a chain. Very festive."

Zoé had pulled on her other boot and was now standing, stamping her feet fully into them. "And we're positive my father is there. Because Anton wouldn't want him too close to the woman, who might ask him his name and then decide *she* wanted him, rather than allow Anton to use him. She probably doesn't want Anton at all anymore, not if she possesses any intelligence. It does make sense."

He didn't want to lie to her. "I can't say I'm completely positive but, yes, it makes sense. The Goose is small, out of the way, yet closer to Redgrave land than the Eagle, and Anton would want to keep him handy. There's also the fact that the Goose has been known to offer food and shelter to highwaymen and other unsavories—for a price—not that Anton would be so foolish as to stay there himself."

"But with a few of those *unsavories* hired to guard him, the inn would be the perfect place to hide my father."

"We'll hope so. In any case, the Society certainly wouldn't want to advertise their presence by staying at the Eagle when they come to dress themselves up like the little devils they believe they are, parade about chanting gibberish and showing off for the ladies being served up to them."

"I don't need another description of what they do, thank you."

"No, I suppose not." Max shook his head, trying to banish the thought of his grandmother, young, undoubtedly terrified, as ever being made a part of such a scene. Murdered her husband? It was a shame she could only kill him once. But then to believe there was no alternative to keeping her grandchildren safe except to destroy her only son in order to stop what her husband had begun, an evil that might otherwise destroy them all? No, Trixie may have pulled the trigger that day, but it was Charles who had really killed Barry.

Zoé was tucking her hair inside the black toque. "Max? I can see you're upset. I'm sorry. I shouldn't be hounding you so."

"No, sweetheart, you have every right. Besides, even without Charfield's description, there aren't that many places to stop, dine, hide their horses before traveling on foot to the Chamber of…to the meeting place. It isn't as if they could have knocked on the door at the Manor and asked for a room for the night. I still can't believe we nearly met the captain there. This might all have been over by now, if we had."

"Or we might all have been very dead, the moment someone from the Society realized where we were heading. Are you ready to mount up? And what are we going to do with all of this?" she asked, indicating the basket and discarded clothing with a wave of her hand.

"Leave it, or be the first Crown agent to go chasing after the enemy with a picnic basket strapped to your saddle."

"And because we'll be back? I'd like to come back here, to the meadow."

"I think that can be arranged. You know, I'm not certain there's a meadow on my estate—the one I haven't seen in over two years. If not, we'll have to create one."

He offered his cupped hands and she put her left foot in them and boosted lithely into the saddle.

"Do you know something, Max," she told him as she smiled down at him. "I think, for all your past declarations that you are no such thing, you're becoming *romantical*."

He swung up into the saddle. "Bloody hell, woman, I've been teasing my siblings, telling them the same about them—especially Kate, who's always said we're the most *unromantical* family in nature. You can't tell any of them what you just said, or else I'll never hear the end of it. Next you'll want me to sit propped beneath some leafy tree while you rest your head against my lap and I read you the poem I wrote about you."

They were nearly back to the dirt track where they'd left—escaped—the manure wagon. "Max, never say you wrote a poem about me."

"Might we please talk about this another time?" he asked, probably nearly bleated. "Otherwise, we're going to have to rouse your father from his bed before we can rescue him." He pointed to the right. "This way. Let's ride."

BY THE TIME Max's circuitous route had gotten them to the point where they could safely hide the horses in the trees behind the Golden Goose and get close enough to the inn and its several outbuildings, Zoé had lost all of the inner glow still lingering after their time in the meadow.

She might say she believed in miracles, and their

afternoon together, the discoveries they'd made, the profound intimacies and truths they'd shared, certainly qualified, considering their past. But she knew the world for the most part revolved around luck, both good and bad, and it wasn't always angels who guided the hand of those forced to roll the dice.

She had her stiletto tucked into the sleeve inside her right boot. She had her pair of throwing knives, plus a third already in her left hand. She resisted the need to turn it over and over in her hand, because that would show Max she wasn't as calm and collected as she needed him to believe.

Max had his pistols—he'd checked them twice before they'd ridden out—and a small, clever, London-built four-barrel pistol that fired two shots at a time. Reasonably accurate. At close range. When it worked. He had a thin but extremely strong rope, complete with knots spaced every twelve inches, coiled and slipped up his arm and onto his shoulder. He also had his strength, his agility and his brain.

They were as prepared as it was possible to be without an army at their backs.

And, in a few minutes, she and Max would once again roll the dice.

"It's not very large, is it? And with very few windows. In fact, it resembles more a small fortress than it does an inn. How do you propose we get inside? From the bottom or the top?"

"It's a basically simple place. The attics are only two large rooms under the pitched roof. Guests share them, lying practically cheek to jowl next to each other. There's only four rooms on the floor below the attics."

"You're disturbingly familiar with the layout of the place, aren't you? What other *service* does the landlord provide?"

He looked at her through the increasing gloom. "Not now, Zoé."

And why not? Hadn't they always joked and sparred, to ease the tension that came before a mission? *"Au contraire, mon ami.* Definitely now."

He flashed her a wicked smile. "Every aspiring young buck has to begin somewhere. The Goose is practically a tradition."

"Ah, I thought as much. All right, please go on. Tell me more about this sanctuary for highwaymen and brothel."

"Not a brothel. Simply several friendly, generous and rather educational barmaids. Now we'll go on. I don't think Anton would chance locking your father in one of the rooms, either. He might call out, alert the inn patrons. With the taproom floor definitely out of the running, that leaves the cellars. And before you ask me how I know about the cellars, as a young man I'd more than once helped carry up small barrels of ale for the barman."

"You could have simply said *down,* you know. But it reminds me to enquire more about your earlier life. And the earl's and Val's, as well, I suppose."

Max grumbled something low under his breath. She thought it might have been *and won't that be wonderful.*

A bit louder, he said, "Remind me to come back here another time and break out one of the windowpanes in the corner room. I scratched my name into the pane with the diamond on my signet ring, directly beneath Gideon's and, for all I know, directly above Valentine's." He put a hand on her arm. "Down."

"Yes, we already—" She looked toward the rear of the inn, to see three men exiting the inn through what must be the kitchens, and quickly went to her belly on the ground behind the bushes they were using as cover. The men were a good twenty-five yards away, and probably couldn't see them, but one could never be too careful. "Sorry. You meant *down*. Where do you think they're going? They're leaving through the kitchens?"

"We need to get closer," Max told her, and she agreed. Together, they made their way from bush to bush, tree to tree, even using the cover of some of the outbuildings, until they were close enough not only to see, but to listen.

"Come on, old man, can't you move those dew beaters of yours faster than that?"

"Hobbled as I am by these ropes of yours around my ankles? Hardly. And so I tell you every night. You weren't a good student as a child, were you? *Vous avez le visage d'un cochon et le cerveau d'une puce.*"

"He's at it again, running his mouth in that Froggie tongue," the second man said. "And not sayin' anything too nice about you, Tom, I wager."

"Papa," Zoé whispered, probably unnecessarily. "He's shackled, wrists and ankles, and he's carrying a—"

"Chamber pot," Max finished for her. "It would seem we've stumbled upon a nightly ritual. Anton never believed in paying well for anything. If he'd crossed their palms with a bit more silver, your father would still be locked in the cellars, and one of the pair of them toting the pot to the privy."

"Hold up. Stand right there, old man," the guard named Tom ordered. "Watch him. Long as we're out here, I might as well put my piss somewhere else than against the wall, eh?"

Zoé watched as her father held up the brass container.

"Full is full, and full is heavy. You do insist in feeding my delicate body with your inferior English food. Slop goes in, slop goes out. *Telle est la vie.* So if you could please first allow me to—"

Tom backhanded her father across the mouth with his filthy paw. "*Parlay-boo* shut your damned potato trap, Frenchie?"

"Mine," she said, claiming the one she'd take, leaving the other for Max.

"*Certainement,* sweetheart. No time for a better plan in any case. Let's just go at them straight on, hope the element of surprise and Tommy-boy's full bladder help us. On three, before anyone else stumbles out here from the inn."

"Simple, but probably effective," Zoé agreed, already crouching down, her weight balanced between the ball of her left foot, the heel of the right, and ready to run. She shifted the throwing blade from her left hand to her right. *One...two...three!*

They ran quickly, quietly, until there was no longer any chance of them not being seen, and then rushed forward together.

"Papa!" Zoé called out. "Get down, get down!"

She should have known better. When had her father ever obeyed an order from his daughter?

In a heartbeat, she was reduced to the role of observer, as her father flung the contents of the chamber pot squarely in Tom's startled-looking face, a move followed close behind by swinging the empty but still heavy pot against the man's head.

At nearly one and the same time, Max disposed of any threat from the other guard by the simple move of ramming him, like a charging bull, and then neatly putting him to sleep with the butt of one of his pistols.

Her throwing knife replaced by the razor-sharp stiletto, Zoé motioned for her father to put out his hands, made quick work of slicing the rope wrapped around his wrists, and then crouched down to repeat the action with those stretched between his ankles. "Ah, perfect, one of my own knives frees me. You're looking better tonight. Somewhat."

She ignored him. "Max? What do we do with them? If we leave them behind, they'll be able to tell Anton about us."

He looked at the man lying prone on the ground. A large man, with a more than ample stomach, and then shifted his gaze to the other one, Tom, likewise unconscious on the ground, only half the size of the other one, but definitely not so pretty. Or sweet smelling.

"*That* travels nowhere with me," he said, pointing at Tom. "We're not going to end the day the same way we began it. Besides, I rather like the idea of Anton knowing it was us." He turned to Monsieur Charbonneau, bowing smartly. "Sir, allow me. I'm Maximillien Redgrave, younger yet deep in the pocket brother of the Earl of Saltwood, and the man who, with or without your kind permission, is to marry your daughter."

"I never expected her to wed the local dustman, so you'll do, if she'll have you, and I imagine she will. Require it or not, you have my permission."

Zoé bit her lip, to keep from laughing out loud. It was going to be interesting, watching these two over the years.

There was noise coming to them from the kitchens now, as the door was pushed open and a fat man in a greasy leather apron and carrying a large, obviously heavy pot, stepped out into the dark. "Slop the pigs, slop the bloody pigs. *He's* a bloody pig," the man was grumbling under his breath.

Max turned quickly to the Frenchman. "Do you ride, sir?"

"I do," her father answered in the midst of kissing his daughter on both cheeks.

"Good, because there's an obvious flaw in our plan. Zoé, take your father, head back the way we came, and I'll meet you there. I'm off to steal a horse."

CHAPTER THIRTEEN

EVERYONE HAD GATHERED in the main saloon by noon, all of them speaking at once, Zoé's father—once again looking his proper best if in borrowed finery—having discovered the irresistible charms of the dowager countess and deep in conversation with her and Richard.

The only ones missing were Rose and Tariq, who were taking their exercise in the Long Gallery, inspecting portraits and works of art on this gray, rainy day, Harold Charfield, who was once more unhappily ensconced in his attic prison, and the earl himself, Gideon Redgrave, and his wife, Jessica.

That last was soon to be remedied when Dearborn, smiling widely, announced his lordship and ladyship's arrival.

"Needed to be in on the kill, did you?" Max asked him as they shook hands and he kissed Jessica's cheek.

"You're not yet finished?" his brother responded in mock surprise. "Trixie assured me you were good at this. But as I can recall a time when you couldn't button your own drawers, I admit to being skeptical." Gideon bowed to Zoé. "*Mademoiselle,* it's a pleasure to finally make your acquaintance in daylight. Allow me to introduce you to my wife—"

"Jessica," the countess interrupted, extending her hand in greeting, and her husband raised his hands in surrender, allowing his wife handle this first meeting in her own way, which was what she'd do in any case.

"Please excuse me as I join Trixie, who has been wildly waving me over to her while I pretend to ignore her, knowing she wants word of how things went for us in London."

"And how did things go in London?" Max asked after his brother walked away. "Did Gideon stare down all the gossips?"

"Not all of them, no. Having the dowager countess of Saltwood attacked midday in the midst of crowded Bond Street, her attacker shot dead? And all with Trixie hanging half out of the coach, blood all over her gown, screaming about cowards, and demanding they look at what they'd done, or words to that effect—and naturally drawing all eyes to her? We never expected all of that to simply fade away quietly. But Gideon has brilliantly turned the thing into an issue of society demanding more watchmen, safer streets in Mayfair, where defenseless women need not to be afraid to step out shopping for a new bonnet without being accosted by dangerous footpads on Bond Street itself."

"Including Trixie in that *defenseless* business? That may have been stretching credulity too far."

"Why?" Zoé asked him. "I would have thought it

quite plausible for society to react exactly as you and his lordship hoped they would."

"If Trixie had been any other woman," Max explained, "they probably would have. Their husbands and fathers would be lining up to speak in Parliament even now, demanding some sort of action. But we're Redgraves. The idea of someone attacking any of us isn't enough to make a single jaw drop, unless it's to gossip about us. But it will go away. Someone else always conveniently comes along to siphon off the crowd's attention. More than once, it has been another Redgrave. Jessica, did Gideon receive my message? I ordered Twitchill not to spare the horseflesh, and use every mount Gideon keeps stored at inns along the way, but it would have been a close-run thing."

"True enough. He actually met up with our coach mere moments before we were going to pull off the road to spend the night in Marsham. Gideon penned a note to one of his friends whose estate is near Bilisington, and sent Twitchill off again, confident the women and children will be safely away by this afternoon. My new husband has some of the strangest friends, but they're all quite loyal. Gideon," she said as he wandered back in their direction. "I was just assuring your brother that you have things firmly in hand concerning the women and children."

"While also informing us that you seem to have the strangest friends," Max added, grinning at his sister-in-law.

"I also manage to have the strangest family. Accord-

ing to Trixie, you've made good use of our prisoner upstairs, deduced the location of the Society on Redgrave
grounds—curse them—and angered this Boucher fellow of yours by not obeying his demand to destroy their
Exalted Leader in order to rescue that charming Frenchman over there. Jessica, darling, I believe we've arrived just in time for the final act, although you and the
other ladies—Kate included, if I have to order Simon
to tie her to her bedpost—will sit in the box to watch,
while the rest of us put an end to this damn drama for
the last time."

Max shook his head. "Home five minutes, and already giving orders. While I'd knock down any man
who didn't believe she's a lady, Zoé will be going with
us tonight. Not to the tunnel, where she was supposed
to assassinate the Exalted Leader last night, but to the
heart of this nest of spiders itself."

Gideon looked at Zoé, whose expression was self-
explanatory. "Very well. I always made it a point not to
take on arguments I know I can't win. The ruins on the
West Run, correct? That's difficult to believe."

"Not when you consider the thing, brother. We don't
go there as a general rule, although Kate did take Simon
one day. We may be lucky no one was there at the time,
to see them, or they felt that they'd adequately hidden
the entrance. At any rate, Trixie long ago ordered the
graves there be attended to, and it was the Coopers who
did that. If this Scarlet, or the woman, came to them
asking for a safe place for their ceremonies—a cave,
whatever—it's logical that someone would mention the

cellars of the burned estate house. God only knows how long they've been meeting there, planning and plotting there, right under our noses."

"I'm not happy, no," Gideon said mildly, and anyone in London, hearing those same words, said in that same way, directed toward them, would immediately begin planning an extended excursion in the Lake District.

ZOÉ LAY WITH her head against Max's shoulder, drawing slow circles on his chest with the tip of one finger. "You didn't tell them."

"The family? No, I didn't. Your father and I decided to wait until this mess is over, and Trixie agreed."

"I didn't agree," Zoé pointed out, sliding one long bare leg across Max's thighs.

"You didn't have to. Val already sidled up to me while we were still downstairs, offering his congratulations. He says he's developed an eye for picking out men who've been beaten over the head by Cupid's shovel… thanks to seeing one in his dressing room mirror every morning. So if Val knows, then Daisy knows, but as a proper governess and chock full of integrity, to hear Val tell it, everything might have stopped there. Except that I saw her whispering into Kate's ear. Trixie may have hoped Daisy would somehow whip Val into shape, but I'd say it will end up entirely opposite to her hopes. Redgraves don't change…they change others. Or corrupt them, depending to whom you apply to for your answer."

"I see. So Kate knows, and Simon knows, and—"

"And if Dearborn finds out we're betrothed it will be all over the estate and halfway to London before we gather downstairs for dinner."

"And the Society? Anton? Will they have heard?"

She waited while Max considered her question.

"Probably. Most likely. It's Dearborn's afternoon off, and he likes to visit the Goose. For lunch. They do prepare a fine goose."

Zoé looked up at him, to see the expression on his face, but for an entirely different reason than Val. She wanted to see if the unflappable Max was lying to her.

"Did he ever take you there? For the fine goose?"

"We didn't have a father, you know," he told her rather defensively. "Somebody had to do it, and Trixie chose Dearborn. Later, when I first went to town, Piffkin took over until he was certain I wouldn't make a cake of myself. Does this mean you're going to demand a full recitation of everything that's happened in my entire life?"

"No. Unless you have something else to confess that's even half so funny. Besides, we have to get up now. We do want to be the first ones in position, don't we?"

"Before Gideon believes he can take charge? I think you know the answer to that." He pulled her up and over him, so that she was lying on his chest. "But I believe we can steal a few more minutes."

"I'm so sorry, but not really, no."

The statement had come from the door to his dressing room.

Zoé drew in a sharp breath even as she felt Max's body stiffen beneath hers, and in the next moment they were rolling across the mattress, away from the dressing room. Tangled in the sheets, they landed hard on the floor, Max on top, and the breath Zoé had taken in was completely knocked out of her.

He hadn't waited any time at all, hadn't wondered how Boucher had made it past the guards and into the mansion, found his way to Max's own bedchamber. You didn't get answers to questions like that unless you lived long enough to ask them.

Max fought to free them of the sheets, and then pushed her, still gasping for air, under the bed.

"Stay here."

Zoé shook her head frantically, unable to speak. *Wait. Don't try to take him on alone!*

But Max was already gone, crawling on his belly toward the trail of clothing they'd left behind an hour earlier as they'd kissed their way toward the bed.

From her position under the high tester bed, she could also see below the trailing bed skirt that didn't quite reach the floor, espy Anton's boots as he, walking slowly and carefully, made his way farther into the large chamber.

The room was bright with sunlight, the window drapes on the far side of the room pulled back, the panes clean and clear as crystal. The slowly setting sun was shining straight into Anton's face. She knew what that was like, had faced the same unfortunate situation herself. It would be impossible for him to make out faces if the person had his back to the sun, but only outlines of their bodies. Blinking, looking away and then back again, didn't help. If anything, such an attempt made the situation worse, and only brought tears to your eyes.

But everyone tried it.

"Sun in his eyes," she whispered frantically as she pushed with her feet until she was against the rear frame, little more than a shadow amid other shadows.

She'd rather liked the bed when she'd first seen it. Max had told her it was a remnant from Tudor times: massive, heavy dark wood polished over and over across the centuries by a thousand hands, turning the wood nearly black. Posts as thick as tree trunks, Tudor red-velvet draperies hanging from beneath the heavy wood frame, supported by the beautifully turned posts.

The draperies had been tied back at each of the four posts for the summer, but not yet replaced with thin muslin because there had been no Coopers in the house to perform the chore, no Mrs. Justis to order them to work.

Still, Anton had to know where she was hiding, might even believe Max to be beneath the bed with her.

It was only a matter of time now, unless Max had another miracle up his sleeve.

Up his sleeve? God, they were both naked as newborns! She'd be damned if she'd die, to have her body found this way! If that was vanity, then so be it. *We're not going to die today.*

She chanced a peek from beneath the bed ruffle. She couldn't find Max. Was there another door somewhere in the room? Some hidden panel? Where was he, where had he gone?

"Max."

Anton's voice.

"Max, you don't really want to prolong this, do you, knowing you can't win? And you, Zoé, hiding under a bed? Is that what I reduced you to in Paris? Look, both of you. Do you really think I'm here to kill you? And how do you suppose I'd do that? I certainly can't shoot you. Think of the noise. I'd never escape alive, and being a martyr to any cause has never been one of my ambitions."

Still Max said nothing, and Zoé believed he wouldn't because he didn't want to give away his position.

"Then why are you here, Anton?" she asked. "Have you come to surrender?"

"My congratulations, *mademoiselle*. As a matter of fact, he has. Not entirely happily, but taking the best option presented to him. He's actually rather accomplished in the art of surrender. Isn't that correct, Sous-Lieutenant Boutilier?"

Before she could even begin to absorb what she'd just heard, above her, Zoé could feel some slight shaking of the huge bed. And then Max's voice, also coming from above her. He'd made it onto the wooden canopy? How had he done that?

"Why, good afternoon, Captain," she heard him say. "At least now we know how our friend Boucher made it so far. Did Jacko send along any of his excellent ham, as I may be feeling a bit peckish."

Zoé rolled her eyes and began uncurling herself from her defensive position so that she could reach for the sheet that had so recently entrapped her. As she did so, she chanced another look from beneath the bed skirt, to see Anton's boots had been joined by another pair.

The captain. The pirate.

She'd better figure out a way to adequately cover herself with a sheet while stuck beneath a bed before anyone else showed up. Lord knew there could be more than a half-dozen yet to come, with her own father bringing up the rear. She wasn't the sort to embarrass easily, but then nothing about her current situation was easy. "Ow!" She'd banged her head on the bottom frame of the bed. "Just to prove my point..." she grumbled.

"Zoé? Sweetheart? You're all right?" Max called down to her. "You can come out now. Use the sheet to cover you, and then if you wouldn't mind tossing me up something to wear?"

"Certainly, *sweetheart,*" she shot back as she struggled to tuck one end of the sheet into the bosom of her makeshift gown. "Where do you keep your hats?"

The captain chuckled. "*Mademoiselle,* you put me in mind of one of my daughters, and make me fear for the day she's completely shed of the nursery. Come along, Boutilier. We'll return to the dressing room for a space."

The moment she heard the sound of the door closing, Zoé was out from beneath the bed, looking up to watch as Max's bare legs appeared over the side of the wooden canopy. "What's going on? Why is the captain here? Why did he bring Anton with him? *How* did he manage to bring Anton with him? Surrender? What a bag of moonshine. How in bloody blazes did you get up there?"

"I only know the answer to one of those questions. The bed doesn't fit entirely against the wall—no, I don't know why. I stepped behind it, as I've been doing since I was a child, and then climbed up to the canopy. I don't fit as well there as I used to, and nearly got myself stuck, which would have been a predicament, wouldn't it? And before you ask, I'd planned to leap down on top of Boucher, all unexpectedly, and disarm him."

They were both busily diving back into their clothes.

"Disarm him? You'd probably have frightened him to death. Did you also leap off roofs as a child?"

"Only the one," he said, grabbing her by the waist to give her a kiss. "You do realize what we've got in the makings here, don't you? A bloodless coup." He kissed her again, but then frowned. "Or something close to that. Come on, let's find out. Captain! You can come back in now."

"I'm not completely buttoned," Zoé complained, turning her back to him.

"One or two may be missing."

Zoé kicked a few bits of clothing neither had bothered with beneath the bed, and then quickly retreated to a couch and small grouping of chairs arranged between two of the large windows. Just before Anton and the captain walked into the room.

She knew it was the captain because she, like Max, had recognized his voice, but that was the only part of him she recognized beyond his tall, slim frame. His hair was gray, to match the beard on his face, and he wore a black patch over his left eye. He walked slowly, his shoulders stooped, making full use of the cane in his right hand.

A sword cane, she had no doubt.

Max remained where he was, one of his pistols tucked into his breeches, his concentration all on Anton.

"Please, Captain," she said solicitously, "you should join me here on the couch."

"He should fall down a deep well filled with rabid bats," Anton Boucher said bitterly. "He's no older than I am, aren't you, *Black Ghost?*"

"Amusing man," the captain remarked, splitting his black coattails before sitting down beside Zoé.

"Someone from your past, Captain?" Max asked at last.

"Something not necessary to the moment, Mr. Redgrave. Suffice it to say our Sous-Lieutenant Boutilier here has seen a year's duty in Haiti, where he made quite a reputation for himself, most especially with the ladies. Not a very good reputation. He barely escaped one encounter with his life, and set sail back to France before certain parties could dole out the justice they believed he deserved. Imagine my surprise in seeing him early this morning, as he was brought to my attention by one of my men, who spied him riding rather recklessly across the Marsh, running toward or most probably from somewhere. Anton Boucher. Sous-Lieutenant

Anton Boutilier. One and the same. We had ourselves a pleasant chat, and then struck a deal between us."

Finally, Max took a seat. "What sort of deal? You don't pull his backside out through his mouth if he co-operates with us?"

"Something like that, yes. Boutilier, or should I say Boucher—it's time the bird sang its little song."

Anton's bottom jaw moved left and right, his lips tightly pursed. At first, Zoé didn't think he would say anything, but then he seemed to realize that, between Max and the captain, he really had no other choice.

"What do you want to know?" Anton asked.

Max leaned his elbows on his knees. "I suppose you could begin by telling us where in hell you were going when the captain's men saw you."

"Away," he answered, shrugging. "West, north, any-where that wasn't here. I know when to cut my losses, Max. France? Not while Bonaparte remains in power, certainly. Remain here, watching the woman destroy everything we could have had? No, I wouldn't even live long enough to watch her fail."

"You're a pathetic little worm, aren't you, Anton?" Zoé said, feeling some sort of weight lifted off her shoulders. "You murdered your own nephew in your supposed great *cause,* and then abandon that cause as if Georges's death meant nothing to you."

"It didn't, you stupid cow. He was no more my nephew than your captain here is a gentleman. He be-lieved he was my partner. The way I heard it, your friend here double-crossed his pirate partner, killed off half his own men and their wives and kiddies before—"

The cane the captain had been resting in his hands came down on the back of the Frenchman's head, and he slid to the floor without another sound.

"That's too bad," the captain said blandly. "Five minutes' time, and in hopes of swaying you to his side, he violated our agreement. You do understand he belongs to me now. Or, should I say, a certain man in my crew who has spent this last decade or more searching for justice."

"Only once he tells us what he knows," Max said. "Unless that cane of yours cracked his skull."

"Merely dented it. Is there some place you may be able to put him until I leave? He's already told me what he knows."

Max looked at Zoé, who knew what he wanted, but was still too amazed at what she felt as she stared at the unconscious form of Anton Boucher to be able to find her voice.

"I don't want him," she said at last. "He's taken enough from us, Max. He can't give us back anything we lost and, killing him, we'd only lose more." She smiled at the captain, this man who had been so many things, but now seemed only to want to be left alone.

"It's nearly over, isn't it? Anton gone, leaving no way for the Exalted Leader to communicate with the emperor. No invasion, no overthrow of the monarchy. Nothing but French soldiers and mercenaries awaiting orders and meeting your men instead. Please, tell us what he told you about the woman."

MAX STOOD UP and shook the captain's hand. "And now you can have him, sir. With our thanks and compliments. He means nothing to us anymore."

MAX DIDN'T KNOW what methods the captain had used, and certainly hadn't asked, to have convinced Anton to be so forthcoming. Although Zoé had said she imagined all he'd had to do was introduce himself before the Frenchman offered him anything he wanted.

The best thing they'd learned was the location of the Coopers, and anyone else the woman had coerced, bribed, blackmailed or otherwise convinced to follow the Society.

The Coopers hadn't been expecting a failure in London with the attempt on Trixie's life. Angus's grandson, known for being fleet of foot, was to have struck quickly, and just as quickly run away, so that nobody would know his identity. But plans fail, and someone like their leader, someone so convinced anything she did was destined for success, don't make provisions for failure.

They'd been forced to gather up their belongings and run. Quickly, without direction. The women to one place, the men to another, to await further orders, and only a few allowed to remain with the woman, only those few she considered her best, the most loyal.

With Gideon in the lead, along with Valentine and

Simon, even Kate and the persistent Trixie, the Redgraves had already ridden off to Newington in the hope of salvaging something of their lives at Redgrave Manor, to bring some of their people home.

People follow crowds, Trixie had told them, and crowds often turn into mobs, but at the end of the day most of them are left wondering *what am I doing here?*

Max hoped she was right.

He and Zoé also hoped Anton hadn't been lying to them about the conditions at the ruins, or how many protectors the Exalted Leader had convinced victory could still be theirs. Even after Anton's defection, the probable loss of French help.

They'd made their way across the dark field, hiding behind the hedgerows until forced to leave their cover and make a mad dash into the copse.

They met no resistance. There were no sentries, no sign of anyone when they located the flat, hidden door beside the largest tree in the copse. The door Anton had sworn led down to the chambers.

Maybe they were gone. Maybe they were all gone.

"Are you ready?" he asked her as he slipped his left hand through a rusted iron ring, one of his pistols gripped in the right. "On three?"

Zoé nodded, and Max counted silently before yanking open the heavy oak door and pointed the pistol down the stone steps that had always led to the cellars below the house.

First the root cellar, and then a door beyond it. Through that and you're there.

That's what the captain had told them, and so far, it seemed his information was correct.

Max took out his flint while Zoé extracted a candle from her boot, and soon they had at least a bit of light to guide them. There was nothing in the root cellar other than the smell of ancient vegetables now more like stone, and still covered in ashes from the long-ago fire.

Nothing else but another door.

This one showed light beneath it.

Zoé pointed to it and Max nodded, yes, he'd seen it. He'd also seen something else, and crouched down to run his gloved hand beneath the door before standing up again to show her what he'd found. It was mostly dry, and sticky when he touched thumb to fingertips, but nobody could mistake what it was.

"Blood?" She leaned in and sniffed at the substance, and then looked at him apprehensively. "Yes, that's blood. And it's fairly fresh. What—?"

He pulled her away from the door. "It opens the other way. I think it could be at least partially barred, though—with a body. Something's happened in there, Zoé. Something Anton didn't share with us."

"He doesn't like leaving anyone behind when he decides it's time to move on," she offered. "Do you suppose he's killed them all? How would he have done that? He said there were at least ten men protecting her."

"Another lie. It has to be, with just enough truth mixed in to keep us guessing." He wiped his glove against his breeches. "Stay here, and hold this," he said, handing her the pistol. "I'm going to put my shoulder to the door and see how far it goes."

"Be careful." He smiled at her. She'd never said that to him before. *Eyes open. Watch for a hidden knife. Follow me.* Yes, that was her favorite. *Follow me.*

"I will, sweetheart," he told her solemnly. "I'll do my very best. But...but if the worst were to happen, please—remember me."

"I could cheerfully murder you myself right now," she shot back, but then smiled. "Oh, go on—go. Or do you want to follow me?"

He kissed her, let her push him away and then approached the door once more. When he put his shoulder against it, the thing moved easily enough, at least as far as to allow him access, but then came up against something that stopped it.

There was enough candlelight to make out his surroundings, so he first checked to make certain there was no one else in what looked to be some sort of antechamber, and then stepped through the opening, waving for Zoé to follow with the candle.

"Scarlet," he told her as they both looked down at the face of his own father, although the man's eyes were closed and he couldn't know their color, and his skin had already turned a sickly shade of gray.

The blood Max had seen first—and there was a lot more on this side of the door—had come from at least a dozen knife slashes on the naked body, and one large, clearly fatal slice to the man's throat.

Zoé bent over the body, holding the candle. "Yes,

that's him, or what's left of him. The man I saw in Ostend. Anton?"

"I think it would have to be. Look, our Scarlet is a tall man and obviously strong. He would have been weakened by all these cuts, but I can't believe a woman like you described would have been strong enough to half sever the poor bastard's neck."

Zoé nodded before holding up the candle and moving farther into the antechamber. "This can't be the main chamber. Only a few bits of furniture and these candles. Most are burned out and the rest won't last much longer. I don't think anyone's been here for hours. Do you see another door?"

To help answer her question, he lifted one of the wooden holders containing a still burning candle, and began walking the perimeter of the room.

On the third wall, his fingertips encountered a long, slim opening. He held the candle to it and its flame was disturbed by air coming out through the wall.

He whistled a quick, soft birdcall to attract Zoé's attention. She seemed to have been distracted by something she'd found inside a cabinet he believed he recognized as one that had once been in the main saloon at the Manor. They'd probably furnished the whole place by raiding the Manor attics.

"Found it," he said when Zoé joined him. "What do you have there?"

"I'm not sure. I used the stiletto to destroy the lock, and this was the only thing inside. It looks like some sort of journal, but it's too dark to actually read it."

"God's teeth, just what we need, another damn journal. Do they never become tired of recounting their exploits?"

She opened the journal and held it closer to her eyes. "Is that what's in here? *Exploits?*"

"Just close it, Zoé. We'll take it with us when we leave. But you're not reading it."

"I don't have any intention or interest in reading it. Neither should you. Or anyone."

"Do I say *amen* now? Believe me, sweetheart, none of us wants to read any more journals, but if we don't find our Exalted Leader, we may have to. I've located the handle. This one also opens into whatever's behind it. Ready?"

Once again she held up the candle, and once again he put his shoulder to a door.

When he picked himself up after the damn thing opened as if the hinges had been greased only that morning, it was to see something he'd never wanted to see in his lifetime.

He saw, having heard Simon's description of the ceremonial rooms that had once existed beneath the dower house, what had to be a pale imitation of the obscenely beautiful chamber that had been home to two generations of perversion.

There were capes lying everywhere, as if discarded in haste, and strange, large masks that would cover an entire head lined up on shelves.

Half-burnt candles flickered against paintings of men and women engaged in strange sexual acts. Statues of naked women, some caught in the grasp of satyrs, a marble boar, standing upright on human legs, "gifted" with male genitals. Max stopped looking and moved on, past the couches, beyond what he recognized as a whipping stool, ignoring the manacles hanging from the walls, only stopping when he came to the deep red velvet draperies that lined the entire rear wall.

Zoé joined him there, slipping her hand into his. "There's no altar, is there?"

"There has to be an altar," he told her, still staring at the drapes. "Help me open these. But get out your knives. Be ready to protect yourself."

"On three?" she asked, and he heard a slight tremor in her voice.

"No. Now."

Together, they pulled back the draperies just enough to see what lay beyond.

"The Exalted Leader," Zoé said, and then turned away.

"You're all right?"

"No, I'm not. It has to be her, doesn't it?"

"You're the only one with the answer to that. Can you manage it?"

Max put his arm around her and they climbed the three marble steps to the Society's last altar.

It seemed to him as if the woman had *arranged* herself to look her best before she left the world she hadn't been able to conquer. She was clothed in sheerest black silk, each fold smooth, without a wrinkle. The mask covering her face appeared to be constructed of real gold molded to match her features. The effect was startling, as was that of the small golden rose depicted in full bloom, a diamond at its center, that pierced her left nipple.

But it was the jeweled dagger protruding from her body just at her heart that took and held his interest.

Zoé stepped up beside him. "She killed herself, didn't she? Like Cleopatra. Even the hilt of that dagger is in the form of a snake."

"From what I've learned about her, I never would have believed she'd kill herself. Shall we take off the mask, get a look at her face?"

Zoé took a deep breath, exhaled it slowly, and then nodded. "Yes, take it off…"

EPILOGUE

IT WASN'T A JOURNAL Zoé had found. It was a diary.

Yet not even that. It was a retelling of a route chosen, a road traveled, a nightmare this strange woman created and called her dream.

But nobody knew that until later, after both bodies had been removed from the ruins and brought to the buttery, to be laid on cool shelves after Simon and Kate oversaw the removal of the tubs resting there. The burials would be swift, at first light the following morning, but for now the Redgraves would assemble, look, hope that one of them, somehow, would recognize the woman.

Trixie, supported by Richard, made her way down the stone steps into the buttery, only to exit again too soon to have taken the time to inspect the faces of both sheet-wrapped corpses inside. "It's Barry, my Barry," she said, sobbing. "God help me, it's my own son all over again. Richard, take me away from here."

Everyone else agreed when they saw the same face they knew only from their father's portrait in the Long Gallery. But nobody knew the woman.

Until Adam, nervously gnawing at his fingernails,

more curious than he was afraid, was the last to enter as Max remained inside, ready to cover the faces after the last person came, looked and left.

The boy approached the man first. "Big one, wasn't he?" he said, his smile rather sickly. But then he walked across the stone floor to take a peek at the woman.

He looked at her for a long time, until Max wondered if something was wrong. "Adam, are you all right?"

The boy raised his hand and gingerly laid it on the body. "Mama?"

THE DIARY REVEALED the rest of the story.

How Clarissa Collier had been introduced to the Society via her new husband. How she'd taken to it in a way Turner Collier first appreciated and then, as the years went on, disapproved of more and more.

He was nearly twice her age, not as interested in what had interested him in his youth, and with his friend Barry gone, he'd actually begun to draw away from the Society. But Clarissa wouldn't let him. Even as more and more of his peers began to die, and new members, young, strong, took their place.

Members Clarissa had hand-picked.

When the new leader was chosen, his face was never seen by any of the older members who now began to wonder if they were becoming increasingly expendable and agreed to most anything, because it might be dangerous to disagree.

Now Collier wanted to leave the Society entirely. Nobody followed the rules anymore. He was the Keeper, and rules were meant to be followed.

Oh, how Clarissa longed for the day the man was rolled into his grave.

But first she had to convince him he was in danger, easy enough to do with help from the new Exalted Leader...the lover she had hand-picked.

Terrified after the failed attempt, Turner Collier had agreed with his beloved wife. They had to protect Barry Redgrave's dream. They'd have to take the bible he'd kept for years, and not turn it over to the Exalted Leader as ordered, but remove it from its hiding place and take it with them as they escaped England altogether. The Society was corrupt; he would not give them the bible.

"But he didn't take it and run," Simon told Max as he stood at the mantel and recited, rather like a schoolboy, uncomfortable knowing Jessica and Adam were in the room, listening. "I saw the ashes, in the cave. Clarissa died still not knowing where he'd hidden the real bible. She believed the information inside it would have made her very, very rich. And untouchable, powerful."

Gideon was nodding. "The coach accident wasn't real. The bodies I saw were real enough—Collier, certainly, and whoever the poor woman was who died in Clarissa's place."

"I think we can all guess the rest. Clarissa followed in our grandfather's footsteps, in our father's footsteps...and made the same mistakes they'd made. She'd begun to believe she was everything she wanted to be. Oh, and according to her last entry, *we* killed her. We destroyed her dream. Although I imagine we had a little help in that direction from your pirate friend, Simon, and even, oddly, from Anton Boucher."

"Is that enough for one night? Anyone curious to know every last detail can certainly peruse this thing at their own leisure."

"Put it in the fire, Max," Jessica said, the first time she'd spoken since entering the room, her arm around her half-brother. "Please."

"TIRED?" MAX ASKED ZOÉ as he leaned over on the bed and kissed her cheek.

"I may never sleep again," she said, even as she snuggled against him. "All the deaths, all the betrayals, all the heartache and degradation…and all the product of one woman? It's nearly incomprehensible."

"One woman following the lead of two men who showed her the way. Did you watch Adam tonight?"

Zoé sighed against his chest. "He came into the room with Jessica supporting him, and left it supporting her. Even Trixie commented on it. She really cares for her *twit,* you know. I only wish we could find this damnable bible. I know your grandmother does, too."

"I know. As long as it exists, there also exists the possibility that someday, somehow, someone *will* find it, read it, believe it all possible and there will be a new incarnation of the Society in some yet unknown time. Please, God, long after I'm gone."

Zoé hated loose ends. Max had always teased her about being too neat, even obsessed with every last detail. But this was important, more than a simple loose end, a single strand that could never be woven into anything of substance.

She had to find that— "Max!" When he didn't respond, she shook him and called to him again. "Max! Wake up! I know where it is."

"Wonderful. Whatever this *it* is, I'm sure it will still be there tomorrow." He turned over and immediately went back to sleep.

"Max!"

He bolted upright, quickly looking around the room. "What? Is the Manor on fire?"

"Yes. That's it exactly," she said, pushing her arms into her dressing gown. "The house is on fire. It started in the Long Gallery. Come with me."

He scrubbed at his eyes, but then climbed out of bed, muttering something under his breath about the perfidies of women as he jammed his legs into his breeches and nothing else.

By the time they reached the huge copper doors, Zoé had begun feeling slightly apprehensive and possibly more than a little worried she was wrong. But when the doors opened, and she and Max and Jacko—who'd been dozing near the kitchens and decided to follow them— stepped inside, her fears calmed.

She was right. She knew she was right.

"This way," she said.

"There is only one way. It's a *hallway*."

"Don't spoil it, Max. Come on, follow the roses."

"Women," Jacko grumbled. "Never wanted one, myself. Haven't seen the need."

"Good on you, Jacko," Max replied, but hastened his step in any case, because at last Zoé had stopped, just in front of the portrait of his father.

"It was the rose," she explained quickly. "The one in her— The one we saw tonight. It made me think of all the other roses. The roses lining this corridor. The rose in your father's cravat. Truly, Max, I think it's the roses."

"They get like this sometimes," Jacko whispered. "Something about the phases of the moon."

"Jacko! You're huge—I mean, you're tall and strong. Can you please try to take down this portrait?"

"I do what I'm told," he said, and stepped in front of the portrait. But it didn't lift up. Instead, as he tugged, it swung open.

"Zoé, you're a genius," Max breathed, holding up the candle he'd brought with him, and they all could see the thick tome resting inside the wall.

Zoé smiled. "Yes, indeed. Are we going to tell everyone else?"

"Tomorrow. Jacko," Max said, looking at the bible he now held in his hands. "You say you're a man who follows orders. What do you say to stoking up the kitchen fire until it's a wild, hot blaze?"

Zoé rested her head against his shoulder. "We start now, don't we? We began before…but we'll really start now."

"Yes, sweetheart, that's just what we'll do."

* * * * *

Don't miss where the adventure all began...
WHAT AN EARL WANTS
Available now from
Kasey Michaels and Harlequin HQN.
Read on for an exciting excerpt...

CHAPTER ONE

London, England
1810

THE EIGHTEENTH EARL of Saltwood, one Gideon Redgrave by name, struck a pose just inside the entrance
of the narrow house in Jermyn Street, looking for all
the world a sketch from the *Journal des Dames et des
Modes* come to life. Not by so much as a flicker of an
eyelid did he give away the fact that he'd no idea he'd
knocked on the door of number forty-seven only to
be ushered into a gaming house. His man of business
would answer for that omission when next he saw him;
the earl didn't care for surprises.

He allowed a curtsying maid of indeterminate years
to relieve him of his hat, gloves and cane, and then
shrugged off his evening cloak, watching as the woman
folded it lovingly over her arm. A gold coin appeared
from his pocket, and he held it in front of her wide-
open blue eyes. A copper coin would do for most, but
Gideon Redgrave believed the gold coin to be an invest-
ment, one that would pay dividends when his belongings came back to him in the same pristine condition

in which they'd been handed over, rather than having suffered the unfortunate accident of walking out the door in his absence.

"Yours if my possessions are safely returned when I leave," he told her, and the maid bobbed her head enthusiastically before scurrying away.

He resumed his pose, meant to have all eyes come to him and their owners too busy being either envious or impressed to think up mischief while he surreptitiously acclimated himself to his surroundings. And the eighteenth Earl of Saltwood's appearance was, without fail, nothing short of enviably impressive.

The superb tailoring of his darkest blue cut-away tailcoat accentuated the snowy perfection of his silk brocade waistcoat, but not so much as it displayed the earl's astonishingly fit physique, broad shoulders, flat stomach and narrow waist. Pantaloons of formfitting buff doeskin clung lovingly to long, muscular lower limbs, ending just at the calf, above silk stockings and low-heeled black patent evening shoes.

His only ornamentation, other than the thin black grosgrain ribbon hanging about his neck and attached to the quizzing glass tucked into a small pocket of his waistcoat, was the small golden rose depicted in full bloom and no more than a single inch in circumference, nestled in the folds of his intricately tied cravat. This latter bit of fancy was a recent affectation, one that had caused comment in some circles, but to date, no one had dared speak of it to his lordship.

Thick, longish hair the color of midnight tumbled over his smooth forehead in natural curls that sent other gentlemen to their valets and the crimping iron to duplicate. Hints of his Spanish mother could be seen in the strong, aquiline nose that saved him from too much beauty, the unexpected fullness of his mouth, the sensual smolder in his dark eyes. There was an earthiness about the man not completely disguised by the trappings of fine clothes, a sense of dangerous energy tightly leashed yet always simmering just below the sophisticated surface.

In a word, the eighteenth Earl of Saltwood was intimidating. In two, if applying to the female population, he was marvelously irresistible.

When he was noticed, and he was always noticed, several of the men who recognized him for what he was, if not who he was, prudently realized they had pressing business elsewhere and quit the room in some haste. Conversations broke off abruptly. Hands stilled in the act of shuffling cards or pulling in chips. The more daring among the players turned their chairs about for a better view of what was sure to be an interesting few minutes, at the least.

One of the hostesses, the term surely taken quite as loosely as the morals of any female in the hall, ran her moist tongue around her lips rather hungrily. She gave her smiling approval of the impossible-to-disguise manly muscle between the gentleman's thighs and took two steps forward, tugging down on the already low neckline of her cherry-red gown before she was grabbed at the elbow and hastily pulled back.

"For Lord's sake, Mildred, control yourself. He's not here for that."

Gideon Redgrave extracted his chased-gold quizzing glass, raising it to one eye, and slowly surveyed the surprisingly well-lit and clean yet faintly down-at-the-heels room before allowing his gaze to halt and hold on the woman who had just spoken.

She advanced on him with some purpose, the light of confrontation in her sherry-brown eyes, her fairly remarkable chin tilted up as if she had somehow raised the battle flag and was announcing her intention to unleash a broadside. But then she stopped, smiled and dropped into a mocking curtsy.

"Lord Saltwood," she intoned quietly, her voice slightly husky, as if she might be whispering risqué endearments in the privacy of a candlelit boudoir, "I've been expecting you. Do you prefer a public airing of our differences, or would you care to retire to my apartments for our chat?"

She was…magnificent. Gideon could think of no other description. Taller than most women, slim almost to the point of thinness, yet subtly curved. Hair the color of flame against the severity of her high-necked black gown, skin the color of finest ivory. The eyes, mocking, the mouth, full and wide…and *knowing*. No sane man could look at her without imagining his fingers tangling in that mass of warm curls tumbling around her shoulders, sinking himself deep between her thighs, plunging into the promised fire as she wrapped long legs up high around him.

Which, of course, would be total madness.

Gideon's eyes widened fractionally, just enough to dislodge the glass, and he deftly caught it by its ribbon and replaced it in his pocket. "You've the advantage of me, madam. You are—?"

"Exactly who you think I am, my lord," she returned, her wide smile frosting only slightly about the edges. "And now that you and your glowering face have served to quite ruin what had promised to be a profitable evening, you will please follow me."

She turned sharply, the scent of sweet lavender tickling his nostrils as her fiery mane, seeming much too heavy for her slim neck, swung about as if in a belated attempt to catch up with her. Her modest gown, a stiff, unyielding taffeta so in contrast to the riot of tumbling curls, rustled as she walked.

"Here now, where do you think you're—?"

She raised her hand to the faintly rotund, gray-haired man who had stepped out from behind the faro table, his eyes on the earl as if measuring his chances of knocking him down. Though he clearly found them miniscule, he straightened his shoulders, no doubt prepared to give his best if asked. "Simply carry on, Richard, if you please. I'm fine."

"Yes, you do that, Richard," Gideon drawled as he and the woman easily made their way through the throng of patrons who had all stepped back to afford them a pathway. He was painfully aware he somehow had been put in the ignoble position of potential despoiler of virgins, which was above everything ludicrous.

"Your employer's virtue is safe with me."

A young man, looking fresh from the country and obviously a fellow with more hair than wit, dared to chuckle at this remark. "There's virtue here? Stap me, I wouldn't have come if it was *virtue* I was looking for."

"Stubble it, Figgins," the man next to him warned, saving Gideon the trouble of having to turn back and waste a dark stare on the impudent puppy. "Don't you know who that is? The fella's a Redgrave, for God's sakes. He spits bigger'n you."

Gideon suppressed a smile. He hadn't heard that one before. But how convenient that his reputation preceded him; it made life so much easier.

He stepped forward as he realized the woman had stopped in front of a baize door, clearly waiting on him to open it for her. Liked to play at the lady, it would seem, straight down to the prim black gown and the erect nature of her posture. Pity for her that her hair and eyes and mouth—and that voice—hadn't been informed of this preferred pretense.

"Oh, please, allow me," he drawled sarcastically, bowing her ahead of him as he depressed the latch, before following her up a long, steep flight of stairs surprisingly located just on the other side of the door.

The stairs were between two walls and just well lit enough for him to be able to enjoy the sway of her bottom as she climbed ahead of him, holding up her stiff skirts, affording him a tantalizing glimpse of slim ankles, as well. Ah, and a hint of calf. Lovely.

The woman was contradiction after contradiction. Buttoned nearly to her chin, yet her slippers were silver-heeled black satin. He could imagine himself kissing them from her feet and then rolling down her hose, just so far, because he enjoyed the feel of silk-encased legs on his back....

He was forced to hold the banister as she stopped, extracting a key from a pocket in her gown and slipping it into the lock. He'd wondered about that, the easy access to the staircase, and how many times in the course of an evening this route might be traveled by patrons and the women.

As if to assure him, she stepped inside the apartments, motioning for him to close the door behind him as she said, "No one is allowed here. We won't be disturbed. Would you care for wine, or would you rather simply be on with it?"

"That's direct, in any case. Be on with what, madam? I had thought I was calling at a private residence, the object conversation. Seeing the nature of this house, the possibilities have become almost limitless. Not that I'm not tempted."

She lit a taper and gracefully moved about the room, lighting candles. "You flatter yourself, my lord, and insult me. I'm not in such dire need of funds. We turn cards here, nothing else."

Gideon sat himself down on a nearby chair, deciding she could remain standing if she so wished, but he was going to make himself comfortable. Redgraves always made themselves comfortable; and the more comfortable they looked, the more on guard any sane person in their midst became. "You might explain that to—Mildred, was it?" he suggested amicably.

He did his best not to blink as she toed off the silver-heeled shoes and kicked them beneath a table as if happy to be rid of them. "I cannot presume to control the world, my lord, only the small portion of it beneath this roof. Mildred and the others make their own arrangements as to what they do outside this establishment."

"That's...civilized. So, a gaming hell, but no brothel. A fine line between disreputable and despicable. Am I to perhaps applaud?"

She looked at him, long and hard, and then reached up both hands and deftly twisted the heavy mass of curls into a knot atop her head before walking over to a small drinks table holding a single decanter of wine.

"I don't particularly care what you do, my lord," she said as she poured some of the light amber liquid into a single glass before turning to face him. "As long as you relinquish guardianship of my brother to me."

"Oh, yes, Miss Collier, the demand presented to me via your solicitor. I can readily see the eminent sense in that. Clearly a fit place for the boy."

"The name is Linden, my lord. *Mrs.* Linden. I'm a widow."

Gideon could not suppress his smile this time. "Of course you are. How very proper. My apologies."

"You can take your apologies, my lord, and stuff them in your...ear," she said, and then turned her back to him as she lifted the glass to her lips. She didn't sip; she drank. He could see that her hand trembled slightly as she lowered the empty glass to the tabletop. The wine was for courage, clearly. He almost felt sorry for her.

Almost.

But then she turned back to him, her eyes shining in the light of the candles. "We've begun badly, haven't we? Are you certain you don't care for a glass of wine?"

"A lady shouldn't drink alone, I suppose. Very well." Gideon got to his feet and availed himself of the decanter. The wine, when he tasted it, was unexpectedly good, when he'd assumed it would be cheap and bitter. "Do you have a first name, madam?"

The question seemed to surprise her. "Why would you— Yes. Yes, I do. Jessica."

"Preferable to either Linden or Collier. Very well. My condolences on your recent loss, *Jessica.* I was remiss in not stating that at the outset."

"My father's death means nothing to me, my lord, as we'd been estranged for several years. But thank you. I only wish to become reacquainted with my brother."

"Half-brother," Gideon corrected. "The son of your

father and your stepmother, also sadly deceased. You have no questions about that sad event?"

Jessica shrugged her shoulders. "No. Should I? When I read about their deaths in the *Times,* an accident with their coach was mentioned. I'm only glad Adam was away at school, and not in the coach with them."

"All right," Gideon said, looking at her carefully. "There's still the matter of a rather large fortune, not to mention the Sussex estate. All of it in trust for your half-brother, who was not estranged from his parents."

"That's also of no concern to me. I support myself."

"Clearly," Gideon said, casting his gaze around the sparsely furnished room. "Bilking raw youths in town on a spree profitable, is it?"

"We don't *bilk* anyone, my lord. We don't allow it. If we see some fool gaming too deep, he's sent on his way."

"Vowing to sin no more, I'll assume, his ears still ringing from the stern lecture you've administered."

Jessica looked at him unblinkingly, her brown eyes raking him from head to toe before seemingly settling on his chest; perhaps she wouldn't be so brave if she looked into his eyes. "I don't like you. *Gideon.*"

"I can't imagine why not. Another man wouldn't have answered your summons. I'll admit to curiosity being my motive for obliging you, but please don't hold that against me."

"And it only took you a month, and then you arrived on my doorstep at this ungodly hour of the night, clearly as an afterthought. Or perhaps your planned evening turned out to be a bore, leaving you at loose ends? I'm sorry, I suppose I should be flattered."

She turned her back to him once more, bending her neck forward. "You may as well be of some use. If you could help with these buttons? Doreen is still busy at the front door, and I'm near to choking."

Gideon raised one well-defined eyebrow as he weighed the invitation, considering its benefits, its pitfalls…her motives. "Very well," he said, placing his wineglass next to hers. "I've played at lady's maid a time or two."

"I'm certain you have played at many things. Tonight, however, you'll have to content yourself with a very limited role."

"You're a very trusting woman, Jessica," he said as he deftly—he did everything deftly—slipped the first half-dozen buttons from their moorings. With the release of every button, he made sure his knuckles came in contact with each new inch of ivory skin revealed to him. Even in the candlelight he could see where the gown had chafed that soft skin; no wonder she longed to be shed of it.

Still, he took his time with the buttons until, the gown now falling open almost entirely to her waist, she stepped away from him just as he considered the merits of running his fingertips down the graceful line of her spine.

"Thank you. If you'll excuse me for a moment while I rid myself of this scratchy monstrosity?"

"I'll excuse you for any number of things, my dear, as long as you're not gone above a minute. You wear no chemise?"

"As you're already aware," she answered, throwing the words at him over her shoulder, bare now as her gown began to slip slightly. "I loathe encumbrances."

She disappeared into another room, leaving Gideon to wonder why a woman who so disliked encumbrances had buttoned herself up into a black taffeta prison. Did she think the gown made her look dowdy? Untouchable? Perhaps even matronly? If so, she had missed the mark on every point.

A widow. He hadn't expected less from her than that obvious clunker; there wasn't a madam in all of London who wasn't the impecunious widow of some soldier hero, making her way in the world as best she could.

And, if he was lucky yet tonight—he would be inevitably, in any case—she was about to *make her way* with him, in hopes of her charms rendering him imbecilic to the point of granting her request to take over the guardianship of her half-brother.

Or, more to the point, guardianship of her half-brother's considerable fortune. A month ago he had roundly cursed Turner Collier for having lacked the good common sense to have altered his decades-old will, leaving guardianship of his progeny to his old chum, the Earl of Saltwood. Perhaps Collier had thought himself immortal, which should hardly have been the case, considering what had happened to his old chum.

But there'd been nothing else for it, not according to Gideon's solicitor, who had notified him that he had gratefully ended his guardianship of Alana Wallingford upon her recent marriage, just to be saddled with yet another ward a few months later.

At least this time there would be no worries over fortune hunters or midnight elopements or any such nonsense.

No, this time his worries would be for reckless starts, idiotic wagers, juvenile hijinks and hauling the boy out of bear-baitings, cockfights and gaming hells such as the one owned by the youth's own half-sister.

All while the whispers went on behind his back. There'd been anonymous wagers penned in the betting book at White's on the odds of Gideon forcing Alana into marriage with him in order to gain her fortune.

Whispered hints Alana's father, Gideon's very good friend, had been murdered within months of naming Gideon as his only child's guardian. There definitely had been suggestions as to whom that murderer might be.

Now there had been a second "unfortunate coaching accident" directly impacting the Earl of Saltwood. And another wealthy orphan placed into his care immediately after that "accident." Coincidence? Many didn't think so.

After all, Gideon was a Redgrave. And everybody knew about those Redgraves. Wild, arrogant, dangerous, if always somewhat delicious. Why, look at the father, the mother; there was a scandal no amount of time could fade from the consciousness of God-fearing people. Even the dowager countess remained both a force to be reckoned with and a constant source of whispered mischief and shocking behavior. Nothing was beneath them, even as they believed nothing and no one above them....

"Shall we return to the wars, Gideon?"

He blinked away his thoughts and turned to look at Jessica Linden, who had somehow reappeared without his notice. She was clad now in a dark maroon silk banyan with a black shawl collar and quilted cuffs that fell below her fingertips. The hem of the thing puddled around her bare feet. Once again her curls tumbled past her shoulders, a perfect frame for her fine, enchanting features. For a tall woman, she suddenly seemed small, delicate, even fragile.

Clearly an illusion.

"My late husband's. I keep it as a reminder," she said, raising her arms enough that the cuffs fell back to expose her slim wrists. "Shall we sit? My feet persist in feeling the pinch of those dreadful shoes."

He gestured to the overstuffed couch to his left, and she all but collapsed into it, immediately drawing her legs up beside her to begin rubbing at one narrow bare foot. The collar of the banyan gaped for an enticing moment, gifting him with a tantalizing glimpse of small, perfect breasts. Clearly she was naked beneath the silk.

The woman was as innocent as a viper.

"How is Adam?" she asked before he could think of a damn thing to say that didn't include an invitation to return to her bedchamber, this time in his company. "I haven't seen him in more than five years. He was just about to be sent off to school, as I recall the moment. What was he? Twelve? Yes, that was it, as I was all of eighteen. He cried so, to leave me."

Gideon began doing quick mental arithmetic. "Making you a woman of three and twenty? A young widow."

"Ah, but positively ancient in experience, and closer to four and twenty in reality. And you? Edging in on a hundred, I would think, if we're to speak of experience. You've quite the reputation, Gideon."

"Only partially earned, I assure you," he told her as he retook his chair and crossed one leg over the other, looking very much at his ease while his mind raced. "But to answer your question, your half-brother is well and safe and here in London. I've hired a keeper for him rather than return him to school before next term."

Jessica nodded. "That's only fitting. He's in mourning."

"He is? Perhaps someone ought to explain that to him. All I hear, secondhand through said keeper, is how fatigued he is with twiddling his thumbs while the entire world goes merrily along just outside the door, without him."

She smiled at that, and Gideon knew himself to be grateful he was already sitting down, for she had a wide, unaffected smile that could knock a man straight off his feet.

"A handful, is he? Good. As our father's son, it could have gone either way. I'm gratified to learn his spirit wasn't crushed."

Now this was interesting. "I barely knew the man, as he was a contemporary of my father's. He was a demanding parent?"

"We'll speak with the gloves off, as I see no sense in dissembling. After all, I've heard the rumors about your own father, and the two men were friends. James Linden, fairly ancient, more than a little mean when in his cups, and a lazy waste of talent, was the lesser of two evils, and here I am. Disowned, widowed, but self-sufficient. Perfectly capable of taking on the guardianship of my brother until he reaches his majority. The last place I want him is anywhere our father wanted him, under the control of anyone he thought *fitting*." She directed a disconcerting glare toward his cravat. "Do you understand now, *Gideon*?"

He touched his hand to the golden rose in his cravat before he realized what he'd done and quickly got to his feet. "You had my pity, Jessica, until the end. I'm many things, but I am not my father."

"No, I suppose you aren't. You haven't yet tried to seduce me, and after all my clumsy efforts to the contrary. Geld you, did he? No, I don't think so. You want me, that's obvious enough."

At last, Gideon understood the whole of it. He waved his hand in front of him, indicating her pose, the banyan, even her nakedness beneath the silk, the glass of wine that had been raised to her lips by a trembling hand; a drink for courage. "You've got a weapon somewhere about you, don't you?"

"Not the complete fool, are you? Very well. Only a very small pistol, holding but a single shot, but deadly, if it became necessary. I can use it to much more advantage than James ever could, even though he taught me. And before you ask, yes, I was willing to trade my body for your agreement to relinquish your guardianship of Adam, within limits, of course." She stood up, chin high, sherry-brown eyes locked with his, her hands going to the silk tie at her waist. "I still am."

He decided it would be safer to be insulted. "And I repeat, madam, I am not my father."

She tilted her head to one side. "You aren't? Your stickpin says differently. That particular rose, by any other name, Gideon, sends out the same stink."

Gideon's jaw set tightly. What in bloody hell was going on here? "You know about that?"

"I know about the Society, yes," she repeated, the light of battle leaving her eyes, to be replaced by a sadness that was nearly palpable. "Among my late husband's many failings was a tendency to run his mouth when he was in his cups. The mark of membership in a most exclusive group of rascals. A flower, in point of fact a golden rose, to commemorate a deflowering, plucking the bud as it were, bringing it into full bloom. But you wear it, you know what it is, what you did to *earn* it."

"The pin was my father's. The rest was rumor or, more probably, bravado," Gideon heard himself saying, even as he hoped he was speaking truth. "It was nothing like that. Only drunken fools and their games, thinking themselves some damned hellfire club. It was all cloaks and oaths of secrecy and more drunkenness and willing prostitutes than anything else. Simply grandiose talk, and all a long time ago."

Her smile was sad, almost as if she pitied him. "So you say. Thanks to James, I never learned for certain. Your father had been long dead by then, your family estate no longer their gathering place. But whatever the Society was, it didn't end with him. You truly profess to not know that? It went on five years ago, it may still go on. If I recall correctly, my father was not too many years above sixty when he died. James was not much younger when we married, and still…capable."

One more mention of James Linden, and Gideon believed he might go dig up the man, just so he could bash in his skull with the shovel. "No. You're wrong. Everything ended with my father's death. This is something else."

"*This*, Gideon? Are we speaking at cross purposes? What is *this*?"

Gideon was seldom the loser in any verbal exchange, but the more he said, the more control of their conversation he seemed to be ceding to her. He didn't much care for the feeling.

"I'll have my town carriage sent for you tomorrow at eleven, to bring you to Portman Square to see your brother. Kindly outfit yourself accordingly."

At last he seemed to shock her, put her off her stride.

But not for long. "Would that include wearing a dark veil to conceal my face, or will the carriage be driven directly around to the mews, and the servants' entrance?"

Not before time, he realized, Gideon decided he'd had enough.

He closed the distance between them in two short steps, taking hold of her right wrist before she could successfully reach into the slightly drooping pocket that had given away the location of her pistol. With his free hand he delved into the pocket and withdrew a small silver pistol, indeed a favorite of cardsharps.

He forcefully turned her hand over and pressed the thing in her palm. "Go on, you idiot woman. I'm about to *ravish* you. Shoot me."

She made no move to close her fingers around the weapon. "You don't mean that."

"Don't I? Are you sure? I can have anything I want from you, Jessica Linden, any time I want it. Most men could. Get rid of that toy before somebody turns it on you. I don't know what all this James Linden of yours taught you over and above honing that sharp tongue of yours, but he should have pointed out that you can't bluff worth a damn."

He saw the tears standing in her magnificent eyes but chose to ignore them. God save him from fools, most especially well-intentioned martyrs who always seemed to think right was on their side and justice would prevail. He turned and walked away from her, exposing his back to her, not stopping until his hand was on the latch of the door leading to the stairs.

"At eleven, Jessica. And if you dare insult me by wearing that black monstrosity or anything like it, I'll tear it off you myself. Understood?"

He'd barely closed the door behind him when the sound of what he presumed to be the derringer hitting the wood brought a smile to his face. He rather doubted James Linden taught her how to do that. No, that was a purely female reaction, and if there was one thing Jessica Linden was, it was female.

* * * * *

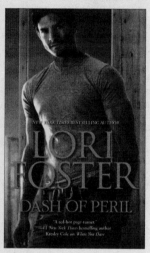

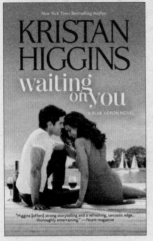

Two classic stories from the *New York Times*
bestselling queen of romantic suspense

LISA JACKSON

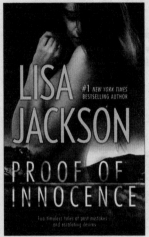

Yesterday's Lies

It's been five years since
Trask McFadden betrayed Tory's
trust, landing her father behind bars.
She'd hoped Trask was out of her
life forever, but now he's returned to
the Lazy W Ranch, claiming to have
discovered a clue that might prove
her father's innocence. For the sake
of her family, Tory's trying to forgive,
but she's finding it much harder to
forget when Trask's presence begins
to stir up feelings she'd thought
were long gone….

Devil's Gambit

Tiffany Rhodes's horse farm was
in trouble long before she met
Zane Sheridan, a breeder with a
shady reputation. Yet she can't help but feel relieved when Zane
offers to buy her out. Though Tiffany doesn't trust him, she's drawn
to him like a magnet. What does this mysterious man want from
her…and can she contain her desire long enough to find out?

Available wherever books are sold!

Be sure to connect with us at:

Harlequin.com/Newsletters
Facebook.com/HarlequinBooks
Twitter.com/HarlequinBooks

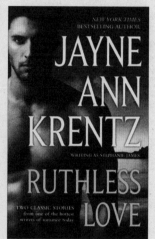

REQUEST YOUR FREE BOOKS!

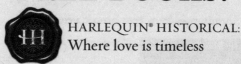

HARLEQUIN® HISTORICAL:
Where love is timeless

2 FREE NOVELS PLUS 2 **FREE GIFTS!**

YES! Please send me 2 FREE Harlequin® Historical novels and my 2 FREE gifts (gifts are worth about $10). After receiving them, if I don't wish to receive any more books, I can return the shipping statement marked "cancel." If I don't cancel, I will receive 6 brand-new novels every month and be billed just $5.44 per book in the U.S. or $5.74 per book in Canada. That's a savings of at least 16% off the cover price! It's quite a bargain! Shipping and handling is just 50¢ per book in the U.S. and 75¢ per book in Canada.* I understand that accepting the 2 free books and gifts places me under no obligation to buy anything. I can always return a shipment and cancel at any time. Even if I never buy another book, the two free books and gifts are mine to keep forever.

246/349 HDN F4ZY

Name _____ (PLEASE PRINT) _____

Address _____ Apt. # _____

City _____ State/Prov. _____ Zip/Postal Code _____

Signature (if under 18, a parent or guardian must sign)

Mail to the **Harlequin® Reader Service:**
IN U.S.A.: P.O. Box 1867, Buffalo, NY 14240-1867
IN CANADA: P.O. Box 609, Fort Erie, Ontario L2A 5X3
Want to try two free books from another line?
Call 1-800-873-8635 or visit www.ReaderService.com.

* Terms and prices subject to change without notice. Prices do not include applicable taxes. Sales tax applicable in N.Y. Canadian residents will be charged applicable taxes. Offer not valid in Quebec. This offer is limited to one order per household. Not valid for current subscribers to Harlequin Historical books. All orders subject to credit approval. Credit or debit balances in a customer's account(s) may be offset by any other outstanding balance owed by or to the customer. Please allow 4 to 6 weeks for delivery. Offer available while quantities last.

Your Privacy—The Harlequin® Reader Service is committed to protecting your privacy. Our Privacy Policy is available online at www.ReaderService.com or upon request from the Harlequin Reader Service.

We make a portion of our mailing list available to reputable third parties that offer products we believe may interest you. If you prefer that we not exchange your name with third parties, or if you wish to clarify or modify your communication preferences, please visit us at www.ReaderService.com/consumerchoice or write to us at Harlequin Reader Service Preference Service, P.O. Box 9062, Buffalo, NY 14269. Include your complete name and address.

HH13R

From #1 *New York Times* bestselling author

NORA ROBERTS

come two classics about not letting your best-laid
plans get in the way of life *or* love.

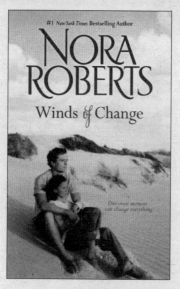

One sweet moment can change everything…

Be sure to connect with us at:

Harlequin.com/Newsletters
Facebook.com/HarlequinBooks
Twitter.com/HarlequinBooks

From *New York Times* bestselling author

JULIA LONDON

comes a brand-new series about four sisters
determined to rescue themselves from ruin when
passion and scandal collide.

Available when

Be sure to c
Harlequin.
Facebook.com/HarlequinBooks
Twitter.com/HarlequinBooks

HARLEQUIN® HQN™
www.Harlequin.com

PHJUL845R1